HOPE
AGAINST
HOPE

HOPE AGAINST HOPE

A Mystery Introducing Alison Hope
and Nick Trevellyan

SUSAN B. KELLY

CHARLES SCRIBNER'S SONS
New York

Maxwell Macmillan International
New York   Oxford   Singapore   Sydney

First United States Edition 1991

Charles Scribner's Sons
Macmillan Publishing Company
866 Third Avenue
New York, NY 10022

Macmillan Publishing Company is part of the Maxwell
Communication Group of Companies.

Library of Congress Cataloging-in-Publication Data

Kelly, Susan B.
    Hope against hope: a mystery introducing Alison Hope and Nick
Trevellyan / Susan B. Kelly. — 1st U.S. ed.
        p.   cm.
    ISBN 0-684-19387-6
    I. Title.
PR6061.E4965H67   1991   91-17430   CIP
823'.914—dc20

10 9 8 7 6 5 4 3 2 1

PRINTED IN THE UNITED STATES OF AMERICA

In Loving Memory of John Graham
1947–1988

*In every friend we lose a part of ourselves,
and the best part*

L'Espoir, malgré moi, s'est glissé dans mon coeur.

HOPE
AGAINST
HOPE

Prologue

Nick saw Alison Hope often that summer. Now whenever he closes his eyes he can conjure her. Sometimes she appears triumphant and self-assured as on the night of her house-warming party – the night Aidan was murdered. Or tired, sad-eyed and frightened as she was the next day, and the next. Now defiant as she looks him in the eye and dares him to call her a liar; now death-mask pale as on the night of the arrest. But, strangely, he sees her most often as she was that day on the road. She is wearing jeans, cashmere sweater, sheepskin jacket and a cross look. So that is the logical starting point: their first meeting. But it may mislead. For when Nick first met Alison, he did not think much of her.

He had the afternoon off. It was already the first of July, but a cold, windy day none the less. He nearly spent his free time at his flat, reading, but then decided on impulse to give himself an outing. Policemen, particularly detectives, are likely to be called out at any moment. He would go where they could not reach him. Then if anyone wanted to rob a bank or mug an old lady in Hopbridge that afternoon, they could do it without his interference.

He turned his old car southwards. There is only one road out of the valley and it twists and turns infuriatingly. Nick longed suddenly for the peace and freedom of the moors above. So when he passed the end-of-speed-limit sign which marks the southern boundary of Little Hopford he put his foot down. But he had to brake almost at once to negotiate yet another blind bend. As he rounded the corner he found

1

the road before him no longer clear. A huge black car was trying to turn left out of the down-at-heel house which occupied the corner site. Fortunately his reactions were swift. He swore a mild curse, hooted, braked, swerved and finished up on the grass verge about twenty yards beyond.

His car, predictably, stalled.

He got out. So did she.

Nick had the habit of observation ingrained in him and during the next few seconds he took in her every detail as surely as a snapshot. He had not yet decided that he didn't think much of her. True: she was not what he'd always thought of as his type; Nick was of medium height and slender build and had mostly been drawn to women of similar physique. This woman was almost as tall as he and big-boned, though lean. She looked glossy and expensive but what really caught his eye was her hair – a long, loose, shining tumble of red. Perhaps it was this mane which brought the simile to mind but he thought that she had the look of a well-groomed racehorse, her long legs covering the ground between them with the grace and speed of a Derby winner.

He resolved at once to forgive her – after all there was no harm done. Racehorses are sensitive creatures – she might well be shaken by the incident. She would be in earshot in a few seconds. He opened his mouth to speak, to reassure, to soothe.

She got in first.

'What the hell did you think you were doing coming round the corner at that speed?' she brayed, having quite different ideas as to what constituted earshot.

Nick didn't think much of her voice, let alone what it was saying. It was loud, upper-class, intolerant. Not a racehorse, then, a mule perhaps.

'I can see what sort of a driver you are.' She made a contemptuous gesture towards his dusty, battered Ford. 'I don't suppose another dent would show on there. But you could have done hundreds of pounds' worth of damage to my Jag. 'I've got a good mind to report you for dangerous driving . . . I've a good mind to call the police.'

She showed no signs of running out of steam and Nick found the performance mildy amusing so he let her rattle on

2

for a while, put his hands in his pockets and heard her out. Years in the interview room had taught him that silence is a powerful weapon and it is disconcerting if you are trying to have a row with someone who will not return the ball. Eventually she ground to a halt and gave him a perplexed look. It seemed the moment to strike his own blow.

'I am the police.'

She might have anticipated a lot of things but not that. She stared, then glared, looking him up and down as if she were thinking of buying him and doubted him worth the asking price. When he judged that she had finished her scrutiny, Nick made her an ironic little bow. It didn't come out quite right as he still had his hands in his pockets.

'Detective Inspector Nick Trevellyan at your service, madam.' She opened her mouth to speak again but this time it was he who pre-empted her. 'And if you're going to be using this gateway a lot, may I suggest you get one of those mirrors put up.' He gestured across the road and her eyes followed his pointing finger as he had known they would. 'Then you'll be able to see if there's anything coming.'

He considered telling her not to let it happen again but she didn't look as if she had much sense of humour. She seemed dumbstruck suddenly so he decided to quit while he was ahead and turned back towards his car. Then he thought of something. She was back in the Jaguar now and had restarted the engine. He ran across and tapped on the passenger window. It wound down with electronic smoothness.

'Yes!' she snapped.

'I wondered if you'd like me to see you out safely.'

She was momentarily at a loss. Then she said, 'Oh, all right.' Grudgingly. As if she were doing him a favour. Alison probably thought that was what policemen were there for – then.

He crossed the road and held up a hand in warning as a large van marked 'Hop Valley Dairies' thundered round the corner. Then he beckoned her out. She gave him a little toot of acknowledgement and sped away up the valley.

So that was Nick's first sighting of his quarry: Alison Hope, the vicar's daughter; Alison Hope, the business woman;

3

Alison Hope, the murderer? Not murderess: once, in the weeks to come, he will call her an adventuress and she will toss her head in scorn and say that he might as well call her a computer-programmess.

No, murderer is a nicely androgynous noun.

He walked slowly back across the road and looked in at the gateway. So someone had bought the place after all these years. A townie with a yen to try country living, she would set herself up as lady of the manor and patronise the locals.

He shrugged and headed back to his car. She would have a job to make that barn of a house habitable after all these years. There would be mice, he thought with satisfaction, probably rats. He got back into his car, whistling, and elaborated on this theme as he tried to restart it – cockroaches, giant spiders, bats? Dry rot? No, that was no good – rot wouldn't leap out of the skirting board and run up her leg. After a few minutes the engine finally caught and he followed the Jaguar, more sedately, up the valley.

Nick's colleagues have many names for him since there is spite and bickering in a police station as in any office. The superintendent, after one of their frequent disagreements, once called him an iceberg: seven-eighths hidden below water where you couldn't see it until you were sinking. But one thing they all agree on: Nick Trevellyan is sea-green incorruptible. He agreed with it himself. But that was before he met the murder suspect with the sea-green eyes.

He is not so smug now.

Chapter 1

Nick forgot about her almost at once – incredible as that was
to seem to him later. It was to be another fortnight before he
saw her again. He went past the house a couple of times. It
was being swiftly transformed from ivy-covered derelict to
the sympathetic restoration – retaining all original features –
so beloved of estate agents. The house was graceful Georgian
and stood three storeys high in an acre of ground.

It was a quiet time at the station. Midsummer: perhaps all
the crooks had sloped off to Benidorm or Majorca for the
duration. If they had gone for the climate, they might just as
well have stayed in the valley. Every morning Nick's radio-
alarm went off and the announcer told him, gleefully, he
thought, that it would be cold and overcast in the west again
today. And every morning, as Nick walked to work, the mist
cleared away from the sea and the sun came out to give a hot
airless day as the inhabitants of the Hop Valley enjoyed
weather little short of a heatwave.

Although perhaps 'enjoyed' is not the word. Nick was
trapped in his office, longing to be free, by the sea or at least
on the open road. Hopbridge police station is late-sixties
concrete and glass and Nick's office is like a set for an amateur
production of *In Camera*. (Some of his 'customers' have
indeed found it a waiting-room for Hell).

Nick is to a large extent his own master. In general no one
questions his comings and goings. He is, at least nominally,
head of CID in this sleepy backwater. Nominally since, if ever
anything really interesting happens, someone from
Headquarters swoops down to dig out the most succulent

5

worms. But even the head of CID finds it hard to justify an unexplained absence in the middle of a crime-dearth. Nick did a lot of paperwork that month.

So when the phone rang one morning he picked it up eagerly even though, by the ring, it was only an internal call. Ten-thirty – just the time when the morning is set to last forever.

'Inspector Trevellyan?' He recognised the disapproving voice of the superintendent's secretary. She disliked Nick – having convicted him of being insufficiently in awe of the boss. 'Mr Grey would like to see you. At once, please.'

Nick put his jacket on and took the stairs, two at a time, up to the fourth floor from which eyrie Reg Grey supervised the policing of the Hop Valley. Their relationship was not without its stormy side but Nick found the superintendent at his mildest that day, in the summer heat, contemplating the bushel of prizes his roses had picked up at the Hop Valley flower show. He had taken off both jacket and tie and Nick felt overdressed.

Reg waved him to a seat and launched in without preamble.

'I want you to go and see Jack Ashcroft.'

'Why?' Nick asked. 'Don't tell me he's been pointing his shotgun at ramblers again. That's not CID work.'

Reg shook his head. 'Oddly enough the boot seems to be on the other foot. He's complaining that someone has threatened him.' Nick tried his best to look concerned. 'I've had him on the phone ranting and raving half the morning. I had to promise him I'd put CID onto it before I could get rid of him. Otherwise we can expect another blast from the crusading *Valley Voice*.'

Police inefficiency – so called – was Jack Ashcroft's hobby-horse and, as he owned the only local paper specific to the valley, the horse got plenty of exercise.

'Have a word with him,' Reg was saying. 'Find out who has a grudge against him.' He looked thoughtful. 'Mind you, it would be quicker to find out who hasn't. He seems to get up everybody's nose.'

'Especially women,' Nick slipped in, mainly to annoy Reg. 'He's the worst type of chauvinist.'

'I don't know about all that stuff,' Reg said, right on cue.

6

'They hadn't invented feminism when I was your age.'

'Right, sir. We'll get round and see him at once.' Nick got up but Reg waved him down again.

'There's another little thing. What you might call a favour to me.' Nick concentrated on not looking incredulous. 'You know that Sergeant Grimm is off on his holidays for the next two weeks?'

Nick nodded. Grimm was the crime-prevention officer.

'I went round to Sir Anton's last night . . .' Reg had spent the last few minutes stuffing tobacco lovingly into his pipe and was now ready to reap his reward. He struck a match and began to puff out clouds of smoke. Nick coughed theatrically, moved his chair as far back as he could and waited patiently. It's no good trying to hurry a pipe addict.

'. . . To have a word about the arrangements for the Police Charity Ball,' Reg concluded at last. Sir Anton Armitage was a lay magistrate with a seat on the Police Authority.

'He's got a charming girl staying with him – a niece of his wife's, I gather. She made a generous donation to the children's home at Hopcliff, very generous.' Reg spent a lot of his spare time raising money for charity and the children's home was his special favourite.

'She's coming to live round here somewhere and she's in urgent need of crime-prevention advice. I forgot that old Grimm was off and I promised her someone would come over today. Well, obviously I can't justify sending you out on a job like that . . .'

You can say that again, Reg, Nick didn't say.

'. . . But I thought, as you can't get to Ashcroft's farm without going through Little Hopford, you could just look in on her on your way back. I really would take it as a favour.'

'OK,' Nick said generously. 'I mean, I'm sure I can fit it in, sir.' Actually he was delighted. All this would get him out of the office for a few hours and it meant that Reg owed him one. 'What's this woman's name and address?'

Reg consulted his diary. 'Alison Hope, Hope Cottage, Little Hopford. Know it?'

Nick shook his head. The name meant nothing to him although it struck him as an attractive name. The civilities on the grass verge had been one-sided.

7

'Probably one of those cottages round the village green,' he said. 'Bill will know.'

At first sight Nick wouldn't seem to have much in common with Bill Deacon. Bill was more than ten years older than Nick and would never rise above his present rank of sergeant. He looked like an ad-man's policeman: six foot two, burly, solid. Nick often thought that Bill looked a bit out of place in plain clothes, since his body appeared to have been designed with a police uniform in mind. But they had been working together for two years now and Nick would trust Bill with his life. He did trust him with his sanity. Bill could be infuriatingly single-minded but Nick found that useful in stopping him from going too far off the track in the wrong direction. Bill had never budged out of the Hop Valley in all his life and he knew just about everyone in it and what they were all up to.

He had been stuck behind his desk all week and was in a garrulous mood that morning. As they waited at the traffic lights to turn over the bridge, he said, 'The Super's in a good mood today, won first prize with his Angela Rippons.'

'With his what?'

'His roses, on Saturday.'

'God, the names they think up!' Nick said. 'Yes, he was in a good mood. Mind you, I know he's a bit irritable at times but I've never actually seen him in a temper.'

'Don't you believe it. You weren't around when Tim Lingfield got done for corruption. That was about five years ago, while you were still at County. You must have heard about it.'

'Vaguely.'

'The Super went up like a volcano. Tim begged to be locked in the cells where the Guv'nor couldn't get at him.'

'What did Lingfield do?' Nick asked, interested now. 'Bribes, was it?'

Bill shook his head. 'He got mixed up with some girl. Her brothers and father had all done time. Well, they got Tim tipping them off about security at various offices and factories round the valley, then they used to rob them. Got away with it for over a year.'

'How did they get on to him?'

'I reckon the brothers got too impatient. They turned over

8

a place just a week after Tim had been round checking their security. Rang some bells somewhere. They set him up after that. He walked right into it.'

'How can a policeman be so stupid?' Nick said hubristically. 'Aren't there enough women around to choose from without taking up with an old lag's daughter?'

'Easy to see you're not married,' Bill said pertly, 'if you think you get a choice in the matter.' He gave Nick one of his sidelong looks – a speciality of his. It got the toughest of their customers trembling in the interview room. Nick knew what he was thinking: You can talk, look at the mess you nearly got yourself into over that Lucy Fielding . . . sir. A lot of insubordination goes on inside a policeman's head – as might be seen during Nick's recent interview with the superintendent. A quiet 'yes, sir' can conceal a Russian novel's worth of dumb insolence. Nick did not begrudge Bill his quota. He changed the subject.

He told Bill about the crime-prevention visit. Bill shrugged philosophically.

'I don't know much about it but I expect we can bluff our way if the Guv'nor wants her kept sweet.'

Nick agreed. 'With a bit of luck she won't take long and we can take a break at the Bird in Hand in Little Hopford. I expect it's just some nervous old maid who's been reading too many sensational newspapers.'

They passed through Little Hopford and rounded the blind corner. Bill said, 'That's it, on the bend here.'

'What? Shit!' Nick said. 'Isn't it one of those cottages round the green?'

'Hope Cottage you said, sir. That's this great ruin on the corner here. Don't know why they call it a cottage at all, looks pretty big to me. The woman who's bought it is a newcomer – no one has met her yet.'

Nick was quite glad to score a point off the Bill Deacon spy network.

'I have,' he said.

Bill made a right turn half a mile south of Little Hopford and took the single-track road which leads eventually up to Threeoaks Hill. After another half-mile they pulled into Jack

9

Ashcroft's yard. Ashcroft farmed a few dozen acres which he had largely given over to whatever would cause him the least trouble. Part of it now housed the valley's only battery hen farm. A dog barked somewhere in the house and Ashcroft was at the door waiting for them before Bill had even turned the car. The yard was potholed and muddy with an overall air of neglect about it. A couple of geese ran shrieking for cover before their wheels, then turned from a safe distance to spit at them. It occurred to Nick that they were the ideal pet for Jack Ashcroft.

He got slowly out of the car, keeping an eye on Ashcroft in case the bellicose farmer decided to set the dog on them. Nick had known Ashcroft at primary school although Jack was two or three years older than he. After that Jack had gone away to boarding school for several years. Nick considered him to be a bully and an emotional cripple. The fact that he knew that Jack had been neglected, if not actually ill-treated, by his wealthy parents did not make Nick like him any better. He would as soon put out his hand to pat a rabid dog as offer friendship to Jack Ashcroft. He was not looking forward to the interview.

Ashcroft is beginning to sound like an ogre. He didn't look it except for a certain ill-humour in his expression. He was about thirty-five; his face was ruddy, his hair reddish-brown. He wasn't at all a bad-looking man though likely to go to seed early. He was six foot tall and quite stocky though not yet running to fat. His voice was loud and, at the best of times, irritable.

Today was not one of the best of times.

'Come in then,' he boomed, standing to one side and ushering them into the house. 'You've taken your time, I must say. It was first thing this morning I rang Reggie Grey.' Ashcroft spoke of almost everyone in these familiar terms – except when he pretended not to know who they were at all. Nick made a hasty resolution not to let Jack get under his skin and put on an all-purpose bland expression as they followed him into the sitting-room.

'Trevellyan, isn't it?' said Jack, who knew Nick's name as well as he knew his own. Nick agreed and introduced Bill Deacon whom he also knew. Policemen are supposed not to be rude to the public – well, not to prosperous landowners, at least – but Nick was only human, so he decided to play Ashcroft at his own game. He looked round the room.

'Had the place done up, Jack,' he said, with mock admiration. This was no less than the truth – the house was looking a good deal smarter than when he had last seen it. 'The woman's touch, is it?' Now that was naughty – the matador eyeing the bull and whipping out his red rag. Implying that some woman had taken him under her wing was the most reliable way of needling Ashcroft. He looked a little embarrassed.

'Well, we're not here to talk about curtains like a lot of girls,' he said unpleasantly.

'OK,' Nick said. 'So, what about these letters?'

'Bloody lunatics. In any decent society people like that wouldn't be allowed. They'd just lock them up – subversives, scum like that – '

Nick had to raise his voice to butt in. 'You've lost me, Jack. Who are we talking about?'

'Didn't Reggie tell you? What the hell do I pay my taxes for? These ARM people.'

'Ah!' Nick saw the light. 'Animal rights?'

'Course. Who else would be threatening me about the hen farm?'

'I didn't know that was what the threats were about,' Nick said in his most patient, don't-frighten-the-old-ladies voice. He knew most of the fringe organisations in the valley but he didn't know much about these ARM people, they were fairly new. He said as much.

'After all, until you started your battery farm there wouldn't have been much for them to protest about in the valley,' he pointed out.

'I've got a right to earn a living, haven't I? And you've got a duty to protect me.'

'Are the letters signed by ARM?'

'No, they're anonymous.'

'It's not actually illegal to send people anonymous letters, you know.'

'They're threatening me!'

'Let's have a look then.'

Ashcroft went to the sideboard and took out a couple of

11

sheets of cheap-looking writing paper. He thrust them in Nick's direction.

'Hang on.' Nick took a pair of thin leather gloves out of his briefcase – he often referred to them humorously as his murderer's gloves – and put them on. Then he took one of the papers from Ashcroft, holding it by the corner. The paper was from a lined A5 pad. The message was in block capitals.

THOSE WHO LIVE BY THE SUFFERING OF OTHER SPECIES
WILL LIVE TO SUFFER THEMSELVES

'Not very specific,' Nick said, handing the paper to Bill, who took it by the same corner with his handkerchief. 'I'm not sure I'd even describe it as threatening. Perhaps it's just a statement of the human condition.'

'Funny, aren't you, Trevellyan? Take a look at this one then.'

The second letter was shorter.

BATTERY CHICKENS. BATTERED ASHCROFT.
BATTERED TO DEATH?

'I think that constitutes a death threat, don't you?' Ashcroft said smugly.

Nick pretended to consider. 'Yes, I suppose so. Quite literate, aren't they? Nice touch of symmetry in both of them.'

'This isn't a bloody Oxford seminar!'

'Got the envelopes?'

'No, I threw them away without thinking.'

'You should always keep the envelopes. There could be hair or something in them. What were they like, cheap stuff like the paper?'

'Er, yeah.'

'You're sure they came through the post?'

'Yeah.'

'Notice the postmark?'

No.'

Not even if it was local – posted in the valley?'

'I didn't notice, I said. Stop barking questions at me. I'm

12

not the one who should be interrogated. Of course they were posted in the valley since it's these ARM people behind it. I did a feature on them in the *Voice*. They're picking on me out of spite.'

'Let's not jump to conclusions,' Nick said firmly. 'If you spot any more, hang on to the envelopes and wear gloves to open them. In fact don't open them at all, bring them straight to us. When and where did they arrive?'

'First one at the newspaper office on Friday, second one here on Tuesday.'

'You've taken your time over reporting them, then, if you think they're threatening you.'

Jack shrugged. 'At first I thought there'd be no point, knowing how useless you lot are. Then I thought I might as well get my money's worth out of the police.'

'Who else might be responsible other than the ARM people?' Nick asked. 'Any enemies?'

'Don't be bloody stupid!' Ashcroft said.

'He's a fine one to talk about spite,' Nick said, as they drove out of the farmyard. 'Did you see that article he did in the *Voice* about lunatic fringe groups?'

'No, I must have missed that one. How seriously are we going to take it, sir?'

'I'm inclined to say they're just trying to frighten him. What do you think?'

'They sounded a bit potty to me. Some of these animal-rights groups get things out of all proportion.'

'They were written by someone literate, educated.'

'I expect educated people have committed crimes from time to time,' Bill said cheerfully. 'Will we get them looked at, then?'

'Sure. I want to know a bit more about these ARM people anyway. If they're behind it, they're probably just a bunch of idealistic kids. We can give them a good scare for wasting police time. Meanwhile we'll get the letters dusted for fingerprints. I loved the look on his face when you said you wanted to take his prints.'

Bill grinned. 'Yeah, he could hardly refuse after calling us in, could he?'

'Let's go and see this Hope woman then,' Nick said, 'and get it over with.'

13

Chapter 2

Bill swung the car into the courtyard of Hope Cottage and pulled up in front of the porch. He pointed at the gate on which the words 'Hope Cottage', neatly lettered on a nameplate, now hung. Nick got out of the car and looked round gloomily.

'It's a bit much, naming the house after herself like that,' he protested.

Bill laughed. 'It's been called that as long as anyone can remember. When I was a boy the two Miss Gordons lived here. They both died in about 1955 and the place has just gone to rack and ruin since then. But it was Hope Cottage then and Hope Cottage in the Domesday book for all I know.'

Nick rang the doorbell. Perhaps the red-headed woman had just been a visitor.

But it was her all right. Ms Jaguar. He realised that he had been confusing her with her car, thinking of her as a big cat. Though the metaphor which sprang to mind then was more canine in nature. The red hair was now plaited and coiled at the back of her head. She was wearing black linen trousers and a cream silk blouse. She looked very cool – as if the hot weather didn't affect her at all – and made him feel rather sticky and grubby. He realised that she was older than he had at first thought, late twenties probably. This thought cheered him up.

She said cordially enough, 'Oh, it's you.'

'Miss Hope? Superintendent Grey asked us to call.'

'Who?' She looked at him blankly for a moment. 'Oh, Reg! You'd better come in. What did you say your name was?'

14

He told her again. She looked at him thoughtfully for a moment as though filing him away in her memory.

'You've brought your minder,' she said. 'There was no need to go to those lengths.'

Nick introduced Bill. Alison Hope shook hands with him and said, 'Now that's what I call a policeman.' Bill puzzled over this exchange as the two men followed her into the house.

'Is it Miss Hope or Mrs?' he asked politely.

'It's all the same to me. It doesn't really mean anything these days, does it?'

Bill's expression made it painfully obvious that he did not agree with this view.

She took them through the house and they went through their paces for her. The whole place was in a state of upheaval; there seemed hardly a window unrotted, floorboard free of worm or dry patch of plaster in the house. Bill began to look more sympathetic. He warned her about the french windows (the architect's gift to burglars), of which there were two sets, and offered gratuitous advice about the rising damp.

Not to be outdone, Nick warned about the conservatory which gave direct access to the house through the kitchen.

There's plenty of cover in the garden,' he said authoritatively. 'A burglar could be on to the terrace and into the house while you were upstairs having a bath. You're so isolated here.' He poked about for signs of a husband. There were none. She wore no rings – which told him nothing, the presence of a ring on the third finger being far more eloquent than its absence.

They reached the kitchen, which had about half the number of floorboards required by popular prejudice.

'You're not living here while all this is going on, surely?,' Nick said.

'No. I've still got my house in London until the end of the month but I'm spending most of the week down here with friends.'

'Oh yes, you're staying with the Armitages, aren't you?' He felt Bill stiffen to attention at the mention of Sir Anton's name. Bill loved a title.

'Molly Armitage is my godmother,' she said. You could

always trust Reg Grey to get it slightly wrong, Nick thought. 'I came down to visit her last spring. I'd been toying with the idea of moving out of London for some time so when I saw a house called Hope Cottage was up for sale, I simply had to see it. I just fell in love with it. Molly says I can stay as long as I like but I intend to move in by the middle of August.'

Nick looked sceptical.

'Oh, it will be more or less ready,' she affirmed. 'The builders have promised it for three more weeks.' He swopped scepticism for disbelief. 'If it isn't ready,' she went on, 'they don't get their ten per cent bonus.'

Hmmm – flashy, Nick thought, keeping the observation under wraps.

When they had finished their tour of the house, Alison Hope led them out on the terrace and they all sat down on the parapet.

'Have a drink?' she said sociably. 'I've got a bottle of chablis in the cool box.' The declined but accepted the next offer of a glass of mineral water. As she handed Nick his glass, their eyes met. He had expected hers to be blue but they were an unusual misty green. She smiled at him. He blushed prettily.

'Well, so much for the house,' she said. 'But more important is my workshop . . . the old stable block,' she explained, seeing their blank looks. 'That's where the valuable equipment will be, more important than a few bits of jewellery and so on. My livelihood.'

'What equipment is that?' Nick asked, on cue.

'All my computer stuff.'

The stable block had been stripped completely bare – stalls and haylofts removed; walls replastered and whitewashed.

'Welcome to the headquarters of Hope Software,' she said. 'Well, soon-to-be headquarters anyway.'

'What will you have here and what will it be worth?' Nick asked.

'Several micro computers of different types so I can be sure the software we develop runs on different operating systems. Printers, disc drives, some tape decks, an air-conditioning unit. Total worth must be well into the thousands, I suppose. Insured, of course, but the insurers will expect adequate

16

precautions and they won't insure work in progress. That's software I'm currently working on. I can't really prove what stage I've got to or how much it might be worth, you see. I keep copies, naturally, but someone might steal it and swipe my ideas.'

Bill whistled under his breath. Nick took care not to. He had a quick look at the place. It was obvious to him that Alison Hope had not bought Hope Cottage on impulse, whatever she said. There were no windows in this stable and the walls were nearly a foot thick. She had chosen well and carefully.

'Well, the door is the weak point,' he said. 'I'm assuming you don't want to replace the old stable door since it would spoil the look of the place from outside. I think your best bet is to install a second, metal door inside it. That will stop anyone breaking in and help the air conditioning function correctly. And you really ought to have a burglar alarm here as well as in the house. And I should think you'd better have smoke detectors – with all that electrical equipment the building could go up in no time.' He thought she looked suitably impressed.

They went back out into the courtyard and he gave her the name of a firm in Exeter which Grimm usually recommended for high-grade security. Bill got into the police car and started the engine – it was way past his dinner-time. Nick was just going to get in at the passenger door when it occurred to him that he had better see Bill safely out of the courtyard. He glanced across the road and saw that a mirror had been put up, nicely angled to show a good stretch of road in both directions. He turned and she was watching him, smiling.

'Don't forget to come to my house-warming,' she said.

'Wonder what she's doing here,' Bill said, pulling up, unbidden, outside the Bird in Hand. 'London lady like her, fish out of water.'

'Oh, I don't know so much,' Nick said. 'Anyway, she's going to be big fish in this pond.'

'Ten per cent bonus for finishing on time! She must have money to burn.'

Nick had thought the same but he was feeling perverse so he said, 'I expect it makes good sense in business circles.'

'She's a tough one.' Bill thought he liked women to be quiet and submissive – a view which would have astonished anyone acquainted with his calmly confident wife and three teenage tomboys. 'Computer software, huh! I can't see her putting up with any nonsense. I bet she's ruthless when it comes to business.'

'Ruthless full stop, I should think,' said Nick, who didn't in the least like submissive women.

'She's not even a pretty maid.' Bill wrinkled his nose.

'No,' Nick agreed. 'I wouldn't call her pretty.'

Chapter 3

'Alison, you look a picture!'

Alison joined the Armitages in their drawing-room one Thursday evening at about seven-thirty and Anton advanced on her with his cocktail shaker and a huge smile of welcome. He patted her on the arm and filled her glass with a rather dry martini. He often patted her on her arm, sometimes on the knee, occasionally on the bottom. Alison didn't mind in the least.

Anton stood looking at her appreciatively. He had been saying to Molly only that morning that they must look out for a husband for young Alison. She must be . . . what? Twenty-nine. Molly had shrugged and said she didn't suppose Alison was much bothered and had implied that if she had had Alison's sort of money thirty-five years ago she might not have bothered either. Anton had retired from the fray, hurt.

To the casual observer the Armitages' mutual devotion was not obvious since their habitual tone to one another was one of brusque sarcasm. But Alison was not a casual observer and took their biting remarks as a matter of course. She had a theory that it was all those years in the diplomatic corps that had done it. If you spent all day gritting your teeth and being nice to people perhaps you had to be brutally blunt with your friends and relations to avoid going screaming mad. Whatever the reason, Molly Armitage could usually be relied upon to say exactly what she thought on any subject.

'Stop leering at Alison like that, Anton,' was what she said now. 'Sometimes I think you're turning into a dirty old man.'

She took her goddaughter by the arm and steered her out

19

on the balcony. The Armitages' Jacobean house perched on the cliff at the mouth of the Hop and the view out to sea, in the evening sunlight, was dazzling. They leant on the rail and looked giddily down the cliff-face as Molly cross-examined Alison about the progress on her house, where she was now spending most of her time.

'There's still a lot to do, of course,' Alison told her. 'But I've fixed the house-warming for the sixteenth of August, Saturday week. I've managed to get hold of most of the London crowd, the ones who aren't away on holiday.'

'You could leave the house-warming until later in the year, I suppose.'

'No. I want to get settled and back to work by autumn. Mind you, the alarms are proving a bit of a problem. The firm I want to use are fully booked up at the moment. But they've got such a good reputation, I said I'd wait. They're the ones that nice police inspector recommended.'

'Bastard!' Molly snapped, to Alison's amazement. It took her a moment to realise that Molly was addressing a seagull which had narrowly missed crapping on her head. They ducked out of range back into the drawing-room, where there was fresh cause for concern.

'Anton! I saw that,' Molly said furiously. Anton had been caught in the act of slipping a cheese straw to Castlemaine, the latest in a long line of King Charles spaniel puppies. Anton came over with his cocktail shaker and topped them both up. The dog trailed after him and sat up to beg at his feet.

'Now look what you've done,' Molly said.

Anton rapidly changed the subject. 'Been meaning to ask you, Alison, if the completion on your place in London went all right yesterday. People cough up the cash, did they?'

'There were no hitches at all. The money is in the bank and the furniture is in a warehouse in Brentford.'

'That reminds me,' Molly said. 'I met James Waddington in Hopbridge today. You remember him, don't you, Alison?'

'Yes, of course.' JW, as he was known, had done the conveyancing of Hope Cottage. 'He must be about ninety.'

'He's sixty-eight,' Molly said severely, 'and he's the best solicitor for miles around.'

'He's the only solicitor for miles around,' Anton said.

'Don't exaggerate, dear.'

'Goodness knows what we shall all do when he finally retires.'

Molly, who was little but fierce, stamped her foot on the floor.

'That's what I'm trying to tell you about if you'd both just shut up for two seconds. He has taken on a partner.'

Alison looked blank and Molly went on to explain. It seemed that the Waddingtons had been lawyers in the valley for generations but James was the last of them. He had said he wouldn't take a partner from outside the family.

'But he's had a change of heart,' Molly said. 'Heard about this young man in London, son of someone James was at school with – you know the type of thing. Been working for a high-powered City firm but he's been ill. Finds it all too much for him. He fancies himself as a country solicitor – bedside manner and so on.'

'Sounds like a euphemism for a nervous breakdown.' Alison hadn't much time for people who broke down under pressure.

'Well, plenty of people are finding the rat race too much these days,' Molly said, with uncharacteristic charity. 'What could be nicer than to settle in a quiet place like this and become a pillar of the local community? After all, Alison, it's what you're doing yourself.'

'I haven't quite made up my mind to vegetate yet,' Alison said dryly. 'Business will still take me up to London quite often and I haven't joined the Women's Institute. Oh, sorry, Molly.'

Molly Armitage, who was the honorary president of the WI for the county, never missed an excuse for a fight. She hit Alison, managing to knock her drink over in the process, and it was some minutes before civilised conversation was resumed.

'So we must make him welcome when he arrives,' Molly said breathlessly, being a bit above her best fighting weight at that time. 'Perhaps he'll be here in time for your house-warming, dear.'

'What's his name, anyway?'

'James did tell me. Thomas . . . or was it Timothy? Then something fairly ordinary. We'll find out soon enough.'

21

The Bird in Hand in Little Hopford was a quiet place which served the local beer, so Bill hadn't needed much persuading to make it their regular watering hole when they were out that way.

'I think I'll push the boat out today,' Nick said that Friday lunchtime. 'Half a pint of Golden Hill, Jos. Bill? Pint?'

'Please.'

Jos Leighland pulled the beer. 'If all my customers were like you, Mr Trevellyan, I'd be in the poorhouse. It's not as if you ever drive anywhere if you can avoid it.'

'Got to keep my wits about me,' Nick claimed implausibly. He didn't care much for alcohol except a bit of wine with dinner, or the occasional glass of beer, but a lot of people seemed to take that as a personal affront.

'No sign of life at Hope Cottage,' Bill said. 'She hasn't got those alarms in yet. I hope the local bloke is keeping an eye on the place.'

'How do you know she hasn't got the alarms in?' Nick asked.

'My brother in law does the odd bit of work for that security firm in Exeter. They're getting a lot of business these days.'

'Sign of the times,' Jos said glumly. 'Few years back no one even bothered to lock their front door round here.' That was true, Nick reflected. They used to get burgled then too.

'They're even getting a new chap in from London to ease some of the load,' Bill went on. 'Hope cottage will be his first project.'

'That'll be one pound twenty,' Jos said. 'You just been out to Threeoaks?' he asked nosily.

'Mmm,' Nick said noncommittally.

'Only I heard he'd had a bit of vandalism up there.'

'Mmm.' *Mind your own business.*

'Paint sprayed all over his hen houses,' persisted Jos, unable to take a hint. 'Pretty ripe language too by all acounts. I bet Jack Ashcroft was livid, wasn't he?'

'Jack Ashcroft was Jack Ashcroft,' Nick said. *Only more so.*

'He was going on in here the other day about these animal-rights people. I mean, we all eat eggs, don't we? No good getting sanctimonious about it. He said he'd shown you some letters he'd had and you hadn't done anything about it.'

'How does he know what I'm doing?' Nick demanded, stung into response. 'He doesn't follow me around all day.'

'He says he know's who's responsible but you won't do anything about it.'

'There is a little something called evidence. We normally try to find some before we get the thumb-screws out.'

'I wouldn't have your job,' Jos said. 'Speaking of Hope Cottage, there's a bloke – .

A head poked round the door and a large, thirsty-looking mouth bellowed, 'Jos, let's have some service in here!'

Jos hurried off towards the public bar. Nick lowered his voice.

'We'll have to take a more serious look at these ARM people. Anonymous letters are one thing . . .'

'We'll have to get Penruan and Miss Halsgrove back on to it,' Bill agreed. 'Find out a bit more about them.'

They had discovered that ARM operated out of a council flat in West Hopbridge. They had sounded pretty harmless – just kids, as Nick had thought.

'They can't get away with that sort of vandalism, kids or no kids,' he said. 'Carol Halsgrove might pass as a possible new recruit. She's never worked in uniform in the valley. They might – '

The saloon-bar door swung open and a stranger walked in. Nick stopped talking abruptly and stared at him – Little Hopford was well off the tourist circuit. The newcomer said good morning and they exchanged a few banal remarks about the weather, which continued fair. He had a cultured voice with an accent which Nick could not immediately place.

Jos reappeared and poured the newcomer a pint of Guiness without waiting for his order.

'The wife has got your room ready for you now, Mr Hope. Did you find the place?' he asked.

Nick choked on his beer, turned it into a cough, and examined the stranger more carefully. Yes, he looked the sort to appeal to a certain type of woman. He had that earthy, gipsyish look – like something out of D. H. Lawrence: hair so dark it was almost black, curling round his face; sooty eyelashes; big brown eyes. Even quite sensible women

23

seemed to have a weakness for his sort – thought they needed mothering.

'I found it,' the man was saying, 'but there was no one there.'

'I did warn you. She hasn't moved in yet.'

'It looks like I shall be renting your room for a few days then.'

'No problem. We only have the one room but I can't honestly claim it's in great demand.'

'Do either of you gentleman know Alison Hope?' The stranger turned his attention to the two policemen and Nick finally identified his accent as educated Irish.

'Yes,' he said cautiously. 'I know her by sight.'

'You don't happen to know where I can find her?'

Bill opened his mouth to speak but Nick kicked him expertly on the shin and answered the question himself.

'I'm afraid not. I believe she's staying with friends in the area. She should be moving into her house quite soon, though. If I see her, who shall I say is asking for her?'

'Just tell her Aidan, she'll know. I'm Aidan Hope.'

So this was the missing husband, Nick thought contemptuously. My God! He might have known she'd fall for the gigolo type. Still, he might as well hang around for a bit and see what Hope had to say. He accepted another beer from him. Bill looked amazed. He had never known the inspector drink more than half a pint at lunchtime and that was a rare enough occurrence. He rubbed his shin thoughtfully.

'Are you holidaying down here, Mr Hope?' Nick asked.

'You might rather say that I'm here on business. Looking for the key that will get me back my wife, if you see what I mean.'

Nick didn't but smiled encouragement. Aidan sank his pint of Guinness in record time and gladly accepted another. These drinks were evidently not his first of the day. He raised his glass.

'Here's to red-haired, green-eyed beauties.'

Nick drank to that.

'I thought Mrs Hope was staying with the Armitages,' Bill remarked, as he drove them back to the station.

'So she is.'

'You told that chap you didn't know where she was.'

'Gosh, yes,' Nick said solemnly. 'I must have been lying then, mustn't I?'

Bill gave him another of those sidelong looks. Nick resolved to speak to him about that – some time when he was feeling a bit less drowsy. Bill said no more beyond: 'Seemed a nice enough chap to me. He would be Mrs Hope's estranged husband, I'm thinking.'

'Looks that way.' Nick sank down in his seat and closed his eyes to indicate that the conversation was at an end.

Chapter 4

Alison was called away to London on urgent business in the second week of August and ended up staying four days. It was with great relief that she pulled the Jaguar into the courtyard of Hope Cottage again on Tuesday, the twelfth. It had been drizzling in London but at Hope Cottage the mellow pink stone was wrapped in heat haze still. She was more than ever sure that she had made the right decision.

The front door was slightly ajar and she left her suitcases in the boot and went into the hall to see what progress there had been in her absence. The builder's foreman poked his head round the kitchen door.

'Oh, it's you, Miss Hope. We've finished the hall and landing, as you see.' She nodded curtly; it didn't do to appear too impressed although she was pleased with the results.

'And the phone people turned up at last. They've put the line in – he indicated a telephone standing on the windowsill, on top of a local directory – 'but they didn't have the jack-plug for your answering machine. They said it wasn't on their work sheet.'

Alison picked the receiver up and raised it gingerly to her ear. She had better celebrate by ringing somebody. She opened the directory in the middle and leafed through the pages. The word *Police* caught her eye. She dialled the number given for Hopbridge police station and asked to speak to Inspector Trevellyan. There was a long pause and she thought the line had gone dead but then he answered.

'Detective Inspector Trevellyan.' Well, she wasn't going to call him that.

She said, 'Hello, Nick Trevellyan. It's Alison Hope.'

'Oh . . .' Rather a long drawn-out *Oh*, she thought. 'What can I do for you, Mrs Hope?' He was obviously still sulking over that day she had nearly bashed into his car. He needn't think he was going to get an apology. Alison never apologised.

'Well, you can cut out the Mrs Hope for a start,' she said firmly. 'You're not going to call me that at my party, are you?'

'Party? Oh yes.'

'I told you you were invited.'

'I thought you'd forgotten, actually, I mean . . .' He wasn't very articulate, she thought disparagingly.

'You will come, won't you? Saturday night. You policemen do get Saturday nights off, don't you?'

'Well, that rather depends, but I think I can safely say I shan't be working this Saturday night.'

'So that's settled then. You'll come.'

'Well, yes, I suppose so.'

Very gracious.

'Thanks very much.'

That's better. 'You can bring your minder too, if you like.'

'I'll tell him but I don't think it's quite his thing.'

'Of course, you can bring your wife . . .'

'I'm not married. I'll come on my own, if that's all right.'

'Yes, of course. We're starting eight-thirtyish.' She went to hang up but speaking of wives had reminded Nick.

'Just a minute! There's a man staying in Little Hopford asking for you. Have you seen him?'

'No, but I've been away for a few days. Who on earth is it?'

'He's staying at the Bird in Hand. I rather think it's your husband. See you Saturday.'

'I'm not – ' she began but Nick had already hung up, 'married either,' she finished to the dead line.

She shrugged. What an odd man he was. He'd got hold of the wrong end of the stick somewhere. Oh, well, whoever this mysterious stranger was, if he really wanted to see her, then he'd turn up at some point. She continued her inspection of the house.

She finished up in the drawing-room. Jenny Tilney, the interior designer, was putting up curtains at the french windows. She was quite a perfectionist, pulling and tugging swathes of material to left and right by such minuscule amounts that Alison could see no difference.

'It doesn't hang quite right,' she said helpfully. Jenny let go of the curtain and turned, very slowly, to look at Alison – every movement of her plump, tense body signalling exasperated weariness.

'It won't go right either if you're just going to hang around criticising all the time,' she snarled. 'I can't work while I'm being watched. I'm an artist.' She tossed her head, which wasn't very effective as her hair was cut very short and spiky. You needed hair like Alison's for really effective head-tossing. Alison did it a lot. Jenny turned deliberately back towards the curtains. Alison wanted to get out on the terrace but Jenny was taking up so much of the french windows that she had to edge precariously past her.

'The customer is always right,' she whispered defiantly as soon as she was out of earshot. Coward, she chided herself. (The last customer of Hope Software who'd offered Alison that truism still woke up screaming in the night.)

The lawn at Hope Cottage spread out from the terrace in all directions. To the south it ended in a group of overgrown hedges beyond which could be glimpsed the top of a dilapidated summerhouse. To the west, running up to the wall which marked the boundary of the main road, was a rose garden. At that time the roses had not been pruned in years and some of them were almost as high as the wall. There was no wall to the east but a small wood ran from the village to rejoin the main road, just south of the house.

The lawn was as dry as could be so Alison didn't bother to change out of her town shoes. She made her way across it to the gap in the hedge and into the summerhouse. The wood had spread over the years and now surrounded the little house on three sides, making it cool and dark instead of the sun trap that had been intended. The sense of peace and solitude was absolute.

She sat down on the wooden bench and closed her eyes. She was still puzzling over what Nick Trevellyan had said. Whom on earth could he have taken for her husband? Then it hit her.

'Aidan!' she said aloud, opening her eyes. 'Aidan Hope.'

'In person.'

Alison leaped out of her skin and back in again when she saw who it was.

'Not a copy,' Aidan added. He sat down beside her and laughed as she pantomimed a woman dying of shock.

'Oh, I'm sorry, sweetheart, I couldn't resist it now, could I? Nobody could. Say you forgive me.' He gave her one of his most winning smiles – taking absolution, as always, for granted.

She took his arm affectionately and he kissed her on the cheek.

'What the hell are you doing here?' she demanded. 'How did you know I was here?'

'There was some stuff in the *Financial Times* a few weeks ago about you. Not a very good picture, sweetheart – you should try to smile. Something about a new silicon valley in the West Country.'

Alison remembered that stupid story. She hadn't been aware that any other computer firms were heading that way and she told the reporter so.

'So as I was going to be down this way I thought I'd look you up. I rang your old place in London and they gave me your address. I've been waiting for you since Friday. As to why I'm here, well, you need me, obviously. Why else would you be calling out my name like that?'

She explained about Nick but not his silly mistake about their relationship.

'Ah, yes. That would be me all right,' Aidan said thoughtfully. 'There was a fellow said he'd tell you I was asking for you. Well, I saw you go past the pub a few minutes ago in that lovely car of yours. Must have cost a good bit, that car. Jaguar, isn't it?'

Alison agreed absent-mindedly that it was.

'And I suppose you get that on the business, so to speak, company car, tax allowable.'

She nodded. It seemed an odd topic of conversation for two cousins who had not met for five years.

'Anyway,' Aidan went on, 'I started to follow you along the road. But then I saw this footpath leading off and I thought that it must go through your garden. I thought it would make a nicer walk on such a fine day.'

'You thought you'd sneak round the back way, you mean.'

'Then I saw you come in here and I thought I'd give you a nice surprise.'

'It was certainly a surprise. Now tell me what it is you're after.'

He looked hurt – one of his little repertoire of tricks. Very effective it was too. It made people curl up with embarrassment and dispense fivers.

'You've a sharp tongue, Alison Hope,' he said reproachfully. 'Can't a man come and look up his long-lost cousin?'

'You were the one who got lost,' she pointed out. 'Don't waste my time with the old family sentiment, Aidan. I'm not a sentimental woman.'

'True.'

'Speaking of families.' A thought struck her. 'Is Judith with you, or has she got long-lost too?'

His face clouded over and she realised her little pleasantry had hit the bull's eye.

'A temporary estrangement,' he said. 'Purely temporary. Judy will come back. She always does.'

'I'm sorry, Aidan. Truly. How is little Daniel?'

If there was one person in this world Aidan really cared about it was Daniel, whom Alison remembered as a charming but sickly child. Aidan gave a genuine smile at the thought of him.

'Well enough. Much the same. He's a nice kid.'

'Believe it or not, it's really quite nice to see you again after all these years.' She wondered why he blushed.

'You remember Adam Knox, I expect,' he said in an apparent non sequitur, wanting to get to the point before she made him feel too guilty.

Alison had to think about it for a minute. Then she remembered – Adam Knox, an actor friend of Aidan's. She'd only met him once. That was the night she had bought Aidan out of the business.

'Oh yes,' she said. 'The soap-opera man. Why? Have you seen him lately? How is he?'

'He's dead, actually. Heart gave out a couple of weeks back.'

'Good God! But he wasn't old.'

'Fifty if you believe the obituary, which I don't. Of course, he was an alcoholic, I don't suppose that helped.'

'Poor old Adam,' she said. She was quite sorry. She was about to be a lot more sorry.

'That's what brings me here really,' Aidan added.

'How d'you mean?'

He told her.

Alison didn't remember Aidan ever raising his voice in his life. He didn't now. She was the one doing the shouting. If she had known they had an audience she would have bellowed more quietly.

'Come on, Alison, be fair.' His tone was all sweet reason. 'It was a joint project.'

'I bought you out,' she screamed. 'You know I did!'

'I don't know any such thing and you just can't prove it, can you. Well, can you? Look, sweetheart, you must be worth a pile now. Look at you: this house, that Jag, those clothes. And what have I got? 'Debts up to my ears.'

'Don't *sweetheart* me. Never thought of getting a job, I suppose?'

'But I have got a job, my love. Joint managing director of Hope Software. I won't interfere in the running of the business. I won't get in the way.'

'No, I'll bet! You were never much in evidence when you did own half the business, when I was struggling to keep it going.'

'Just a little salary and a few perks, that's all. A nice car like yours maybe, share options . . . You wouldn't want a nasty scandal just as you're thinking of forming a company and going for a stock-market listing, would you? I can just see the headlines in the *FT* with yet another unflattering photo. "Cruel Cousin Cheats Childhood Companion". Or Callous – yes, that's even better than Cruel. It isn't even inaccurate. Of course, we weren't childhood companions but it has a nice alliterative effect and why spoil a good headline just because the facts don't fit?'

He was holding her arm and she wrenched away from him, almost knocking him off balance.

31

'I'll see you in hell first, Aidan Hope!'

She ran back across the lawn. At least that bloody curtain woman wasn't anywhere around to see the state she was in, she thought thankfully. She jumped into the Jaguar and roared away back up the valley.

Jenny Tilney was there when Alison got back to the house on Friday. Alison almost bumped into her when she opened the front door. To her amazement Jenny smiled at her.

'What d'you think?' She stepped back from the window.

'Very nice,' Alison said feebly.

'You made the right decision not going for Austrian blinds, too fancy.'

'Have you done my room?'

'Yes. I think you'll be pleased.'

'Only I was planning to spend the night here. I see the furniture's arrived at last.'

'Is that all of it, then?' Jenny looked unimpressed.

'I just had a little town house in London,' Alison said, wondering why she was explaining herself to Jenny. 'So long as there's something to eat off and something to sit on and a bed for me to sleep in, I'll manage for a bit.'

Jenny lost interest and turned back to her blind.

'Well, I'll just adjust this, then there's only the two middle bedrooms left. I'll do those this afternoon.'

'Thanks. Excuse me.' As Jenny clambered gracelessly onto the windowsill and began fiddling with the ratchet, Alison consulted the phone book and dialled.

'Is that the Bird in Hand? I'd like to talk to Aidan Hope, please. Tell him Alison. Thank you.'

Jenny Tilney went off to lunch shortly after, spluttering out of the courtyard in her Mini. The man who was parked a little way along the road watched until she was out of sight.

Alison went through the double doors into the drawing-room. She sat down on the chaise longue which gave her a clear view through the french windows into the garden. She put her feet up on it and gazed round her with satisfaction. With her furniture and belongings finally installed, Hope Cottage was home at last – perhaps for the rest of her life.

And bloody Aidan Hope wasn't going to spoil things.

The doorbell rang a few minutes later. She went to answer it. A Transit van was parked in the courtyard, with the words 'E & D Security' painted on the side. On the doorstep was a small balding man, in early middle age, carrying a clipboard.

'Mrs Hope? I'm Ian McCarthy of E & D Security Services. You asked us to call.' He had a nice voice, she thought, all rounded vowels and rolling Rs.

'Can I see your identification?'

McCarthy pulled a card out of his pocket. 'You've got the right idea,' he said, as she had intended. 'A lot of people just let anyone in.'

She made a fuss of examining the card. 'Right, well, you'd better come in.' She stood aside to let him through the front door. He sidled into the hall.

'There's something needs looking at right away,' he said. 'No bolts on the door. It's a good solid mortice lock but you could do with bolts top and bottom. You must have a chain too – isolated place like this.'

'I was thinking of getting an entry phone.'

'Even better. We can supply those. I'll put that down on the list, shall I?' He started scribbling on a checklist on his clipboard.

'Do you live here alone?' he asked. 'Only it makes a difference to what we might recommend. If you have a man about the house or a big dog, say . . .' He laughed.

'I live alone.'

He spent well over an hour in the house going over the buildings very thoroughly. His recommendations for the workshop seemed sensible and he made no effort to sell her unnecessary extras. Alison was very pleased with McCarthy.

Finally he finished his tour and said, 'Right, I've got several jobs up this way, so I shall be in the area for the next few days. I shall drop you in a complete list of everything we've identified that's needed with a price and an idea of when we could do it and how long it will take.'

'The sooner the better,' she said and implied that she had other estimates to consider – which she hadn't, having been too lazy to organise any. He glanced at his watch and she realised that she was expected to offer some refreshment.

'Er, would you like a cup of tea?' she asked. 'It's Earl Grey,' she added to prompt the answer no.

33

'That would be most welcome. I'm parched, to tell the truth. I talk too much.'

They sat in the kitchen and exchanged banalities as the kettle boiled. Then he said, 'Would it bother you if I smoked?'

'No, not at all.'

She almost revoked this permission when he produced a pouch of tobacco and some cigarette papers from his pocket. He proceeded to roll the thinnest cigarette she had ever seen. He puffed at it quickly, not giving it time to go out.

'I'm sure I knew a chap called Hope once,' he said. 'Still, it's not that rare a name, is it? What was his first name? . . . Let me think, something unusual. He lived down Notting Hill way a couple of years back.'

'Wasn't Irish by any chance, was he?'

'Yes, I believe he was.'

'That would be my cousin, Aidan.'

'Aidan, that was it. I didn't know him very well. I doubt he'd remember me. Whatever happened to him? Still in the Gate, is he?'

'He doesn't live there any more as far as I can make out. He's staying round here at the moment.'

'Well, what a coincidence! Of course it's nice to have your family close by.'

'Oh, Aidan and I aren't at all close.'

'So he's not staying with you, here?'

The correct answer to this, as Alison well knew, was: 'Bit nosy, aren't you?' Instead she answered civilly that Aidan was staying at the pub. She reflected wryly that she must be losing her nerve.

'Well, I must be off,' he said, leaving most of his tea. 'Thanks very much, Mrs Hope. You'll be hearing from us.'

Chapter 5

Alison woke that Saturday to a misty but fair morning which promised well for her house-warming. The caterers arrived early as there was much to do. A lot of old friends and business associates were coming down from London and making a weekend of it. She'd invited quite a few of the locals too although she wasn't sure how the two groups were going to mix. Something told her that tonight was going to be the end of an era.

She had also invited Aidan Hope. She had spent hours with her solicitor in London on Wednesday morning and none of them had been encouraging. Considering the vast sums of money she'd paid him over the years, he might at least have been able to tell her what she wanted to hear. But no. There was a partnership agreement and Aidan had a copy of it – signed and sealed. She could not prove that the agreement had ever been terminated. Those were the simple facts. Conciliation, said Jake Trowerbridge, compromise; honeyed words. Poor Jake should have known his friend and client better after all these years.

Oh no, Jake, she said to herself that morning. You're getting me mixed up with someone else. I'd rather tear my tongue out than talk sweet to Aidan now.

When she'd finished with Jake she made her way to the Tottenham Court Road and bought a miniature tape recorder with a powerful microphone. It should be possible in the course of the evening to get Aidan to admit that he had sold his share. Not in front of witnesses – he was too shrewd for that – but for the benefit of a small piece of Japanese technology. It would not be easy. Casting her mind back over their encounter in the garden she realised that even then, when he had her completely off her guard, he had not admitted that he was trying it on.

She put the tape recorder in her pocket and went round talking to some of the caterers. Then she retired to her study and played it back. She would probably get only one chance to pull this off so she mustn't screw it up. After some trial and error, the results proved satisfactory. She locked the tape recorder away in her desk.

By seven o'clock everything was ready and the caterers had retired to transform themselves into waiters. Alison went upstairs to bathe and change. It was half past eight by the time she came down again. She went into the drawing-room, flung the french windows wide open and went out on the terrace. She had had floodlights installed in the grounds but had decided not to use them tonight. They illuminated most of the garden and it wouldn't bear too close a scrutiny at the moment. She had placed flares, garden torches and candles in the least scruffy parts of the grounds and had instructed the caterers to light them as soon as night began to fall.

She slipped off her new evening sandals and examined them critically. They were really not at all comfortable. She had much better go upstairs and change them for her old black ones or she would be crippled by midnight. But at that moment the front doorbell rang. She pushed the sandals out of sight under a sofa and went to welcome some early arrivals.

Nick let himself in at the open front door and followed the sound of the music into the drawing-room. He glanced round, hardly recognising the building site of a month ago. The only people he could see whom he knew were Sir Anton and Lady Armitage and Reg Grey. Everyone else looked very smart and metropolitan.

Alison, naturally, was the focus of attention, standing in a group of people near the window. She was eye-catching in black, a single strand of pearls her only adornment – except for her hair, gleaming like newly polished copper, which was tied loosely back with a velvet ribbon. Her shoulders were bare and lightly freckled: in the artificial light they looked golden.

She spotted Nick almost at once and made her way over to him. Black was certainly her colour, he thought, showing off her hair, eyes and creamy skin to perfection. He told her so. She looked surprised. But not as surprised as Nick.

'Thank you,' she said gracefully. 'It's nice of you to say so.' She knew how to accept a compliment, he thought. She looked him up and down. It has a habit of hers – a business tycoon's trick – designed, he supposed, to discomfort, so giving her the ascendancy. He just stood meekly and did his best not to look discomforted. He must have succeeded because she soon gave it up. He decided to get his own back by teasing her a bit.

'I haven't changed that much since you first stared at me like that, have I? That day on the road outside, about six weeks ago.'

Alison went very slightly pink. 'I was hoping you'd for-gotten about that. I'm not very good at apologising, so I won't. I'd only hold it against you. I'll just say that I was in a furious temper that day because one of the builders was botching something up and I was in a hurry to get to see his boss. You were so nice to me. I felt a real rat.'

'Forget it.' He smiled, liking her.

'I didn't know policemen were allowed to wear glasses.'

'Oh yes, equal opportunities for women, ethnic minorities and the myopic.'

'Don't they get in the way?'

'Ninety-nine per cent of my job is just wandering round asking people nosy questions. I take them off if I have to wrestle a dangerous criminal to the ground.' It was his well-rehearsed reply to that question. Policemen got asked a sur-prisingly small range of questions – have you got the time? where is the post office? don't your glasses get in the way?

She laughed uncertainly. 'I'm not sure when you're being serious.'

'Rather a common complaint, I'm afraid.' Many women had accused Nick of being inscrutable. He claimed that it was an occupational hazard but the truth was that it came natur-ally to him. He changed the subject. 'Here, this is for you.'

37

He had wanted to bring her a house-warming present but had no idea what would be suitable. Then, that morning, as he was walking along Bridge Street, near his flat, he had seen the very thing in an antique (or junk) shop window.

'Just a little house-warming present,' he said, thrusting the parcel into her hands.

Alison pulled off the wrapping paper impatiently and gave an exclamation of pleasure. Nick had been rather pleased with his find. It was a print of Hope Cottage, showing the house from the courtyard. A groom held the head of a horse for a disdainful young woman, in full hunting regalia, to dismount.

'Why, it's the nicest house-warming present I've had,' she said.

'I just happened to see it by chance,' he said truthfully. 'I'm glad you like it.'

He watched her as she stood examining the picture. She wasn't a beautiful woman, nor even pretty – as Bill had so ungallantly pointed out. She had strong features and a long nose. But she certainly had something. Vitality: that was it – an appetite for life. Her scent was deliciously, expensively, musky. She was smiling up at him now and he realised that she was barefoot, which was why she seemed shorter than before. She was clutching a black velvet bag tightly as if she expected to be mugged at any moment. He realised that she was speaking again and made an effort to concentrate on what she was saying. He found the exotic scent distracting.

'There's someone over here I want you to meet.'

She led him over to a table against the far wall where the barman had obviously given up all idea of being allowed to serve Aidan Hope, who was copiously helping himself.

'I think you have met,' she said, 'but not been properly introduced. Aidan, this is Nick Trevellyan; Nick, this is Aidan Hope . . . bane of my life, a well-known troublemaker . . . my cousin.'

Her cousin! That had not occurred to him. He had dismissed the idea of a brother since there was no physical resemblance. A cousin. He smiled at Aidan with something approaching liking.

Alison said, 'I'll catch up with you later,' and went off to greet some new arrivals.

'Let me get you a drink,' Aidan said and began pouring Nick a glass of champagne without consulting his preference. 'It's all right, laddie,' he said to the barman, 'we can help ourselves. Don't you worry about us.' Appropriating another full bottle, he turned his attention back to Nick.

'I remember now, the pub. It must have been about a week ago.'

'What brings you down here?' Nick asked. 'Aidan, is it? Unusual name.'

'Not in Ireland. I've come to see Allie on business. The firm is half mine, you see: Hope Software, I mean – my brainchild actually. Surely Allie must have mentioned me, her partner.'

'Well, I hardly know her really.'

'Not many people do.' Aidan moved a little closer and muttered 'At Cambridge we used to call her "No Hope".'

Nick wanted to enquire further into that but couldn't think of the right question. Instead he said, 'So you're staying here now, are you? At Hope Cottage?'

'No, I'm still at the pub. It's a bit of a dump but I won't be there for much longer.'

'There must be masses of room here,' Nick said, in surprise. 'Five bedrooms, not to mention the attic floor.'

'You seem to know the place well for someone who hardly knows Allie,' Aidan said.

Hello, Nick thought, unexpected alertness.

'I had what you might call a guided tour a few weeks ago,' he explained or rather didn't.

'Well, we don't want to live in each other's pockets, do we? Even if we are cousins.'

'It seems odd that she didn't seem to be expecting you,' Nick said demurely, sipping his champagne. He wasn't sure what to make of this man. He'd had ten years of practice in sizing people up and Aidan Hope didn't fit into any of the usual categories. His intuition – his policeman's nose – told him that there was a sharp intellect behind these moist brown eyes.

'I wasn't sure when I could get away,' Aidan was saying. 'I was over tying up a business deal in Ireland, you see. Got it all signed up faster than I thought. Couldn't get hold of Allie to let her know I was coming.'

'Still, I expect we shall be seeing quite a lot of you round here from now on.'

'Oh, I don't think so. I shall be back off to London as soon as Allie's signed a few papers. There's so much to do that end. We can't all indulge ourselves playing the country squire. I don't know how you all stand it down here. What do you do for excitement?'

'Oh, my job gives me a bit of excitement.'

'What job is that?' Aidan asked dutifully.

'I'm a policeman.' Nick spotted an imaginary acquaintance across the room, excused himself to Aidan, who had suddenly gone very quiet, and left him to it. He exchanged a few polite words with the Armitages before stepping out on the terrace. A few minutes later he noticed Alison take Aidan by the arm and lead him out of the room. He was not pleased to see that Jack Ashcroft had arrived.

He was even less pleased an hour later to find himself stuck talking to Ashcroft and Reg Grey. Jack was holding forth, as usual, on his favourite topics although he had not yet said anything offensive to either policeman. Nick was wondering how best to get away when Ashcroft switched the subject suddenly. He nudged Nick in the ribs and nodded his head to where Alison was now standing by the french windows talking to a good-natured, pleasantly rounded girl called, Nick had earlier discovered, Janine.

'Pretty little pair of birds. Why are they wasting their time gossiping to each other, I wonder?'

'I don't think they are gossiping,' Nick said. 'When I came past just now they were talking about databases.' Whatever they were.

'You were dancing with that bird earlier, weren't you, the one with dark hair? Nice tits. Any luck with her?' Honestly, he was like something out of a play, Nick thought. Sir Jasper, probably.

'She seems a very nice girl,' he said politely. 'Her name's Janine.'

'Is she as friendly as she looks, though, that's what I'd like to know? Is it worth my while asking her to dance?'

'If you want to dance, then yes,' Nick said, playing dumb.

Ashcroft gave him a pitying look. 'You're not queer, are you?' he asked abruptly.

Nick had no doubts on that subject but he pretended to consider the question. Ashcroft's face with its boozy breath was pressed close up against Nick's waiting for an answer. Nick thought of offering him a kiss but decided that Reg wouldn't like it. It didn't hold much appeal for him either.

'I don't think so,' he said, affecting a slightly worried expression. Ashcroft gave him a sharp look, unsure if he was being mocked, then resumed his theme.

'I don't know what to make of our hostess, though.' He undressed Alison with his eyes. 'She's got a good body, I'll give you that, nice legs. But I'm not sure she'd keep a bloke warm in bed. What d'you reckon?' The total lack of response from his audience did not deter him in the least.

'No,' he pronounced decisively, 'freeze your balls off you as soon as look at you. I like a woman to have a bit of flesh on her anyway, something to get your teeth into. It has to be the brunette. Here.' He thrust his empty glass at Nick as if he were a waiter and headed off across the room.

Reg and Nick watched his progress in silence, then Reg said, 'I've never had much time for this women's lib business but I do see what you meant about him, Nick.' They watched Jack steer Janine off towards the terrace with a hand on her bottom.

'You don't suppose he meant that literally, about the teeth?' Nick asked.

'Wouldn't surprise me. But then I spent two years in the Vice Squad so it's hard to imagine what would. Why, once . . .'

For a moment Nick thought Reg was about to expand on his years in the Vice Squad – an experience he had hitherto kept better guarded that the crown jewels – but then Alison came towards them and Reg's anecdote disappeared into the mists of might-have-been.

Alison made a face. 'I don't think much of your friend's manners.'

'He's not our friend,' Nick pointed out, 'and you must have invited him.'

'Yes, I suppose I did. Somebody introduced us and I found

41

out he lived only a mile away so it seemed the obvious thing to do. He was polite enough at the time.' She looked at Nick. 'Why are you holding two empty glasses?' He gestured helplessly. 'Put them down and come and dance with me,' she suggested. Nick looked around for somewhere to stow the glasses, then handed them to Reg, who gave him an odd look.

It was now about ten-thirty. Aidan Hope had reappeared and was still laying into the champagne.

Nick led Alison along the terrace until they found a spot which was not too crowded. The music was quite slow and he put an arm around her waist and drew her close to him. She had grown taller again.

He glanced down and said, 'Oh, you've put some shoes on now. Good – I won't have to worry about treading on your toes.' She put her hands on his shoulders and he noticed that she no longer carried the evening bag.

After a few minutes Alison said, 'I must go and replace some of the lights. Come and help.' She led him into the kitchen and handed him a pile of flares. She picked up a box of garden candles and led the way out through the conservatory.

'The caterers are supposed to be doing this but I think they've all had too much champagne.' She looked a little flushed herself and her eyes sparkled in the half-light.

'It may not be worthwhile,' Nick said. 'It's going to rain in a few minutes.'

'Surely not, it's been a lovely day.'

'It's been a very close day. There's thunder in the air. I can sense it.'

'What gifts you country folk have,' she said mockingly. 'I rang the Met office this morning. There were no storms forecast.'

Nick shrugged and changed the subject. 'Is country life all you hoped for, Alison, now you've had a few weeks to get to know it?'

'It's not really what I expected. I haven't seen a single forelock-tugging peasant in all these weeks.'

'They're all indoors watching television,' he said.

'Seriously, I can see you think I'm a townie, but I grew up in the country. I knew it wasn't going to be Ambridge.'

'Where was that? Where you grew up.'

'Shropshire, the Welsh Marches, near Ludlow.'

'It's rural there, all right. What made you retire to the West Country instead?'

'I'll let *retire* pass. I've no family up there now – my parents are both dead, you see. And I like to be near the sea. I think I'm going to like it here. You haven't always lived here, surely?'

'Oh yes, I have. Except for three years at Oxford, I've been here all my life.'

'Oxford man?' She looked him over again. 'Whatever made you become a policeman?'

'I always intended it, since as long as I can remember. Not here, though, I was going to go to London after finals and join the Met.'

'Why didn't you?'

'Plans change,' he said evasively. He was not about to tell his life story to Alison Hope. How Ruth had told him, exams safely over, that she was going to marry someone else, sending him running home to the West Country to lick his wounds. Nor how, once back in Hopbridge, he had experienced an unexpected sense of homecoming; nor how, three months later, it had occurred to him with a rude shock that he could no longer remember Ruth's face very clearly.

'I was at County HQ for the first few years,' he told her instead, 'then a couple of years ago they sent me here – back to my home town.'

'What did you read at Oxford?'

'French and Italian.' It had never come in very useful although, when he had been at County, they had sometimes dragged him in to talk to a French national who'd sneaked off the boat with half a kilo of cannabis or a pet white rat.

'Is an inspector important?' she asked.

'It depends who you're talking to. A beat constable and the chief constable might give you very different answers.'

'I'm sure the chief constable would be very tactful and say all his men were vital.'

'Exactly. While the beat constable would tell you I'm quite surplus to requirements.'

Alison laughed and led the way along the edge of the wood, replacing flares as she went, until they reached the hedgerow.

'Come and have a look at my favourite statue,' she said.

They passed through a gap in the hedge to where a statue guarded the entrance of the ramshackle summerhouse. It was of a half-naked woman, curved and rounded in a way which was no longer fashionable. She lacked one arm.

'I call her Semi Venus,' Alison said proudly. Actually it was Persephone since her remaining hand held a pomegranate but Nick didn't think it was the moment to enlighten her.

'She's a fine-looking woman,' he said aloud. And so are you, he added – but only to himself. What would you do, Alison Hope, if I were to kiss you? Are you waiting for me to kiss you or am I completely misreading the signals? Is it worth the experiment? Nick had had his share of women over the years but he was never quick to assume a woman's interest. Probably she was just flirting with him to keep her hand in. He put the remaining flares down on the pedestal just in case.

Back at the house a lot of noise and shouting had broken out. They ran back to the gap in the hedge. They were just in time to see Aidan Hope punch Jack Ashcroft in the stomach.

Chapter 6

Ashcroft doubled up, staggered a few feet across the terrace and was sick over the parapet. Nick began to run back to the house, Alison following a few feet behind. Ashcroft lay on the flagstones, a look of stunned disbelief on his face. Aidan was poised over him for another blow, just waiting for Ashcroft to straighten up. None of the onlookers seemed capable of movement. Nick grabbed Aidan by the arm and dragged him bodily back into the house. Alison looked in concern at Ashcroft, who was being sick again.

'I haven't finished,' Aidan said drunkenly. 'I'm not done with him.' He began to struggle. Reg Grey appeared beside them and took hold of Aidan's other arm.

'That's enough,' he said mildly. 'Calm down now. You've given him a nasty shock. Let it go.'

Alison came in through the french windows, Ashcroft trailing miserably behind her, and looked at them quizzically. Nick made a quick decision.

'I'll take Jack home. It'll only take me a few minutes. He can't drive in his condition.'

'Thank you,' Alison said. 'I'll take care of Aidan. I think he should get home too.'

'Perhaps he should lie down for a while, in a spare bedroom or something,' Nick suggested.

'No!' she said sharply. 'Once he moves in I'll never get rid of him. He's going back to the pub.'

'I can come back for him, afterwards,' Nick offered. 'It's only at the Bird in Hand, isn't it?'

45

'No,' she said again. 'I'll walk him back along the footpath. The fresh air will do him good. He's a bit groggy.'

'Do you want any help?' Reg Grey asked of nobody in particular.

'Just out to my car perhaps,' Nick said, taking him at his word. 'It's only a mile. He can pick his own car up in the morning.'

Nick and Reg bundled Jack Ashcroft out of the front door and into Nick's car. He got in and started the engine.

'Don't you dare be sick in my car, Jack.'

Neither man spoke during the short journey. As they reached Threeoaks Farm there was a rumble of thunder and it began to rain quite heavily. Nick took Ashcroft's keys off him and opened the farmhouse door.

'Come on, Jack, time for bed. You'll feel much better in the morning.'

'I'll get that Irish pig for this,' Jack said sullenly. 'He didn't have to go mad like that.' He slumped down on the sofa and moaned softly to himself. Nick switched on the electric fire. He couldn't let the silly fool catch his death. He'd only come back to haunt him.

'I'll make you some coffee, Jack. Black, I think.'

'Just fuck off and leave me alone, will you.'

Nick glanced out at the downpour. He didn't intend to catch his death either. 'Nothing I'd like better, but I'll make us both some coffee first.'

By the time Nick got back to Hope Cottage it was half past eleven. The storm was over and the rain had ceased as abruptly as it had begun.

He went back into the house. The windows were still closed against the elements. The caterers had produced another case of champagne and some more food and the party looked set to go on all night. He stood leaning against the drawing-room doorway. Nick leant against things a lot, usually with his hands in his pockets – it had been purgatory when he was in uniform.

Alison came down the stairs and he stood watching her descent. She had changed and was now wearing a navy-blue dress with a white collar. She looked like a demure schoolgirl. Ashcroft had been right about one thing – she did have good legs.

'I got soaked,' she said indignantly. 'It did rain after all.' She indicated the black dress which lay, dripping, over her arm.

'Is your cousin all right?' Nick asked.

'He wasn't as shaken as he made out. I left him at the end of the footpath. It was pouring down and I didn't want to get any wetter than I already was.' She shook her damp hair. 'Thanks for getting rid of Ashcroft. You're nice, aren't you?' Damned with faint praise, Nick thought ruefully. When did the *nice* man ever get the girl?

'What on earth was the row about?' he asked to distract attention from his niceness.

'God knows. Didn't Ashcroft say? Aidan isn't the easiest man in the world to get on with but I've never known it come to blows before.' She set off along the hall in the direction of the kitchen.

'Jack Ashcroft could have picked a quarrel with Albert Schweitzer,' Nick said.

It was well after midnight and most of the older guests had gone. Reg Grey showed no signs of leaving – he'd got nothing to get home for. His wife had left him more years ago than anyone could remember – opinion divided as to whether he had noticed or not. He was quite happy, smoking one of his pipes and slurping champagne as though it was his normal tipple.

'Really a beer man myself, but its not bad, this stuff,' he told Nick. Nick felt a sudden surge of affection for him. He seemed to be the little friend of all the world that night, ministering to Jack, being nice to Reg.

The storm had left the night air cool and fresh. Alison reopened the french windows and the guests spilled out into the gardens once more.

Since Reg was blowing smoke all over him, Nick edged him out on the terrace as soon as he could. The storm had brought out the scent of the flowers and Reg instantly set off to examine Alison's rose garden, dragging Nick with him.

'Some of these strains have gone out of fashion and you hardly see them any more,' he enthused. 'It's really interesting.'

47

'It's really muddy, Reg,' Nick said good-naturedly. He turned, hearing his name being called.

'Nick! You're wanted on the phone,' Alison called. 'It's your minder – Sergeant Deacon.' Reg and Nick exchanged looks.

'*Work*,' Nick said resignedly. They both set off for the house at a run. Nick picked up the receiver in the hall.

Bill Deacon's voice said, 'Sir? I'm really sorry to disturb you. Lucky I remembered where you were. We've had a call from the constable in Little Hopford. He's at the Bird in Hand pub. They've got a body, one of the guests.'

'Accident?' Nick suggested hopefully.

'No, sir. He's had his head bashed in.'

'Wait a minute. They only have one room to let at the Bird in Hand, and we know who's staying there.'

'That's right, it's that Irish fellow we were talking to that day.'

'Aidan Hope! Christ!' Nick was temporarily stunned into silence. It wasn't often a murder victim turned out to be someone you were chatting to a couple of hours before.

'OK,' he said after a moment. 'You take charge out there. I'm going to stay here for the time being. I want you to send a couple of constables out to me, at Hope Cottage. Make one of them a WPC, if you can. When they get here I'll join you at the pub.' He hung up and explained the situation to Reg Grey in a low voice.

Reg said, 'We're staying here for the time being?'

We! It was an awkward situation and Nick hoped to God that Reg wouldn't try to take charge. He said, 'Yes, sir. I'm not leaving here until I can get the names and addresses of everyone here tonight, especially the ones who witnessed the quarrel between Jack Ashcroft and Aidan Hope. Will you stay here and make sure that no one leaves while I break the news to Miss Hope?'

'You're in charge, Nick. Glad to help. It's nice to be back in the field after all these years.'

Nick found Alison back in the drawing-room.

'Don't tell me,' she said, 'you've got to leave.'

'Can I have a word with you, somewhere quiet?'

She looked at him in surprise. 'Sure. Let's go into the sitting-room next door, shall we?'

Nick shut the door of the empty sitting-room firmly behind them. He didn't usually get lumbered with the job of breaking the news to the bereaved so he was a bit out of practice, but he owed it to her to tell her without delay. He decided to jump in with both feet.

'I'm very sorry, Alison, but I've got some bad news for you. That call was about your cousin.'

'Aidan?' She looked puzzled. 'But he's not been gone long. Has he had an accident?'

'There's no way to break it gently, really. He's been found dead at the pub.'

Alison was silent for a moment, trying to take it in.

'He was a useless bugger,' she said at last. 'But I was fond of him in an odd sort of way. We had our differences but I certainly didn't wish this on him. How did it happen? It wasn't something horrible like choking on his own vomit, was it?'

Nick sighed. He obviously wasn't very good at this. He'd have given a lot for a motherly WPC at that moment. He took a deep breath.

'I'm not making myself very clear. Your cousin has been murdered.'

Alison reeled and he sprang forward in case she should faint, cursing himself for not making her sit down before he told her. But she recovered herself and stepped back, feeling for the window seat. She sat down heavily on it.

'I must ask for your help, Miss Hope,' Nick said briskly – from the little he knew of her he thought she would best be kept occupied. 'I'm expecting two constables here at any moment. They will have to take the names and addresses of everyone at the party. In the meantime no one may leave the house. In fact I'd like you to collect everyone in the drawing-room and keep them there. The party's over, I'm afraid.'

'You can't think it has any connection with the party!'

Nick shrugged. 'This was the last place he visited, the last place he was seen alive perhaps. Quite a few people must have witnessed the quarrel he had with Ashcroft. I shall want to know the details. Will you help me?'

'Yes, of course. I'll tell everyone there's been an accident.' She got up and walked past him stiffly, back out into the hall.

49

He followed her. She passed Reg Grey without a word and went into the drawing-room.

Reg looked questioningly at Nick. 'She's taking it coolly, I must say.'

'She was pretty stunned, actually. But I think she wouldn't like to let it show – not to strangers.'

Fortunately Reg Grey, with unusual tact, did not offer to accompany Nick to the village. Nick left the constables collecting details.

'I want two lists,' he told them. 'One of everybody at the party and one of people who witnessed a fight at about a quarter to eleven. Then you'd better let them go. Don't let anyone go upstairs, though. Or anywhere else except to the cloakroom to get their coats. I may want to search the place later. Miss Hope will just have to wait down here until I get back, I'm afraid.'

Chapter 7

Nick reached the Bird in Hand at one o'clock. Bill was waiting for him at the foot of the stairs which led up to Aidan Hope's room.

'I couldn't get hold of DC Penruan, sir, so I left a message for him. The SOCOs are up there now and the photographers have already finished. Do you want to take a look at the body?' The question was rhetorical and Nick did not bother to answer it but started up the stairs. No, he didn't want to look at a dead body – who does? But look at it he would.

'Who found him?' he asked.

'Jos. He's waiting in the bar with his family. Their rooms are up here too and I couldn't let them up just yet. It's this door on the right.'

Nick nodded and pushed open the door with his elbow. Bill laid a hand on his arm.

'He's a bit of a mess, sir.'

Nick took a deep breath. 'OK,' he said and went in.

The tiny room was full of bodies. Considering the disadvantage Aidan Hope started off with, being the only dead one, he had succeeded remarkably well in making himself the centre of attention. He was lying face down on the bed, dressed in the same clothes he had been wearing at the party – black jeans and a green and white checked shirt. They were still damp from the rain.

Nick put his hands in his pockets. He always claimed that this was a reliable method of not touching anything he shouldn't. He moved closer to the bed and looked down at the remnants of Aidan Hope's head.

The back of his skull had been smashed in by several blows and the blood was congealed into a patch of dark red with white specks. Nick's first horrified thought was that these were pieces of brain but then he realised, with relief, that it was foam from the pillow. For Hope's bedroom had been ransacked, as if by a maniac: every drawer and cupboard stood open, its contents strewn about the room; bedding and clothes were scattered everywhere; the pillows had been ripped open.

Nick stared at the corpse for a few minutes, unable to tear his eyes from it, then turned away at last. He felt sick.

'Somebody had it in for him,' Bill said inadequately. 'They must have hit him a dozen times. They weren't taking any chances.'

'Panic, maybe.' Nick stared at the floor, anything rather than at the lump on the bed. 'He was pretty drunk when last I saw him. I think he just lay down here and went to sleep, or even fell unconscious. Killing him must have been the easiest job in the world.'

'You saw him this evening?'

'Yes, he was at Hope Cottage. We'll have to get back there tonight.'

'Sir!' One of the SOCOs jumped up like a man who has just discovered a tenth planet orbiting the sun. 'I think we've got our murder weapon.' He lifted some of Aidan's clothes from the fireplace and pointed to a heavy glass ashtray which was lying face down in the grate. It was square with sharply pointed corners. The base was stained a reddish brown. He sniffed at the shirt which had been lying on top of the ashtray.

'Blood, definitely.' He held the shirt out towards Nick in his rubber-gloved hands. Nick turned away.

'I'm prepared to take your word for it, Harrison! Get the photographer back to get pictures of the ashtray before you move it.'

'Yes, sir.'

'Well, that's something,' Nick said to Bill. 'And it's also clear that the room was ransacked after the murder, not before. So Hope didn't get back earlier than expected to find his room being burgled and have a fight with the intruder. The intruder murdered him deliberately and then turned the room

52

upside down.' But in search of what? They might never know. The victim wasn't in a position to tell them what was missing.

'Do you know what time he left the party?' Bill asked.

'It was ten to eleven.' He told Bill about the fight. 'He would have been back here by eleven.'

'Did he come back alone?'

'No, Alison Hope walked him back, at least as far as this end of the footpath. She didn't come into the pub, according to her. What time was the body found?'

'Quarter past twelve.'

'Why was it found?' Nick wondered. 'Surely in the normal course of events he wouldn't have been disturbed until morning.'

'Right. Jos Leighland closed at midnight – he had an extension tonight. He was locking up, checking everything was OK out the back. Then he noticed that the window pane was broken.' Bill gestured to the window. It stood wide open and, when Nick crossed to the opening and looked out, taking care not to touch any part of the window or sill, he saw that it had a hole the size of a saucer in it, a few inches from the catch, just big enough for a man's hand.

'Nice neat hole,' he remarked. 'Professional job.'

'Jos came up here, knocked and called out. Got no reply, of course. So he opened the door, took one look, bolted out and dialled 999.'

Nick stayed by the window. He was glad of the fresh air.

'Did he see Hope get back here last night?' he asked.

'No, this part of the building leads directly off the passageway, as you saw. You don't have to go through either of the bars to get to it. It's only locked up at night and Jos had given Hope a key and didn't expect him back until late as Hope had told him he was going to a party. Do you want to talk to him yourself tonight?'

'No, leave it until morning. Have they finished out in the passageway yet?'

'Yes, and the bathroom. There's just the one which the family and the guest room both use.'

'Tell Jos to get off to bed then, if he thinks he can sleep. Doc Brewster should be here at any minute, then we'll get back to Hope Cottage.'

There was something Nick wanted to check; something was nagging at his mind.

A few minutes later there was a flurry of activity in the passageway as Mike Brewster – the regular police doctor – made his entrance, bending his tall frame through the low doorway. He looked as if he'd just come from a party himself.

'I don't know why people can't get themselves killed at civilised hours,' he said callously, by way of greeting. 'I've just got back from a dinner party and I was looking forward to my bed. Ugh, what a mess. Head wounds bleed a lot,' he added, unnecessarily.

Dr Brewster looked at his watch. 'Half past one, now. He hasn't been dead all that long. A couple of hours, I'd say. He's nice and warm still.'

'We already know the time of death within an hour and a quarter,' Nick objected. 'Can't you pin it down any closer than that?'

Mike looked interested. 'Shouldn't think so,' he said, to nobody's surprise. 'Got a witness, have you?'

'Yes, me. I was one of the last people to see him alive. The body was found less than an hour and a half later. And it would have taken him ten minutes to get back here. Cause of death?'

'Don't ask stupid questions, Nick. He's been bashed on the head with something heavy and sharp. Only the postmortem will show if that was the cause of death.'

'I know,' Nick said patiently. 'But you must have some first impressions.'

'Well, there's plenty of blood, which implies he was alive when his head got split open. That's as far as I'm prepared to go.'

'When can you fit him in?'

'I'm not doing it tomorrow, or rather today, if that's what you mean. My Sundays are sacrosanct even if yours aren't. Get on to the coroner's office and he'll get done first thing Monday morning, don't you worry. I don't need him any more. If the photographers have finished you can wheel him away.'

Nick nodded to the waiting ambulance men who bundled Aidan unceremoniously into a body bag and took him out.

54

'Leave a constable here overnight,' he told Bill. 'Arrange for him to be relieved first thing tomorrow. Everyone else back to Hope Cottage with me.'

Alison was sitting dismally in an armchair in the drawing-room, her head buried in her hands. Apart from a woman detective constable only Janine and her man friend were there. He was sleeping fitfully on the sofa. She was confirming Nick's earlier judgement of her by comforting Alison and generally making herself useful.

'Is the superintendent still here?' Nick asked DC Halsgrove in a low voice.

'No, sir. He said he wouldn't wait.'

'Thank God for that! Got all the names and addresses, Carol?'

'Yes, sir. I've let everyone go as you said. Apparently Miss Hope had offered to put these two up for the night.'

'All right, I shall need you in a minute.' He turned to Alison. 'I should like your consent to search the house, Miss Hope.' She looked at him, bewildered.

'This was the last place Aidan Hope visited before his death,' he explained. 'He didn't stay in this room all evening so I should like to have a look round in case there is anything here of use in my investigation. If you agree to the search, anything I find will be taken away and may be used in evidence. You are not under suspicion at present and you are not obliged to give consent.' Since he then classed Alison as a friend, Nick gave her the full rigmarole. He wished he hadn't since Janine picked him up on it sharply.

'How could she be obliged to give consent? It's a contradiction in terms.'

'I agree,' Nick said gravely. Obviously someone at the Home Office hadn't had their educational advantages. 'What about it, Miss Hope?'

'What sort of thing are you looking for?'

'I don't know unless I find it. Probably the whole thing will be a waste of time, but it's possible that the murderer was here, at this party, tonight.'

She made a weary gesture which he took for assent. Bill and the constables followed him out into the hall.

'Search Miss Hope's bedroom suite and the guest room, since they'll be in use tonight,' he told them. 'Oh, and her study. The rest must wait until tomorrow.'

'Are we looking for anything in particular?' Bill asked.

'Well, you could keep an eye out for a black velvet evening bag. I suppose it will be in Miss Hope's bedroom or dressing-room. Bring it to me if you find it. I'll be in the drawing-room.' That was what had been nagging.

'I must have that consent in writing, Miss Hope,' Nick said, when he got back to her. 'I'll write it out for you and just ask you to sign it, shall I?' She nodded.

'I shall be leaving some constables here overnight, and I shall be back myself early tomorrow. You will be quite safe here. Is there anybody you would like me to telephone for you?'

Alison shook her head. 'I'll be OK. I've given Jan and Peter a bed for the night. I think I'll go up myself.'

'In a minute, when my people have finished up there. I'll take a full statement from you tomorrow but I'd like to ask you a few questions now if you feel up to it.'

Janine got up. 'I'll make some tea,' she said. He smiled at her gratefully. 'Would you like some, Nick?'

'Please.' He sat down opposite Alison, who gave him the ghost of a smile.

'Times like this I wish I smoked.'

'I know what you mean. Miss Hope, you told me earlier you left your cousin at the end of the footpath. Is that correct? You don't want to change that statement?'

'I wasn't making a statement,' she said sulkily. 'I was just talking to you. But I don't want to change it. I left him where the footpath comes out to the road.'

'What time was that?'

'It must have been just on eleven. What time did he die? I suppose you won't tell me that if I'm a suspect.'

Nick leant back in his chair and looked at her for a moment.

'We don't know,' he said at last. 'It's unlikely that we shall know for sure even after the postmortem. The pathologist won't be able to pin it down any closer than the times we already have. And what makes you think you're a suspect? I just said you weren't under suspicion.'

'"At present" you said. You're searching my house, questioning me.'

'Pure routine really.' A useful formula and true enough in this case, as far as he knew. 'After all, you're a very important witness. It looks as if you were the last person to see him alive.'

'Except the murderer!' Alison said, with a brief return to her usual spirited delivery.

Yes, of course, Nick thought, that was what I meant.

Janine came in with a tea tray and poured out two cups. 'I'll be in the kitchen if you want me.'

'Thank you,' Nick said, 'but I shall talk to you tomorrow.'

'Are you all right, Alison?'

'She's all right.'

Janine looked uncertain but, realising that he was waiting for her to go, she went out again.

'Should I send for my solicitor?' Alison sipped her tea without tasting it.

I'd much rather you didn't. Just tell me what happened. If you've nothing to hide then you've nothing to worry about.

'That's entirely up to you' was what Nick actually said. 'One thing I must ask, Miss Hope, we would like to take your fingerprints, for elimination purposes. Sergeant Deacon will take them before we leave if you could just be patient a few more minutes.' This time he didn't tell her she needn't consent. He had done enough to make his own life difficult.

At that moment Bill came into the room and said, 'Excuse me, sir, was this what you were looking for?' He held up the black velvet bag. Nick glanced quickly back at Alison but she was not looking at them.

'Where was it, sergeant?' he asked deliberately.

'In Mrs Hope's dressing-room, sir. In . . . um . . . her underwear drawer, sir.' The image of Bill poking through Alison Hope's underwear might have raised a smile in normal circumstances.

Alison looked up at this, saw the bag and made a gesture of protest. Nobody took any notice.

'There's a tape-recorder in it,' Bill went on. 'A miniature. Nice bit of workmanship.'

'Take it in to the station,' Nick said. 'We'll get it transcribed in the morning.'

'Now wait a minute . . .' Alison began.

'I'll give you a receipt for it, Miss Hope.' He thought for a moment that she was going to make a fuss, then she subsided back on to her chair with a sigh.

'I can't find anything else that's likely to interest us,' Bill said.

'We'll search the rest of the house tomorrow.'

While Bill took Alison's fingerprints, Nick had a last word with the uniformed constable who would be keeping an eye on the place overnight to make sure that neither Alison nor her guests went into any of the rooms which had yet to be searched.

Nick left his car at the house and Bill drove them the three miles back to Hopbridge in silence. They had the roads to themselves until they got into town. As they reached the turning to West Hopbridge, two fire engines – silent red giants – were waiting to turn out on to the bridge, heading for home.

'One of those high-rise council blocks been struck by lightning,' Nick suggested.

'Someone smoking in bed, more likely,' replied Bill, who had the suburban home-owner's prejudice against the unmortgaged.

They pulled into the police station, where the night relief seemed to be enjoying its usual slack period, and went up to Nick's office. He was shivering.

'It's freezing in here.' He was still in his shirt sleeves. Bill, who had been called out from home after the storm, was well wrapped up. Nick rummaged in a filing cabinet and found a sweater, which he pulled over his head.

'That's better.' They sat down. 'Nice early start tomorrow,' Nick said. 'Hadn't made any plans for Sunday dinner, had you?'

'Huh!'

'First thing is to get hold of Hope's next of kin.'

'That'll be Mrs Alison Hope, surely, sir?'

'Sorry, Bill. My brain must have seized up. We were misled there – he's Miss Hope's cousin, not her husband. But there is a wife since he mentioned her that day in the pub, remember? We'll ask Miss Hope about that first thing.

'Two, get that tape transcribed.'

'Odd thing that. What do you reckon it is?'

'Miss Hope was carrying it in that bag when she went out with Aidan during the party. They were gone for quite a while. Then when she came back she wasn't carrying it. Obviously she wanted to record something, their conversation presumably, and I'd very much like to know why.'

'Three?'

'Three, have a long chat with Jack Ashcroft. He came off much the worse in that fight and he did actually say he'd get even with Hope over it.'

'Odd thing that,' Bill said again. 'Ashcroft being such a big, belligerent sort of bloke. Hope was quite a little chap.'

'Jack talks a good fight. He relies on his nasty tongue and his reputation. Put him in a real scrap and he keels over. He was swearing revenge when I left him last night, but then he would. We'd better get a search warrant sworn out as soon as we can haul a JP out of bed in the morning. Someone can bring it out to us at Hope Cottage. Get one for there and the pub and Threeoaks.'

'Any ideas yet, sir?'

'Not one, Bill. What I can't get over is that the whole thing happened almost right under my nose. It makes me look a complete idiot, doesn't it? Which reminds me that you'd best take a fresh set of prints off me – just in case.' Bill duly obliged. 'Get off home now,' Nick told him. 'Susie will be worried.'

'Asleep more like.' But Bill got up and put his coat on. They arranged for him to pick Nick up at his flat early the following morning.

Bill Deacon went home to his suburb of Hopbridge. Nick lived just round the corner from the police station in the Market Square. He didn't feel at all sleepy at that moment. He picked up the tape recorder and turned it over in his hand a few times. Then he rewound the tape and started it. Alison's voice came out first, unmistakable in its self-assurance – its certainty of her place at the top of the tree.

'I want to talk some more about what you said.'

'Been thinking it over, have you? Been to see your fancy lawyer, I bet. What did he say?'

59

'Let's be civilised about this, Aidan. I don't want to quarrel with you. Of course I can prove that you don't still own half the business but it could take a long time and drag through the courts for years. I'm sure we can come to some sensible arrangement.'

'That's my girl.'

'After all, since Adam's death you and I are the only two people who know for sure that I paid you off five years ago.'

'You're the only person who thinks that, lovely. I have no recollection of it at all. You must have been dreaming.'

Nick rewound the machine and played the same passage again a few times. The more he heard it, the less he liked it.

'Lawyers, courts, quarrels,' he said aloud, 'how horribly familiar. I shall be wanting a few details, Miss Alison Hope.'

He left the tape with the desk sergeant with orders that it should be transcribed with all urgency. He walked round the corner to his flat, fell into bed and slept, untroubled by the macabre image of Aidan Hope, until Bill's ringing at the doorbell wakened him.

Chapter 8

Their first call on Sunday morning was at the Bird in Hand. Detective Constable Penruan was already waiting for them outside the sealed room.

'Any trouble during the night, Paul?' Nick asked him.

'As quiet as the grave, sir.' Paul Penruan had a gift for the *mot injuste*.

'All right,' Nick said to the landlord, who was grumbling at being woken early. 'Let's go somewhere for a quiet chat.'

They went into the bar. Nick asked the questions while Bill made notes of what was said.

'How long had Aidan Hope been staying here?' he began.

'About a week. He arrived that day you saw him here.'

'Did he give a reason for staying in the neighbourhood?'

'Well, he said he was related to that Miss Hope up at the big house.'

'You know her?'

'Everyone knows her by now. Plenty of money and not mean with it either.'

'Had she been to see Hope here?'

Jos thought about it. 'No,'. he said at last. 'She has been in but not in the last week. She rang up, though, asking to speak to him. Friday morning it was.'

'Did you hear any of the conversation?'

'Well, just this end, naturally. He said something like "OK, see you tomorrow then". That's all.'

'How did he sound? I mean, was he shouting or speaking angrily or anything like that?'

'Not at all. I never heard him raise his voice all the time he was here.'

'Did anyone else come in asking for him?'

'No. No, I'm sure not.'

'You told me the other day that Jack Ashcroft had been in. Does he often drink here?'

'Not really. He drinks in the Gordon Arms at Great Hopford as a rule. He comes in occasionally.'

'Been in during the last week?'

'No, definitely not.'

'What time did you last see Aidan Hope alive?'

'It must have been just after eight o'clock. He said he was going to a party. He didn't say where and I didn't ask. He didn't have a car so I suppose if I'd thought about it I would have assumed it was at the big house. But I didn't think about it.'

'And you didn't see him come home?'

'No, I assumed he'd be pretty late because he was a drinking man, was Hope, and I thought if he was going to a party with free booze he wouldn't be in a hurry to get back. The room we let and our own living quarters have their entrance from the alleyway with a locking door, so I gave him a key and said I'd be locking up at about half past twelve and he could let himself in.'

'Is that door kept locked normally?'

'Not while we're open. Just at night.'

'You had an extension last night, I believe.'

'There was a party,' Jos said defensively. 'Eighteenth birthday. We had a whole crowd in, not all of them local people. So don't ask me if I saw any strangers, because I saw dozens. We had a disco so there was an almighty row and we had the extension so nobody went home until gone midnight. I don't normally worry much about the guest room. It's up to whoever's staying there to keep it locked. You wouldn't expect them to keep anything worth stealing in there.'

'All right,' Nick said mildly. 'No one's blaming you for anything. What time did the disco start?'

'About nine.'

It had been his lucky night. The murderer's, not Aidan's. A lot of noise, plenty of non-regulars around. 'So what happened at closing time?' Nick asked.

'We were that knackered we decided to leave most of the clearing-up until this morning. I went round to lock up. I always check out the back, what with the storeroom and all. I saw the broken window and thought I'd better investigate. When there was no answer to my knock I tried the door. It wasn't locked. That's it. I found him, I dialled 999. I wish I'd never set eyes on him.'

'What did you make of him?' Nick asked curiously. 'What sort of a man was Aidan Hope?' He hadn't been able to make Aidan out so he was keen to find out what other people thought of him.

Jos looked oddly wary. Probably no more than the old superstition about not speaking ill of the dead. He cleared his throat.

'He seemed all right at first – very friendly sort of bloke. But as I got to know him, I took a bit of a dislike to him, nothing you could put your finger on. Like, he was a troublemaker somehow. Or not even that, but the sort of bloke trouble follows about. Know what I mean?'

Nick nodded. He knew what Jos meant.

'OK, I won't bother you any longer,' he said, getting up. 'My sergeant will take your fingerprints since they're likely to be in the room, and he'll want the name and address of the person whose party it was. We shall want a written statement from you too, as soon as it's convenient. I'll have to call you for the inquest since you found the body. Otherwise I'll be in touch if there's anything else.'

Nick warned Jos against talking to the press. He knew they would soon be there, given their nose for trouble. He explained that he didn't want the victim's name released until the widow had been informed. He told Jos to make sure all his family and staff understood that. Jos nodded. Nick and Bill went back up to the dismal room.

Bill said, 'Leighland's got a pretty daughter, about twenty. Hope may have made a nuisance of himself there.'

'In which case Leighland will never admit it,' Nick said realistically. 'I'm not sure that Hope struck me as a womaniser, but we'll check up if anyone noticed Jos absent from the bar at any time after eleven.' They looked out of the window.

'It's a small window,' Nick said. 'You'd never get through it, Bill.'

'No, sir.'

'It was cut from the outside by the look of it. Perhaps the intruder thought it safer to come in this way rather than risk being seen going up the stairs. It's nice and dark out in the car park. He could have looked through the window, seen Hope flaked out on the bed and broken in, knowing that there was no danger of his raising the alarm. But he would have to be quite a small man to get through it. Ashcroft wouldn't make it, for one.'

Nick called DC Penruan in. 'How tall are you, Paul?'

'Just about six foot, sir.'

'Do you think you could get through this window?'

Penruan looked doubtful. 'Probably not. If I could it'd be a hell of a squeeze.'

'We might try it later, when all the technicians have finished, but I'm inclined to agree with you. Not a big man then, no bigger than me probably.'

'Or a woman would do it easily,' Bill said – a thought which had occurred to Nick but which he had left unvoiced.

'Did they find any prints on the window or the sill?' Nick asked.

Bill made a face. 'Yeah . . . but they'll certainly turn out to be Hope's and Leighland's. Even the ransacking had a certain method in it. There was nothing amateurish about this job.'

'Except the way his head was bashed in?' Nick suggested.

'Maybe. But whoever did this was well prepared. I reckon it had been carefully planned.'

'They couldn't know that Hope was going to get drunk, start a fight and come home early.'

'But they knew he'd come back here eventually and they waited for him. He just made it easy for them. You can plan a murder and leave the precise timing to circumstances.'

A thought struck Nick. 'Jack Ashcroft is the one person who could have known there was going to be a fight. Let's take a look around outside, shall we?'

The Bird in Hand was orginally two buildings with an alleyway passing between them. As a result you walked through the front door and found yourself virtually in an open passageway. Doors led off on both sides, the saloon bar to the left as you came in from the road, the public to the right. If you went straight on you came to the car park and a modern block, with a flat asphalt roof, containing a storeroom. The storeroom roof ran under Aidan Hope's window. The stairway to the living quarters and the guest room ran from the passageway. If you came in from the road you had to pass the saloon and public bar doors to get to it. But from the car park it was the first door you came to.

'Wouldn't there have been a lot of toing and froing between the two bars, though?' Nick wondered aloud.

'The saloon was booked for the party,' Bill explained. 'And Jos was behind the bar in there himself with his daughter and the usual barmaid. His wife and a relief barmaid handled the normal trade in the public. So no one would have any reason to go from one to the other really. It would have been pretty quiet out here.'

'If our man used the stairs I should think he came in from the car park end. It would be a needless risk to come through the front door and past the two bar doors. If you waited for the right moment you'd be out of the car park and up the stairs with very little danger of being seen.'

'But the murderer came in through the window, surely, with even less danger of being seen.'

'That rather narrows our range of subjects, though, doesn't it? Let's not dismiss the stair route for the time being.'

'Anything more to do here, then?' Bill asked.

Nick glanced at his watch. Well after nine. 'Not for the time being.'

They would have to put out a public appeal to anyone who had been at the party the previous night, and had seen anything, to come forward. But they couldn't do that until the widow had been informed.

'We'll leave Penruan in charge here,' Nick said. 'I want to get over to Hope Cottage. Tell you what, we'll walk it and take a look at that footpath on the way. Get one of the constables to run the car over for us.'

The footpath was now closed off by a piece of barbed wire and the presence of the local PC who had attracted a small audience

65

of young boys. He stood aside for Nick and Bill, moving the wire for them, and they looked into the tunnel of branches.

'They started this end, sir,' Constable Moore said. 'At first light. They're about half-way up now.'

Hope Cottage was not visible from this point at this time of year but they could make out the shapes and sounds of the officers carrying out a fingertip search of the path.

'Mostly moss,' Nick said, shaking his head. 'We'll get no footprints off that. It's not even very wet, the branches saw to that.'

'Let's see how long it takes to walk up it, anyway,' Bill said.

'It would take longer at night. You'd have to mind your footing. It'd be as dark as pitch in here. Remind me to ask Miss Hope if she took a torch.'

The path curved away due south from the road through a mass of overgrown ashes and willows. The vegetation had recently been cut back to make the path passable and they picked their way easily up it. Half-way along they came to a small clearing where a rickety wooden bridge crossed a narrow tributary of the Hop. Here they caught up with the searchers. Nick stood on the bank of the river and surveyed the bridge.

'If you were crossing that you'd automatically put your hand on the rail, wouldn't you?'

'Pretty well.'

'It's all right, sir.' PC Harrison, in green waders, emerged from the banks of the river looking unreasonably cheerful for a man who had been up half the night and was now getting covered in mud. 'You can touch it as much as you like. They're finished there. Couple of handprints, couple of footprints – all largely obliterated by the rain. We haven't found a thing, except a few bits of litter.'

'He needn't sound so pleased about it,' Nick muttered as he and Bill crossed the footbridge.

They reached Hope Cottage at about nine-thirty. Nick's car was still parked in the courtyard, as was Jack Ashcroft's Rover. Janine opened the front door to their ring.

'Hello again,' she said. 'Alison's up. She's been up for ages actually – I don't think she got much sleep. She'll see you in her study upstairs.'

66

Nick thought it typical of Alison Hope to take the initiative and tell him where she would graciously receive him. He was tempted to haul her in for questioning but the chances were that she had spoken to her solicitor and knew that he couldn't force her down to the station without arresting her. And he wasn't ready to do that yet.

He said, 'I'd like a quick word with you first, if I may, Miss . . .' He realised that he didn't know her surname.

'Baxter,' she supplied. 'But you might as well go on calling me Janine.'

'It won't take a minute, Miss Baxter. Let's go into the sitting-room, shall we?' He held the door open for her. 'I just wanted to know if you witnessed the fight between Jack Ashcroft and Aidan Hope last night.'

'Oh yes, I did. I saw the whole thing.'

'But do you know what the fight was about?'

'Ah, no, I can't help you there.'

'Just tell me what you saw, then.'

'I'd been dancing with Ashcroft. That was a mistake – he's quite the most obnoxious man I've ever met.' Nick found himself nodding and stopped himself. 'Well, I finally managed to give him the brush-off and he went over to the bar and got himself another drink. Aidan Hope was there too.'

'Did you know him?'

'Yes, but I hadn't seen him for years. I heard Ashcroft say, "Hello, I'm Jack Ashcroft" quite loudly but then they started talking quietly and I didn't hear any more. There was no one else near them.'

'Not even the barman?'

'No, he'd gone off somewhere, to get some more supplies, I suppose. Then suddenly Aidan started shouting and swearing at Ashcroft and sort of pushing him – you know, the way people do – pushing at his chest as if to emphasise what he was saying. So Ashcroft backed away out on to the terrace. Aidan followed him. Ashcroft started to bluster a bit and then Aidan hit him in the stomach. Jack doubled up and lay there as if he couldn't quite believe it was happening to him. Aidan sort of stood over him while waiting for him to get up so he could hit him again. Then you came running up from the garden and grabbed him by the arm.'

67

'Did you happen to notice if anyone was missing from the party for any length of time?' Nick asked. 'Say at least half an hour between eleven and twelve-thirty.'

She thought hard. 'Not apart from you, no.'

'All right, that's all,' he said. 'Is your friend still here? What's his name?'

'Peter North. He's still asleep.'

Nick looked down the photocopied list of names and addresses. Janine Baxter, an address in west London. He turned over a couple of pages. Peter North, same address.

'He's not on the list of people who witnessed the fight,' he commented.

'No, that's right. After I escaped from Ashcroft's clutches I remember wondering where Peter had got to and looking around for him. He certainly wasn't in the room when the fight broke out.'

'Where was he?'

'I found him in the dining-room eventually, having a snooze.'

'We won't disturb him then.' He smiled at her. 'Thanks very much for your help, Miss Baxter.'

'I haven't been any help at all,' she said realistically.

'Well, thanks for coping so well last night, then.'

'Are we free to go, Peter and I?'

'Yes, certainly. We've got your address and phone number.'

'Only I'll stay as long as I can if it will help Alison but I'm seeing a client first thing tomorrow morning. Oh, dear.' She looked tired and unhappy suddenly and Nick thought that Alison Hope had one good friend at least. 'I'll show you up to the study.'

'Don't bother, we know the way. Is my woman constable here this morning?'

'Yes, she arrived quite a while ago. She was in the kitchen just now, dispensing tea and sympathy all round.' Yes, Nick thought, and keeping her ears and eyes wide open.

'Would you mind sending her up to the study?' he said.

'I'll go and find her.' She went out and disappeared along the corridor.

'Nice, sensible sort of girl,' Bill said approvingly, as they went up the stairs. 'Wish all witnesses were like her.'

Carol Halsgrove caught them up before they reached the landing.

'Good,' Nick said. He would need the indispensable Carol.

He knocked on the closed study door.

Alison's voice called, 'Come in.'

Chapter 9

She didn't look as if she had slept. She was sitting on the window seat with her back against the shutters and her feet up on it, looking out over the garden. She wore blue jeans and a thin, black cotton sweater. Her feet were bare. Her hair was loose and hid half her face. She did not look round.

'Good morning, Miss Hope,' Nick said. 'I just want to establish a few facts about last night.' She did not reply. 'We shall be carrying out a more thorough search of the building and the grounds today. I shall obtain a search warrant for that purpose as soon as is practicable; meanwhile I'd like permission to make a start.' She nodded her head.

'My sergeant will keep a record of our conversation,' he persevered. 'You do not have to say anything unless you wish to do so, but what you say may be given in evidence. Do you understand?'

'Yes.'

He couldn't wait any longer for her to invite him to sit so he draw up a chair to the big leather-topped desk. Bill sat at a small table and opened his notebook. DC Halsgrove waited silently by the door.

'Will I have to identify the body?' Alison asked suddenly.

'I think that would be best as we don't seen to have any closer relations to hand. Do you mind?'

'Well . . . I'll do it. Is he . . . um . . . how was it done?'

'They'll tidy him up before you see him, don't worry.' Nick did not answer the question. 'Can you tell me his full name and address?'

'Aidan Daniel Hope, but I don't know his address. I got the

70

impression that he didn't have a permanent home at the moment.'

'Can you tell me who his next of kin is?'

'He had a wife and a son.' She was already speaking of him in the past tense, Nick noticed. 'It usually took them a while to get used to that.

'Of course. I remember now that he mentioned a wife. What's her name and address?'

'Her name's Judith but I don't know where she is at the moment. They had separated – temporarily, he said. She wouldn't have had much money so perhaps her family is the best place to try.' That was a blow.

'You wouldn't happen to know her maiden name?' Nick asked. Smith, probably.

'Oh yes,' she said unexpectedly. 'It was Cooke, with an "e". She came from Exeter originally and her mother still lived there five years ago. I've no idea of the address, though.'

'Get on to the police in Exeter,' Nick said to the constable. 'We shall have to track her down. Then get the search started.' DC Halsgrove went out and he turned back to Alison.

'You knew her well?'

'Once.' She looked round at last. 'We went up to Cambridge together, eleven years ago almost exactly. We became very friendly. Two little provincial girls, first time away from home. Then I introduced her to my cousin.'

'So you had known your cousin all your life, obviously.'

'Not obvious at all,' she said, tossing her head scornfully. 'My father's only brother married an Irish woman, went to live in Dublin and was converted to Roman Catholicism. As the men in my family were mostly in the church, including my father and grandfather, that caused quite a breach and they lost touch.'

Alison Hope, the vicar's daughter? Nick smiled very faintly to himself. He would never have guessed that. She went on.

'I met Aidan for the first time in my life when I went up to Cambridge. He was two years ahead of us, me and Judith, in his final year reading maths. He was a sure bet for a first and I think King's had a fellowship lined up for him.'

Nick sat back in his chair, fascinated. What a waste of a life. 'What happened?'

'Judith happened. I met Aidan at some party, people made a joke about our having the same name. We were pretty staggered to find out that we were first cousins, as you can imagine. We barely knew of each other's existence. I introduced them. Judith wasn't pretty but she had a lot of charm. She could twist the men round her little finger. It was uncanny to watch. They started out not taking much notice of her, just being polite. Then you'd see their interest being engaged, almost visibly. Aidan was handsome and brilliant so she set her sights on him.'

She paused – looking back over the years. Could she have been jealous? Nick wondered. Had her best friend run off with a man she had earmarked for herself? The green-eyed monster – could it survive for more than ten years?

'Go on,' he said.

'Oh, just the usual sordid little story. She got pregnant – absurdly careless and unnecessary. They got married. The funny thing was he wanted to marry her. She was the one who was angry about it all. He wouldn't hear of her having an abortion, though – he still called himself a Catholic in those days. He almost failed his finals. I think they gave him a third out of pity. But he doted on her and the boy. I got the impression he was desperate to get her back, even last week.' She sighed heavily. 'What a waste of a life!'

'Would you call your cousin a womaniser?'

'God, no! Not at all. Too pissed as a rule, I should think.'

He took her through the events of the evening.

'After you went off to take Jack home I walked Aidan back along the footpath.'

'Did you talk to him?'

'Yes, of course, a bit. He was pretty far gone.'

'What about, Miss Hope?'

'Oh, just nothing really – the party, the storm.'

'Did he tell you what his quarrel with Ashcroft was about?'

'I asked him but he said it was about nothing at all and laughed.'

'Did your cousin know Jack Ashcroft before last night?'

'Why should he? He was a stranger round here.'

'I just wondered if he'd mentioned it. Go on with your story.'

'I was going to walk him right back to the pub, but then it came on to rain so hard that I left him and hurried back to the house.'

'How far along the footpath did you leave him?'

'Right at the far end, where it comes out into Little Hopford. We could see the pub, all lit up and noisy. I just stepped out on the grass verge. The state Aidan was in he might have rushed out in front of a car.'

'Did you see him enter the pub?'

'No, I turned back straight away. At least the trees gave some shelter from the rain.'

'See anybody at all in Little Hopford?'

'No. After all, no one would have come out in that downpour, would they? They'd have waited for it to stop.'

'Did you have a torch with you?' he asked.

'No, I didn't think. That was stupid, it was pitch black out there.'

'What time did you get back to the house?'

'It must have been nearly ten past eleven.'

'Who saw you arrive?'

'No one. I came in through the conservatory and the kitchen and straight upstairs to change. The french windows were closed by then and I remember noticing that someone had drawn the curtains so no one would have seen me cross the garden. You were the first person I saw when I came back down.'

'But that was at half past eleven!'

'Yes, I know. I had a quick shower – I was really drenched.' Nick looked at her unwaveringly. 'No one told me I'd need an alibi!' she snapped.

'I'd like to take the shoes and the clothes you were wearing for examination,' he said.

There was a short silence, then she said, 'You can have the shoes, but I put the dress in the washing machine straight away.'

'What!'

'I slipped in the mud by the river bank coming back, there were mud and grass stains on it. When I changed I decided to wash it before the stain dried in.' Nick could almost feel Bill tensing up at that moment as he sensed a quick arrest and pats

73

on the back all round. 'It was expensive,' she said, suddenly on the defensive. 'I didn't want it ruined by a stain. You saw me!' she added. 'I had it with me when I ran into you.'

'Best to leave mud to dry, then brush it off,' Bill said. He was hunched over his notes and Alison was treated to one of his sidelong looks, but she wasn't watching.

'Maybe, but grass can stain quite badly. I thought it best to wash it at once.'

I'll bet, said Bill's face.

'All right,' Nick said, tiring of this laundry debate. 'We'll take the shoes, and we'll take the clean dress too. Have you seen any strangers hanging about lately? Anyone at your party you didn't know? Anyone at the party who had any connection, business or personal, with Mr Hope?'

She answered no to all of these. 'But you must realise I hadn't seen or heard from Aidan for five years – I wouldn't know what business or personal connections he had.'

Nick stared at her in surprise. 'Five years! But he was your business partner.'

She started up from the window seat, her lethargy gone suddenly. There was anger in her face as she walked across to the desk. She leant towards him – her palms flat on the desktop – and spoke slowly and deliberately.

'*Was* my partner. Past tense. I bought him out five years ago.'

'That's not the impression he gave me last night, Miss Hope,' Nick said coolly. 'He gave me the impression it was very much present tense. That's also the impression he gave me on that tape you made.'

She looked at him uncertainly for a few seconds. She had thought him so nice the previous night. Different. A bit odd, perhaps. There was a sort of barrier he kept up about himself and she had thought it might be fun to get behind it and see what was hidden there. So she had flirted with him outrageously and the wall had begun to crumble. Today he was another person altogether and the fortress was impregnable. His face was a blank mask and she could not tell what he was thinking. Whom was she trying to kid? She knew exactly what he was thinking. Him and that hefty sergeant of his. Shit.

'You said I didn't have to say anything.'

74

'Quite correct. Do you want to send for a solicitor?'

She thought for a moment. 'Look, I think it's best if I tell you all about it,' she said in the end.

'I think that would be very wise.' If Nick was relieved, no one would have known it from his face. She sat down again and began.

'When I left university I got a job with a software house in London working mainly with business micro computers. I'd been there a couple of years when I happened to run into Aidan one day. He didn't seem to have been doing anything since graduating. He was just drifting about, working some-times – more often not. He'd taken an interest in computers at Cambridge – the maths department had one.

'He said, why didn't we set up on our own instead of making enormous profits for other people? I could see the sense in that but I was a bit dubious about going into business with him. Still, I knew that he hadn't always been like that and that he really did have a brilliant mind. So Hope Software was born. I had a bit of money my parents had left me and we used that to buy our first micro.

'Aidan was quite enthusiastic at first. But things didn't work out as well as we'd hoped. It was a bit slow getting off the ground. He began to lose interest. The work was too easy for him really. He did less and less and I was getting pretty fed up. Also we didn't make enough to pay ourselves very well. I could manage, but Aidan had a child to support.

'One night I was at his flat in Ladbroke Grove and we went out for a drink. We met Adam Knox, an actor Aidan knew – Aidan was the sort of man who knew everybody. We went back to his place. I got the impression that he was a hard drinker and we all put away quite a bit that night.

'Eventually we got round to talking about the business and Aidan said he wanted out. I said I'd buy him out – I was pretty drunk too or I probably wouldn't have done it. I gave him a cheque for a thousand pounds. It was the last money I had left in the world. After that he took off. I didn't see him again until last week.

'That Christmas was the turning point for Hope Software. Suddenly every little boy in the country wanted a home computer to play games on. I started doing games as well as business packages. That year the business made a profit – not a big one, but it just grew and grew from there.'

'Then Aidan reappeared out of the blue?' Nick guessed.

'He turned up here asking for half the business. Adam Knox died, you see, a couple of weeks ago. He could no longer say that Aidan had sold out.'

'You must have got something in writing!'

'I never saw him again after that night. I tried to contact him the next week but he'd gone off, presumably to give his creditors the slip and spend my thousand pounds. As far as I know he never went back to that flat in Ladbroke Grove, although he seems to have lived in the area again since then.' She hesitated, puzzled. Who had told her that? 'When I couldn't find him I didn't bother any more.'

'So his turning up like that was a nasty shock to you.'

'I was furious. But not furious enough to kill him, if that's what you mean.'

There was a knock on the door and Carol Halsgrove came in and whispered to Nick that there was a messenger outside.

'I'll come down,' he said. 'Excuse me a moment, Miss Hope. Sergeant?'

They went downstairs. A motorcycle was drawn up in the courtyard. The search warrants had arrived along with the transcripts of the tape. Nick leafed through the closely typed pages, then handed it silently to Bill, who read it through carefully.

'I call that pretty damning,' Bill said.

She was still sitting on the window seat in the study when they got back a few minutes later. Nick sat down again, the transcript on the desk in front of him.

'So, what about this tape, Miss Hope?' he resumed.

'I was coming to that. I thought if I could get Aidan to admit that he was trying it on and get it on tape I would be in a better position. I invited him to the party. He got here quite early and I left him soaking up the champagne for a couple of hours. Then, when I thought he was well sozzled, I brought him up here. I pretended that I wanted to bargain with him. Played him along, you know. He was too clever to fall for it, though.'

76

'Is this a true transcript of the conversation?' Nick handed the papers to Bill, who took them to her. She glanced through them. It was much the same as the snippet he had listened to the previous night: Alison feinted; Aidan parried.

Until the end. When Alison had lost her temper and shouted, *You're storing up a lot of trouble for yourself, Aidan. I'm not going to let you get away with this.*

'Yes.' Her voice faltered. 'I suppose it's correct.'

'What did you mean about not letting him get away with it?'

'I meant that I would make him drag me through the courts. I knew he couldn't afford it. At least I thought he couldn't. After I switched the tape off, as we were leaving the room, he said something like: "Don't think I can't afford to take you to court, I'm in funds at the moment. Better if we can settle it between us."'

'What did you make of that?'

'I thought he was bluffing. Aidan's never been in funds in his life.' She passed the papers back.

'Did you consult a solicitor about your cousin's claims on you?' Nick asked.

'Yes, straight away.'

'I'd like the name and address of your solicitors.'

'Trowerbridge and Colman in Covent Garden. Jake Trowerbridge is a personal friend.' Bill wrote down the address and phone number.

'What did Mr Trowerbridge say?' Nick asked.

'If memory serves he said, "We're up shit creek without a paddle, Alison."' Nick noticed Bill was writing that down too.

Oh, God! Alison thought in anguish, why had she told him that? Some sort of crazy bravado? Policemen were nice, avuncular men, in reassuring uniforms, who told you the time and helped old ladies across the road. She had never come across policemen like these before: men with sharp eyes and sharper questions, who sat there looking innocuously like businessmen in their grey suits. They did mean business. They were not exactly . . . user-friendly.

'Why did you hide the tape yesterday evening?' Nick asked.

'I didn't *hide* it. After I'd left Aidan I realised my feet were cold. I went into the dressing-room to find my evening sandals. Then I thought I didn't need the recorder any more so I just stuffed it into the nearest drawer. I can't see anything sinister in that.'

Nick did not comment but got up and said, 'That's all for the present, Miss Hope. I shall have to ask you not to leave the area without my authority.'

She gasped. He could feel her glaring at him but he did not look up and meet her gaze. He shuffled through the transcript papers on the desk instead.

Finally she said, 'Am I being accused of murder?'

'You're not under arrest, if that's what you mean. The victim was your cousin, he was killed shortly after leaving your house. You were the last person to see him alive – as far as we know. You had the opportunity to kill him and now it is clear that you had had a serious quarrel with him – serious enough to constitute a motive.'

She said nothing and he turned abruptly to leave the room. At the door he stopped and said, 'You'll be notified when they're ready at the mortuary for you to identify the body. My constables will be here all day, searching the house and grounds. If you think of anything you want to add to your statement – or change – Miss Halsgrove knows how to get hold of me. I repeat that you are not, at present, under arrest.'

'And the Super may well be asking why not,' Bill grumbled as they made their way down to the police car. '*Up shit creek without a paddle! She's either very stupid or very clever and somehow I don't think she's stupid.'

'Or just very innocent?' Nick suggested.

'Or that, I suppose,' he said grudgingly. 'Where to know?'

'We'll pay a little visit to Jack Ashcroft.'

A handful of local newspaper men had gathered outside the gateway to Hope Cottage. They recognised Nick and Bill. Bill had to slow down and hoot to get them out of his way. They swarmed round the car, all shouting at once.

'Inspector Trevellyan, is it true that the murdered man is this Alison Hope's husband?'

'Was he really bludgeoned to death?'

'Are you anticipating a speedy arrest, Nick?'

Nick wound down the window. Camera flashes were going off all around him. 'I have no comment to make at present. I shall be calling a press conference when the victim's next of kin has been informed.'

'So he's not Alison Hope's husband?'

Nick wound up the window without replying. Bill lurched out of the yard, sending one young reporter jumping out of the way.

'Ghouls!' Bill said succinctly.

Chapter 10

'She's got no motive,' Nick said, as they headed for Threeoaks Farm.

'I don't call half of this computer business no motive myself,' Bill said acidly.

'But she's not his heir, Bill. He's got a wife and kid. If half the business belonged to him, then it now belongs to the wife and son. She's no better off than she was yesterday.'

Bill considered this and decided he wasn't having any of it. 'She might have thought that the wife didn't know about Hope's claims; that once he was dead no one would question her right to the whole business any more.'

'Well, the wife's going to know about it now, isn't she?'

'Only because you spotted that missing handbag.'

Nick changed tack. 'I thought your theory was that the whole thing had been carefully planned – a professional job, you said.' Actually it was Nick who had used the word "professional" but that was what subordinates were for – to act as repositories for unlikely theories.

'That was before I saw that tape transcript,' Bill said. 'You already knew about that. I wondered why you cautioned her.'

'I listened to a bit of it after you'd gone last night.'

'You might have told me,' Bill said grumpily.

It sounds as if Bill and Nick are always squabbling. But that is how they operate. Bill puts forward a theory and Nick shoots it down in flames. Or vice versa. Mostly vice versa.

Bill swung the car to a screeching halt in front of Threeoaks Farm. 'He's been pretty quick about getting those hen houses repainted, hasn't he?' he remarked.

They got out of the car and made their way across the muddy farmyard. Nick hammered on the front door for several minutes before he got any reply. Ashcroft finally opened the door, wearing nothing but a grubby dressing gown.

'What d'you want? Oh, not you again.' He wrapped the dressing gown tighter around himself as if he thought Nick might be about to get the electrodes out. Nick walked into the house past him. Ashcroft looked startled.

'Here . . .' he said nervously.

'I want to know what your quarrel with Aidan Hope was about,' Nick said.

'Who? Never heard of him.'

'Aidan Hope,' Nick repeated patiently. 'He punched you in the stomach last night, remember?'

Ashcroft clenched his fists. 'That Irish pig. Is that his name? He won't get away with it.'

Nick sat down. 'What was the argument about, Mr Ashcroft?'

'Here, what is all this?' Ashcroft said suspiciously. 'Since when do you lot interest yourselves in a little harmless punch-up?'

'Aidan Hope was found murdered not two hours after your little harmless punch-up,' Nick said bluntly. He watched Ashcroft's reaction very carefully. Ashcroft gaped at him and slumped on to the sofa, looking dazed.

Nick clapped his hands slowly. 'Very convincing, Jack. Now I want a full account of your movements after I left you here last night.'

'Don't the police call people *sir* any more? I don't have to answer your questions.'

'How's the head?' Nick asked sympathetically. 'I can shout a bit louder if it'll help you to hear my questions. On the other hand you can refuse to co-operate and send for your solicitor – all of which will delay your getting back to your nice, warm bed.'

'Bastard,' Ashcroft said, half-heartedly.

'You quarrelled with Aidan Hope just before he was murdered.'

Ashcroft looked genuinely astonished and said reasonably,

81

'If I murdered everyone I quarrelled with, the valley would be strewn with corpses.'

'What was the quarrel about?'

Ashcroft scratched his head. 'I hardly know. He just flared up at me about practically nothing.'

'Practically nothing being?'

'I'd been dancing with that dark-haired bird. She'd been giving me the come-on and then backing off at the last minute. Typical bloody woman.' Nick wondered what Janine would have made of this version of events. 'So I gave it up as a bad job in the end and went off to get another drink instead. The paddy was there at the bar, seemed friendly enough. I said something about bloody women and he said yes, they give you a hard time, and I said at least I wasn't married which was something and was he? He said his wife had left him. I said he was well off there. That all women were bloody tarts, he was better off without her. You know the type of thing.'

'Little soul of tact, aren't you?'

'He just went berserk.'

'Is that all there was to it? Two grown men starting a fight over that like a pair of kids?' Bill said, in disgust.

'That was it.'

'Did you know Aidan Hope before he came to stay here a week ago?' Nick asked.

'Never seen him before in my life.'

'What did you do after I left you here, just before eleven-thirty?'

'I went to bed.'

'Any witnesses?' The question didn't go down well.

'Yeah, when you brought me back here I had half a dozen topless floozies hiding in the cupboard. Thought you'd have noticed, being a detective. But I forgot – you don't like women, do you?'

'You didn't go out again?'

'You may recall that I left my car in Little Hopford. It must still be there.'

'You have another car, a Land-Rover. I've seen it.'

'Oh, that, yeah.' Ashcroft gave him a shifty grin.

'After I left you last night you could simply have got into

82

your Land-Rover, driven down to the Bird in Hand and killed Aidan Hope.'

Ashcroft shrugged. 'Well, I didn't. I didn't even know he was staying there, did I?'

'Yes, you did. I mentioned it to Miss Hope as I was taking you out.'

'I wasn't listening. I was concentrating on not throwing up.'

'I'd like to take a look at that Land-Rover . . . sir.'

'Have you got a search warrant?'

'Yes, thanks. Give him his copy, sergeant.'

Ashcroft merely glanced at the warrant. 'OK.' He opened the window and bawled, 'Gary! Ouch! I wish I hadn't done that.' A young man with blue overalls and acne appeared from the hen houses.

'Show these . . . gentleman the Land-Rover,' Jack said, through the window. 'I'm going back to bed,' he added. 'I feel rotten. So if that's all – '

'Not quite. I'd like to take a look at your shoes and your clothes.'

'Which ones?'

'All of them, but especially the ones you were wearing at the party last night.'

Ashcroft meekly led them into his bedroom, which looked like the Augean stables before Hercules got his dustpan and brush out.

'My God!' Nick said, awe-struck. 'Why don't you open a window occasionally? And the bed looks as if you've been holding an orgy in it.'

'I don't sleep well – I toss and turn a lot. Now are you going to search the place or just hurl personal abuse at me?'

They started looking. Nick hoped he wasn't going to catch anything nasty.

The shoes Ashcroft had been wearing the previous night were very muddy. 'It was muddy in the yard, when I got out of your car,' he said.

'I'll take those for examination,' Nick said. Bill put them in a transparent bag. They went through the rest of Ashcroft's shoes and confiscated two more pairs. They found surprisingly few clothes.

'Where are the rest of your clothes?' Nick asked.

'That's the lot, I don't have that many. You can search the other cupboards, if you don't believe me.'

'I intend to. Now you can go back to bed, sir, but I don't want you to leave the valley without telling me.'

'Balls!' Ashcroft went so red that Nick thought for a moment he might combust spontaneously. 'You've got no rights at all and you know it. You want to order me about – you arrest me.'

'If only,' Nick said to Bill, as they left the house.

'He was surprisingly co-operative, though, wasn't he? For him.'

'Suspiciously so, I would have said. At least we've got his fingerprints, which is handy. I doubt if we'd have got them off him otherwise.'

They followed spotty Gary across the farmyard.

'You're not thinking of buying it, are you?' he asked, 'because it's rubbish. Don't let the old bastard tell you different.'

'I don't want to buy it,' Nick said. 'Why? What's wrong with it?'

'Doesn't bloody go.' Gary opened a barn door and pointed to the Land-Rover, half hidden behind some stacked-up straw bales. 'It's on its last legs. Been broken down for the past two weeks.'

'Are you sure about that?' Nick said sharply.

'Yeah, course. I had to look at it but I'm not a mechanic, am I? And the garage wouldn't fix it. The old bugger already owes them so much money for servicing his car and the farm machinery. They said either he paid what he owed or he got no more credit out of them.'

'Which garage does he use?'

'Sillington's in Great Hopford.'

'John Sillington lives next door to his garage,' Bill said. 'We ought to be able to catch him in, Sunday morning.'

'All right,' Nick said. 'We'll have a word with him.'

John Sillington was at home and seemed more than ready to help. He was in the middle of a Sunday-morning sherry party with his in-laws and Nick got the impression that he welcomed any diversion, however bizarre. He took them over to his office on the garage forecourt. He pulled a buff folder out of a filing cabinet and threw it on the desk.

'That's Ashcroft's unpaid bills, hasn't paid me a penny for the last six months. Then he has the cheek to ring me up a fortnight or so ago, "Johnnie old chap,"' Sillington did a passable imitation of Ashcroft's plummy voice. '"Wondered if you could pop up and have a look at my old Land-Rover." I said I'd just love to, the minute he'd paid me the six hundred quid he owes me. He laughed and rang off.'

'So you don't know if the Land-Rover really had broken down?'

'No, but it wouldn't surprise me.'

'Have you seen him driving it these last two weeks?'

'No, but he's stopped buying his petrol here to avoid aggro about his bills every time and he doesn't have to come past here to get anywhere.'

'Well, thanks for your help,' Nick said.

'Any time.' Sillington sat down at his desk and gave no sign of any intention to get back to his house.

'Well, at least we know Ashcroft reported it broken down a fortnight ago,' Bill said in response to Nick's complaint that the visit had been a waste of time. 'He'd hardly have been planning the murder of Aidan Hope for the past two weeks, would he? What with Hope only turning up out of the blue a week ago.'

'We'll get the Land-Rover looked at, see if it's really out of commission,' Nick said.

'He could have walked it, just about.'

'Just about, he was pretty drunk.'

'Are you sure, sir?' Nick thought for a minute. He saw what Bill was getting at. 'Only it's not hard to pretend to be drunk, especially if everyone expects you to get drunk.'

'I saw him actually drinking, steadily, for some time.' It had seemed an awful lot to Nick but it was hard for him to tell, not being a drinking man himself.

Bill duly made this point. 'He's used to it, though, isn't he? And he might have had a full stomach – eaten a heavy meal or lined it with milk, say. Being sick can sober you up quicker than almost anything as well.'

85

'We'll keep it in mind as a possibility,' Nick said readily. 'It's not as if we've got much else to go on at the moment.'

'Mind you,' Bill said, 'there's a lot of truth in what he said. If he killed everyone he quarrelled with the valley would be depopulated in no time.'

'He quarrels with a lot of people but this time someone quarrelled with him.'

'How do you mean?'

Nick tried, rather incoherently, to explain what he meant. Ashcroft liked to pick fights but he liked to choose his time and place. Also his antagonist, preferably someone weaker than he. His victims did not usually punch and humiliate him in front of a crowd of people.

'Yes, I see what you mean,' Bill said unconvincingly.

Nick was prepared to admit that it was not one of his better efforts.

'Let's pick my car up and get back to base,' he said.

'So, what's everybody doing at the moment?' Nick asked, fidgeting with his collection of biros. Bill didn't answer. He was used to his boss's rhetorical questions. He said they helped him to think.

'DC Halsgrove is staying at Hope Cottage for the time being,' Nick duly answered himself. 'Until we've finished searching the place. We'll have to get her back here soon. She'll have to work her way through the list of people who witnessed the fight to see if anyone knows what it was about.'

'That's going to be a long job.'

'It doesn't sound as if we shall get much joy there either, according to Miss Baxter. We shall probably only have Ashcroft's word for it. It sounded plausible enough, knowing Jack, but it could be complete fabrication. He's had all night to think of it. What did you make of his reaction when I told him about the murder? I was watching him like a hawk. He put on a pretty good show. Was he genuinely surprised, d'you think?'

'I'd have said so, but who can tell? Was Miss Hope genuinely surprised? That might be a better question.'

'She seemed stunned, certainly. Also I just told her he was dead at first, I didn't mention murder. She assumed there'd been some sort of accident or illness.'

86

'Clever move, if she did it. But then she struck me as clever, so that's no help.'

'Penruan's seeing the birthday man, as soon as he's finished at the pub, right?'

'Yeah, getting names and addresses of all the people who were at the party.' Nick groaned. 'Then they'll start interviewing them all.' Nick groaned some more. 'Everyone else is doing house-to-house in Little Hopford or manning the incident room at the church hall.'

'All that will take forever. Here's a real needle-in-a-haystack job for you then, Bill.'

'Sir?'

'Find out if Jack Ashcroft and Aidan Hope knew each other previously.'

Bill looked glum and shook his head. 'Can't be done.'

'There's no getting away from it,' Bill said later that morning. 'Miss Hope is our most likely bet.'

'She could just about have done it from the timing point of view,' Nick agreed. 'She left the party with Hope at ten to eleven. They reached the pub at eleven. Supposing she watches Hope go into the pub, then hangs around until there's no one in sight and nips up the stairs. She walks into the room without knocking. Hope is lying flaked out on the bed, face down. She picks up the ashtray and brings it down on the back of his skull. Does it a few more times to make quite sure.'

'What about the hole in the window?'

'Maybe done on purpose to mislead us.'

'The SOCOS checked – it was definitely cut from outside.'

'So maybe she came in that way. Maybe she thought it was safer than the stairs. Maybe Hope had locked his door. She looks quite athletic and there are empty beer kegs stacked against the storeroom. You can climb onto the roof quite easily. In which case we need to allow a bit of extra time for that, I think. Anyway, then she ransacks the place. Why?'

'Either to make it look like a burglary gone wrong . . .'

'In which case she did it very ineptly as it was obvious that the murder was done first, if only from the specks of foam in the wound.'

'. . . Or she was looking for Hope's copy of the partnership agreement.'

'He'd hardly have had it with him,' Nick protested.

'But he would, sir. He had no fixed home at the moment, remember. It stands to reason that he would carry his valuables about with him. Like Jos Leighland said, no one would expect to find anything worth pinching at a pub like that.'

'Either way that sort of mess would have been taken quite a time to make. Ripping open pillowcases and mattresses. I think we have to allow at least ten minutes for her to kill Hope and search the room. More like fifteen, giving her time to hang around until the coast was clear both coming and going. That takes us to eleven-fifteen. It would take her at least five minutes to get back, even if she ran all the way. Eleven-twenty. I saw her at half past, by which time she'd showered and changed. She'd certainly changed, she can't prove she showered.'

'The shower was wet when I looked for that bag last night,' Bill offered, 'and there were wet towels draped around.'

'So the timing was very tight indeed. I'm not saying it was impossible. We shall see if there are any traces of asphalt on her shoes and if anyone saw her near the pub last night. And if there's any blood on that dress, they ought to find it, despite the washing. Also, if she was looking for the agreement and she found it, then it must be at the house somewhere, or hidden along the path. In which case we shall find it.'

'Unless she just destroyed it right away.'

'Not so easy. There are no fires at this time of year.'

'Tear it up and flush it down the loo maybe,' Bill said, with a shrug. 'I don't think we can put too much emphasis on not finding it.'

The thought that he might be able to send PC Des Harrison down the sewers quite bucked Nick up.

'Now how does the timing fit Ashcroft?' he said, with renewed energy. 'I left him at eleven-twenty-five. He would have waited until I was safely out of the way. Then if he had a car he could have been in Little Hopford in five minutes. If he had to walk, it would take at least fifteen. Call it eleven-forty-five. I'm inclined to think the murder was done before midnight. After that Jos Leighland would have been calling time and the place would have been swarming with people. It would have been rush hour out in the car park. And the body was found at quarter past.'

'During the rainstorm's, the most likely time – there'd be no one about in the car park then – which puts it early, between eleven and twenty past.' Bill leant forward eagerly. 'Besides there's no way Ashcroft could have got through that window, he's a good six feet and stocky with it. So why cut it from the outside?'

Nick buried his head in his hands. He was beginning to feel the lack of sleep. He took his glasses off and rubbed his eyes.

'We're not getting anywhere,' he said wearily. 'Let's find out what the postmorten comes up with before we go any further on timings. Then I want to talk to Judith Hope, see if she knew what her husband was up to.'

'What about the other party guests?' Bill suggested. 'Almost any of them could have nipped down the footpath once the rain started. No one would notice if someone was missing for half an hour. In a house that size they could be almost anywhere. Someone could have slipped away quite easily.'

'I could have done it, come to that,' Nick said. 'I was away for more than half an hour, as Miss Baxter pointed out, taking Ashcroft home. I made him some coffee because – well, because I was in a good mood, I suppose. I felt sorry for him, God help me. But he'd never be able to remember how long I stayed, or what time it was – not in his state. And if he did remember he probably wouldn't say.'

Bill smiled. 'Well, I've got your prints,' he said placidly, 'if I run short of suspects.'

Nick yawned. Bill glanced at his watch in what he imagined was a surreptitious manner.

'Yes,' Nick agreed. 'Definitely lunchtime.'

'Why don't we both go back to my place? Susie'll give us some dinner. You'll think better on a full stomach.'

'Sure it'll be all right?'

'Yeah, course. There's always masses on a Sunday.'

'You talked me into it.' In the middle of a murder enquiry – particularly one that was all in the family, so to speak – Nick often found himself yearning for a glimpse of normality and families didn't come much more normal than the Deacons.

'I'll give Susie a ring,' Bill said. 'Tell her to expect us. That'll give our Sarah time to put her best frock on.' Bill's eldest daughter, fourteen-year-old Sarah, had an ill-concealed crush on Nick, much to the unkind merriment of the rest of the family. Nick was obliged to walk a tightrope of being kind to the girl without fuelling her adolescent fantasies.

The phone rang. Nick picked it up.

'Penruan,' he mouthed. 'What! Where was it exactly? Yes, all right, bring it with you when you come.' He hung up.

'They've got the partnership agreement,' he said, whipping the rabbit out of the hat before Bill's very eyes.

'What! Along the footpath?'

'No, it was in Hope's room all the time.' Couple of herrings in the hat too, by the look of things.

Bill puffed out his cheeks in a pantomime of bewilderment. 'So she didn't find it. Maybe she thought she'd already stayed too long.'

Nick stamped on that one. 'It wasn't even hidden. It was in the inside pocket of his jacket, hanging up behind the door, all the time. So I don't think it was that our murderer was looking for.'

Chapter 11

Nick's phone rang late that afternoon. It was Carol Halsgrove saying that Alison Hope wanted to speak to him.

'OK,' he said. 'How are the searches going?'

'Just about finished, sir. Nothing very interesting, though.'

'There's no point in your hanging about there much longer then. As soon as the last lot have packed up, get back to the station – soon as you can.'

'Yes, sir. I'll put Miss Hope on.'

'Hello, Miss Hope?' Nick said.

Alison came on the line. Her voice was confident and businesslike.

'Two things, inspector. You asked me if I had seen any strangers about. I don't know if he qualifies as a stranger, but there was a man from the E & D Security people – the ones you recommended. His name was Ian McCarthy.'

'But presumably you were expecting him, so he wasn't exactly a stranger.'

'No, but he was asking questions about Aidan.'

'What sort of questions?' Nick asked sharply.

'Very casual. Said he used to know someone called Hope, would he be a relation by any chance? I told him where Aidan was living, too. I didn't really think anything of it at the time, but now it strikes me as odd.'

It struck Nick as odd too. Very interesting. 'Give me his name again,' he said, reaching for a pen.

'Ian McCarthy was the name he gave me, and the name on his ID card from the security firm.'

'Description?'

'Shortish, balding brown hair, florid complexion, blue eyes, forty-fivish.' She'd be convincing in the witness box, Nick thought, scribbling hard. Less good in the dock perhaps.

'Anything else?'

'Well, he had a Scottish accent, at least I assumed it was Scottish – what with his name. There wasn't anything else about him, except that he smoked filthy-smelling roll-up cigarettes.'

'I'll check it out. What was the other thing?'

'Molly Armitage rang me.' Was she reminding him that she was well connected? Because if so she was barking in the wrong forest. 'She's heard about the murder. It made the local news this lunchtime. No details apparently but they mentioned Hope Cottage. She wanted me to go and stay with them for a few days. I refused but she persuaded me to go for dinner tonight. If I can have permission, that is.'

'You're not under arrest,' he repeated. 'You can go out and about. I just don't want you to leave the country, at all, or to leave the valley without telling me.'

'You'll know where to find me when you've got your warrant.'

She put the phone down quite hard.

Molly rushed to open the door to Alison and hugged her until she could hardly breathe.

'My poor darling, how could such a terrible thing happen? How are you?'

'I'm all right, Molly. Or I would be if I didn't have such a nasty feeling that Nick Trevellyan thinks I did it.'

'Nonsense!' Molly said vigorously. 'He's a perfectly sensible young man. He can see at a glance that you'd be incapable of such a thing.' Alison smiled faintly, resolving to take Molly along next time she was being interrogated.

'Nonsense!' Molly repeated a little less dogmatically, recalling the time when Alison had tried to drown Sophie Armitage in the paddling pool at the British Embassy in Cairo. She had been four at the time and Sophie had dismantled her Lego castle while she was having her afternoon nap. That didn't count, surely.

'I did hate him for a little while just before he died,' Alison confessed.

92

'I hate all sorts of people but I don't go around murdering them.' Molly lowered her voice. 'There's someone else here. I just about forgot I'd invited him with all the excitement – I mean with the terrible news. It didn't seem quite kind to put him off as he doesn't know anyone round here.'

'Whoever is it?'

'That solicitor I told you about, James' young partner.'

'Um, well. I may need a solicitor before long.'

Molly led her up to the drawing-room. Anton and the other man stood up as they came in.

'Alison, this is Thomas Howard. Thomas, this is Alison Hope I was just telling you about.' The two shook hands.

Thomas said, 'I'm so sorry to hear about this dreadful thing that's happened to you, Miss Hope.'

She gave him a weak smile. 'Please call me Alison, and I'd rather just talk about something else this evening, if you don't mind.'

'I reckon what you need is a little drink,' Anton said.

'Nothing too strong,' Alison warned – she knew Anton's notion of a little drink. 'I don't want to be picked up for drunken driving on top of everything.' They all laughed uncomfortably. She sat down in an armchair facing Thomas Howard while Anton fetched her a weak gin and tonic. Castlemaine promptly came and sat at her feet.

Molly said, 'Seriously, my dear, and before we drop the subject for the rest of the evening, shouldn't you send for Jake Trowerbridge?'

'Alison shook her head vehemently. 'Squealing for a solicitor, particularly a London solicitor, is going to look more like an admission of guilt than anything. Just because I haven't got an alibi that doesn't make me a murderer.' She sipped her drink defiantly. 'Cheers,' she said.

She surveyed Thomas covertly over the top of her glass. Hmm, not bad. He was about thirty and rather a good-looking man. He was over six foot tall, of athlete build – he looked as if he might be a sportsman. His hair was very fair and a little lank – a lock of it kept falling over his eyes and whenever it did he would brush it back impatiently or toss his head boyishly. His eyes were a watery blue. Alison had a weakness for big blonds. He looked a little pale. She remembered that he had been ill. He had begun to chatter politely about the valley, Waddingtons and the weather. Alison took this as a sign of good breeding, respecting her wish not to discuss the murder. She found herself beginning to enjoy the evening.

'When did you arrive, Thomas?' she asked.

'A couple of days ago. I'm just getting settled in, ready to start work later this week.'

'Where are you going to live?'

'I've rented a cottage on the outskirts of Hopbridge – the area they call Easterbank – this end of town. It's only ten minutes' walk from the office. I shall be buying a place when I get settled, of course, but I thought it best to have a base to look around from first, while I get to know the area – see where the best houses are. Lady Armitage says you have a lovely house. I haven't been over to Little Hopford yet. Are you keen on interior design and all that?'

'Has DC Halsgrove got back from Hope Cottage yet?' Nick asked.

'Yes, sir. I sent her off to have a bit of a break, she's in the canteen now.'

'Better take a break yourself, Bill. Tell her I want to see her when she's finished, will you?'

Carol Halsgrove tapped on the door twenty minutes later and came in. 'You wanted to see me, sir?'

'Sit down, Carol. It's been a long day.' He smiled at her. She was a lively, petite woman of twenty-seven. She had been at HQ and had transferred to Hopbridge at the same time as Nick so they'd worked together for years. She was very bright and conscientious and he respected her judgement. He wanted her judgement now on a matter where he wasn't sure he could trust his own.

'You've been with Alison Hope for most of the day, Carol. What do you make of her?'

If the question surprised her she did not show it.

'I can't help liking her, sir. But that's not the sort of thing you mean, is it?'

'It might be. What do you like about her?'

'She's . . . clever and independent and . . . tough.'

94

'You admire those qualities in a woman?'

'In anyone,' she said, putting him firmly in his place, 'male or female'.

'So do I,' he said with a smile. 'But surely it's those very qualities which make her our most likely suspect. Whoever killed Aidan Hope acted quickly, opportunistically, ruthlessly and competently.'

'I should think she's got a hot temper,' Carol said uncertainly, 'but hitting an unconscious man from behind? I can't see that, sir.'

'No, that's a fair point and one I shall bear in mind. Of course you didn't get anything out of her all day? No, don't worry, I didn't expect it. If she is a murderer, she's too clever for that. Well, thank you, Carol. I'm going to reward you for your useful opinions by giving you a really rotten job.'

'I know,' she said cheerfully. 'Talk to all the people who were at the party.'

'I'm afraid so. With a bit of luck Sunday evening will be a good time to get hold of them. Right. For the ones who said they witnessed the fight I want you to get some details out of them – make sure they really did see it and are not just repeating what someone else saw. If there is anyone who falls into that category they may be trying to cover up the fact that they were absent from the party. See if anyone knows what the fight was about – it could be important. For both sets find out if they noticed anyone missing for any length of time between eleven and twelve, any length of time being not much less than half an hour.'

Carol looked doubtful.' Then she gave him a cheeky grin and said, 'People are always slipping off at parties, sir. Usually for half an hour or so. For quite innocent reasons – as far as we're concerned, that is.'

'Then they will find their amorous activities a little less private than they had hoped, I'm afraid.' He wondered if he sounded as priggish to her as he did to himself.

'But it means a lot of them will lie about it.'

'I know, Carol. We shall have lots of conflicting reports to sift through. Just do your best, as always.'

'If I do get any names of people missing at the relevant time, should I ask them about it?'

'No. If I can establish any genuine absences I may have to pay a personal call.'

Nick was beginning to see why people lied to the police. If that fight had broken out five minutes later: and where were you when this fight started, Mr Trevellyan? I was kissing Alison Hope in the garden, officer. Oh? I'll put you down on my list then.

The evening wore on and Alison found she was forgetting her troubles, sometimes for minutes on end. Thomas was very good company. He seemed genuinely interested in the computer-software business and asked several intelligent questions about the various packages available to solicitors. Molly Armitage was looking insufferably smug. It wasn't until after dinner that they really got on to the subject of Thomas' profession.

'Aren't you going to find it rather boring after life in the City?' Alison asked. 'You won't find any high-powered deals being conducted down here, you know. In fact it's hard to think what James Waddington really does. What does a country solicitor do?'

'Well, it's rather like being a GP instead of a specialist. You do a bit of everything: conveyancing, wills, swears, divorces, debt collecting – which is a bit sordid; evicting people – which is even more sordid. But you also get to do a bit of criminal law – even advocacy in the magistrates' courts – which is not something you ever get in the City. I hope I'm not being indiscreet in saying that JW has rather let the practice run down. I'm hoping to drum up some new business once I get established.'

Molly looked startled. 'You're hardly going to persuade people to move house or get divorced more often, and I don't know about swears, whatever they are. And you can hardly go about telling people to make wills. Most people round here haven't much to leave and anyway they don't want to think about dying.'

'Back on the subject of death again, Molly,' murmured Anton.

'I really don't mind talking about it in the abstract,' Alison said. 'It's the particular which worries me.'

'I think I can persuade people to make wills,' Thomas said. 'You'd be amazed what ill-conceived ideas people have about the intestacy laws. Little better than old wives' tales, most of them.'

Anton nodded in agreement. 'It's rather a complex subject in Britain – most places the wife just gets the lot.'

'Isn't that what happens here?' Alison asked. She knew perfectly well that it wasn't but thought a suitably feminine display of ignorance would please Thomas. You frightened men off if you let them realise too soon that you were much cleverer than they were. It went down well.

'By no means,' Thomas said with a little, patronising laugh. 'But I'm sure you've made your will, Alison, a sensible business woman like you.'

Alison went rather pink. 'Well, Jake has been on about it to me more than once. But I keep putting it off.'

'There,' he said, 'I rest my case. You can have the privilege of being my first customer if you like.'

'What happens if I don't make a will then?' She opened her eyes wide and hoped she wasn't overdoing it. Apparently not.

'Let's see. You're not presently married, I gather, no children?'

'No. I've never been married.'

'Illegitimate children have the same rights as legitimate ones these days. OK, parents? Brothers and sisters?'

'Both my parents are dead. I'm an only child.'

'Sounds like plenty of fees for a solicitor to sort your estate out then. I suppose you're going to tell me next that there are no other descendants of your grandparents either, in which case every penny you have will go to the crown.'

Molly coughed.

Alison said, 'I did have a cousin, until today.'

There was a stunned silence. Thomas looked mortified.

'I'm just so frightfully sorry. I got carried away pontificating about my pet subject.'

'It's OK. Don't worry about it.' She should have had more sense than to let that subject run on. She was beginning to feel about as welcome at a dinner party as Banquo's ghost. They all began to talk about something else.

97

Thomas and Alison left at the same time after Molly had failed to persuade Alison to say the night.

'Really, Molly, I'd rather be at home. All the police have gone now.'

'That's what worries me. At least while they were there you had some protection.' Somehow Alison didn't think that's what they had been there for.

'You need a dog,' Molly went on rather wildly. 'One of Castlemaine's full brothers is still looking for a home.'

'I'll think about it, Molly.'

'She wants an Alsatian, not a bloody lap dog, you silly woman,' said Anton.

Thomas helped Alison on with her coat and saw her to her car. As he was closing the driver's door for her he said, 'As we're both new around here perhaps we might see some of the sights together.'

'Yes, I'd like that.'

'I hope I wasn't insensitive this evening. Everything seemed so normal. I kept forgetting.'

'So did I, for which many thanks.'

'Can I phone you then?'

She pulled out one of her business cards. 'Yes, give me a ring, any time. I'm not geared up for work yet and I can't leave the valley without getting Interpol chasing after me.'

'There are very strict limits to what the police can do without arresting you. Would you like me to . . .?'

'No!' she said. 'I'm not a criminal and I'm not going to start acting like one.'

'Bravo. I think there's only one road up the valley, isn't there? So I'll be behind you as far as Hopbridge. Not that you won't outrun me in your Jag.' He shut the door and got into his own convertible Golf.

They drove off in convoy.

Chapter 12

When Nick arrived at the police station at eight-thirty the following morning, Bill was already hard at work.

'I've been on to the coroner's office,' he said virtuously.

'I'm surprised he was up this early,' Nick said sarcastically. Coroner's office was a rather flatulent title since, for the purpose of investigating sudden deaths in the valley, the crown was represented solely by a local solicitor who fitted it in between his other engagements, both business and social.

'He was having his breakfast.' Bill grinned. 'He's given the OK for the postmortem. He says he'll open the inquest on Wednesday morning. He's in the magistrates' court until then.'

'Suits me. With a bit of luck we'll have made an arrest by then.'

Enter Reg Grey.

Reg arrived at the station at a quarter to nine every working morning. Not taking your men by surprise was the most reliable method of not witnessing small breaches of discipline, so Reg was always punctual and usually went straight up to his room to have a nice cup of tea before descending at nine o'clock to an orderly station office to review overnight developments. This morning, however, he went straight up to Nick's office instead – determined to take a personal interest in the Hope case.

'Don't get up,' he said, as he walked in without knocking.

Bill, who was occupying the only respectable chair in the office – apart from Nick's – promptly vacated it and Reg sat down.

'Any developments on the Hope murder, Nick?'

'We're not ready to make an arrest, sir, if that's what you mean.'

'I see that the press are still not giving the man's name.'

'That's right. The police in Exeter are trying to find the widow, or at least her mother, but, as they pointed out to me at great length, it isn't easy.' They could have contacted at least another ten Cookes during the time they had taken pointing it out.

'We're sure she's in Exeter?'

'No. Only that her mother was living there five years ago. If they haven't turned her up by the end of the day we shall just have to release his name and appeal for her to come forward. It's not the way you'd want to hear about your husband's murder, though, is it?'

'We can't afford to be too sensitive.'

One allegation Reg was quite safe from, in Nick's opinion, was that of being oversensitive.

The phone rang. Bill answered it and listened. He put his hand over the mouthpiece.

'Talk of the devil. Exeter.'

'Excuse me, sir.' Nick picked up the phone.

'Trevellyan. Yes, excellent. As soon as possible. Thank you.' He hung up.

'That's it. They've found Judith Hope. They're sending her up by car so we can expect her before lunchtime. Call a press conference, Bill. Now the widow's been informed, we can release some details. Someone at that birthday party at the pub must have seen something.'

'Right you are.'

Since they had now started behaving as if he wasn't there, Reg got up. 'Well, I've got a meeting at HQ, which will occupy most of the day, so I'll leave you to it but I want to be kept informed on this one, Nick.'

'Sir.'

'I'll brief the assistant chief constable. I expect he'll want to send someone more senior in.'

'Sir.' No. No. No.

'It's not even as if you have the advantage of local knowledge, the victim and his family being newcomers. Oh yes, and I've told Inspector Burcombe to take over on this ARM business, as you've got your plate full for a bit.'

'I'd have thought it could wait,' Nick said, puzzled.

'No. Burcombe will handle it. Anything else you need?'

'Just twice as much manpower, sir.' This was a standing joke and Reg duly laughed and went out.

Bill rang the press, the local radio station and the TV news office in Taunton. After several calls he had fixed the conference for midday.

'Get me that security firm on the phone,' Nick said.

'E & D Security said that their Mr McCarthy was out on the road. He spent most of his time driving around and no, they didn't have any way of getting in touch with him. He usually rang in during the afternoon, if the inspector would care to call back then. No, he hadn't worked for them long but he came from a London firm with the highest references. Nick took the name of the London firm and shouted for DC Halsgrove.

Bill was reading through such technical reports as they had received.

'No prints on the ashtray except Leighland's, and they were pretty smudged, showing that someone had held it afterwards.' Nick often wondered why they bothered – as if the murderer hadn't got the sense not to leave prints. 'No prints in the room except Leighland, Mrs Leighland and Hope himself. A few hairs – some dyed blond, that's Mrs L most likely, some dark. None red. No footprints worth a damn in the car park. It's not made up round the edges but at least a hundred people traipsed over the muddy bits before the body was discovered.'

'Is there anything useful in there at all,' Nick interrupted, 'or is it just a catalogue of negatives?'

'Only that the ashtray was definitely the murder weapon and that there are smudged footprints on the asphalt roof, where it hadn't quite dried out.'

'That's better.'

'Size seven.'

'Quite small. Certainly nôt Ashcroft. What size does Miss Hope take?'

101

'Six and a half.'

'Close.'

'Doesn't match any of hers. Window break was a neat, professional job, like you said.'

Did Alison Hope's talents include being a glazier? Nick wondered. They could get on to the DIY shops in the valley, to see if anyone had bought a glass-cutter lately. But if it was her, she'd have more sense than to buy it locally. Waste of time but it had to be done.

Mike Brewster appeared at half past eleven. He sprawled his long body on a rickety chair, his feet stretched out before him until he was almost diagonal. He yawned.

'It's being typed up,' he said, as soon as Nick opened his mouth.

'Anything useful?'

'Nothing to add to what I said on the spot. The body was of a man aged between thirty and thirty-five, a little undernourished but otherwise healthy. He had consumed a large amount of alcohol not long before death but no more than many another man out for a Saturday night's partying. It certainly had no connection with his death, which was caused by a brain haemorrhage brought about by a blow to the back of the head with a sharp object. Unconsciousness would have been instant, with death following very shortly. He wouldn't have made a sound – didn't know what hit him.'

'We do,' Nick said. 'Why didn't the murderer bring a murder weapon with him, Bill? It points to an opportunist crime.'

'Always safer to use a weapon which can't be traced back to you,' Bill said dampeningly – he took their devil's-advocate game too far at times.

'But he couldn't know there would be such a handy instrument just waiting for him,' Nick insisted.

'He – or she – probably had a weapon with him – or her – but chose to use something on the spot instead.' Bill emphasised the second pronoun meaningfully each time. He hadn't actually said yet that he'd made his mind up – Nick was supposed to be the brains of the outfit – but he didn't need to. He put on his long-suffering look, the one which said: We could have arrested her yesterday, beaten a confession out of her and had today off.

'I am still here, you know,' Brewster said. 'Would you like some coffee, Mike? Thanks, don't mind if I do.'

'Can you pin the time of death down any closer, Mike?' was the question he got instead.

Brewster shook his head. 'No. If he'd had a proper meal that evening it might have helped but you told me yourself that he was just nibbling at party food all the time. I stand by what I said last night. He was wet, which would have depressed his body temperature. Alcohol also depresses the temperature. Ther are too many variables for me to pin it down between eleven and twelve-fifteen.'

'Off the record, though, you must have some instinct. I won't tell anyone.'

There was a long pause. It was like trying to cajole a Sally Army major along to a booze-up with promises that there would be a stripper. Nick had plenty of time to refine this into an epigram to pass on to Bill afterwards before Dr Brewster spoke again.

'Earlier rather than later then, but that really is off the record.' He gave Nick a furtive look as though wondering if he was recording all this to be used against him. Which reminded Nick that he still had Alison Hope's tape recorder. He took it out of his drawer and put it on the desk so that he wouldn't forget to give it back to her. The paranoid pathologist jumped six inches off his chair.

'Would the murderer have got blood on himself?' Nick asked, pressing home his advantage. 'I mean, would it have spurted up?'

'Not if he was careful. If he had a sitting target, as it appears he did, he needn't have got any blood on himself at all, except a bit on his hands or gloves.'

'All washed away by a nice, hot shower,' Bill murmured.

'Not really a woman's crime, is it?' Nick said with distaste.

Mike Brewster clicked his tongue. 'Funny. I could have sworn you were the same Nick Trevellyan who was lecturing me about sexism in the pub the other day.' He got up. 'Well, thanks for the offer but I'll go down to the canteen.'

There was a good turnout at the press conference as the story was big enough to make the nationals. Nick made a brief statement to the effect that a man identified as Aidan Hope, an Irish citizen, had been found dead in his room at the Bird in Hand public house in Little Hopford in the early hours of Sunday morning, following a blow to the head. The police were treating the case as murder. It was obvious from the questions Nick was asked that, while he had observed the prohibition on releasing Hope's name, Jos Leighland had spoken freely on everything else he knew. There was no chance of keeping secret the way Hope had died.

No, no arrest was yet contemplated.

Yes, there was a widow who had been informed and was on her way to the valley.

Yes, it was true that Hope's room at the pub had been ransacked after the murder took place. The police would like to hear from any member of the public who had been in Little Hopford on Saturday night and had seen anything at all which might give the police a lead.

No, Inspector Trevellyan had no theories yet and was pursuing the usual course of interview and elimination. House-to-house enquiries were being carried out in Little Hopford.

No, County Headquarters were not being called in at this stage, let alone Scotland Yard. Nick had no authority to say this but as Reg had gone off without leaving any explicit instructions, he pleased himself.

Fortunately Judith Hope arrived while the press conference was still in progress and was able to enter the building unseen. The press men left, unaware of her presence, to camp outside Hope Cottage.

Nick made Judith Hope comfortable, offered his condolences, which she accepted, and some tea, which she declined. She was not at all what he had expected. Alison's description of her had led him to expect some sort of vamp. Here was a perfectly ordinary, housewifely woman. He was no longer in any doubt that Alison Hope had been jealous of her friend.

She did not cry. Her eyes were a little puffy but otherwise there was no outward sign of grief. Nick thought her rather drab in her woollen cardigan and sensible skirt. Her hair was almost as red as Alison's but looked as if it needed a good wash. He noticed that she had green eyes too and remembered suddenly what Aidan Hope had said that day in the pub – something about red-haired, green-eyed beauties. Whom had he meant? Surely not this woman. There must have been more between him and his cousin than she was letting on. Had their quarrels been not solely about business after all?

Perhaps it was not strange if the two women, ostensibly friends, had been rivals – being so alike. Judith was also tall but quite painfully thin. She wore the sort of defeated look he had seen so often on the faces of women from the council estates of West Hopbridge. Defeat born of no money; no time to themselves; no affection or consideration; unwanted children. Judith Hope had a child.

'I hope your son is all right, Mrs Hope,' he began.

'He was very fond of his father.' Her voice shook and she rummaged in her bag for a handkerchief and blew her nose. 'He's staying with my mother. He'll get over it. He's nine – they're very resilient at that age – not like at our age.' Nick realised with a jolt that she must be – what? twenty-nine, thirty? She looked much older.

He decided to concentrate on a few facts for the moment until she was at her ease.

'Will you be staying at Hope Cottage?' he asked.

'God, no, I hardly know her now. I'll find a bed-and-breakfast place in town. I'll stay until the funeral. When will he be released for burial?'

'Not immediately, certainly not before the inquest is opened on Wednesday. Do you want him cremated round here?'

'Buried. He was a Catholic – not a very good one. They're not supposed to be cremated. I'll get him buried here. Who identified the body?'

'Miss Alison Hope.' Judith nodded. 'We can arrange for you to see him if you like.'

'No . . . no thanks.'

He said gently, 'I have to ask you where you were on Saturday night, Mrs Hope. It's pure formality.'

'I was at home, my mother's home that is, all evening.'

'Who else was there?'

'Mum, Daniel and our neighbour, Mrs Collier.'

105

'May I have Mrs Collier's address, please?' Judith gave it. 'What time did she leave?'

'Oh, it must have been well after eleven. She can talk the hind leg off a donkey. It was pouring with rain at about eleven o'clock so she waited until it stopped, then went home.'

'I understand that you and your husband were separated, Mrs Hope.' She dabbed the handkerchief to her eyes. He said, 'Take your time, there's no hurry, at your own pace.'

She bowed her head. 'He disappeared back in May, just went off one day. Left me with no money to pay the rent or anything. I had to leave our flat. His creditors were harassing me.'

'Creditors? Do you know who they were? Any names?'

'Some.'

'Could you make me a list of any enemies your husband might have had, any creditors who had threatened him, that sort of thing? Anyone with any sort of grudge.'

She nodded and gave him a tight-lipped smile. 'He had a knack of making enemies.'

'So you left London,' Nick prompted.

'I went to stay with my mother in Exeter.'

'When was that?'

'About the twentieth of May, I should think.'

'He told Miss Alison Hope that the separation was just temporary.'

She looked angry suddenly. 'Not as far as I was concerned. I can only take so much.'

'So you have not seen your husband since the beginning of May?'

'I've seen him all right. He turned up in Exeter a couple of weeks ago and hung around outside the house for ages until I agreed to speak to him.'

'What did he want?'

'To tell me about some wild scheme he had for making money – or rather getting money out of Alison.' Bill and Nick exchanged glances.

'You mean his claim that half of Hope Software was his?'

'Oh, you know about that.'

'Yes, but I'd like to hear your version, or the version your husband gave you.'

106

Judith's story tallied with Alison's. Adam Knox had died and there were no other witnesses to her arrangement with her cousin.

'He knew Alison had come down to the West Country to live,' Judith said. 'We read about it in the paper some time in the spring. He seemed to think all he had to do was come up here and she'd just hand over half the business to him.'

'What did you make of this plan?' Nick asked.

'Aidan lived in a fantasy world – cloud-cuckoo-land. Not that Alison couldn't have helped us, being her only relations. I thought she might give him something out of pity.'

'Was that the last you ever saw of him?'

'Yes, but he rang me on Friday. He seemed quite cock-a-hoop – said that Alison was going to come round. He said he was going to some party at her place on Saturday and he was going to sweet-talk her then. Sweet-talk Alison! Moonshine.'

'What makes you say that?'

'You might as well try and *sweet-talk* a bag of nails. All these years, she could have helped us, but she didn't.'

'Miss Hope claims she lost touch with you and your husband.'

'Oh, well, it must be true . . . if she says so.'

'What is your opinion of your husband's claim to half the business?'

Judith dismissed the question with a wave of her hand. 'I've no opinion. They never involved me in the business from the start. I might have had a say in it. It's all academic now, isn't it?'

Nick looked at her hard. Hadn't she realised the implications?

'Had your husband made a will, to your knowledge?'

'Aidan! Should he have made a will saying who he left his debts to?'

'Then he died intestate?'

'I assume so.'

'But don't you see, Mrs Hope, you are his heir. Your son too if the estate is substantial – which it would be if it included half the assets of Hope Software. It is hardly academic.'

Judith stared at him in amazement. 'Who's been telling you this rubbish? The partnership agreement they drew up between them provided that each would inherit from the other if either of them died. I told you they left me right out of it. Even if he did own part of the business when he died . . . she owns it all now for sure.'

'She's a cold woman, that Alison Hope,' Bill said when Judith had gone.

'You think so?'

'Yeah, don't you?'

Nick thought of his own reaction to her that day on the road, and what Jack Ashcroft had said about her at the party. But she had not been cold to him that evening.

'I think she can hand out the freeze treatment when she wants to,' he temporised.

'I don't just mean her manner – that's stuck up all right. But she must be loaded and she didn't do anything to help her cousins, and them with a little kid too.'

'Let's have a look at this agreement, then.' Penruan had brought it back with him late on Sunday night but Nick had only glanced at it, checking the headings and the signatures. It had not occurred to him to read it in more detail. Bill produced Aidan's copy of the agreement and Nick leafed through it. Through the legal obfuscation he judged that was Judith had said was correct.

'Get me Miss Hope's solicitor on the phone,' he said. 'He doesn't know we've seen the agreement. Let's see what he has to say about it, shall we?'

Bill looked out his notes, dialled the London number and asked for Jake Trowerbridge.

'Blows a hole a mile wide through your no-real-motive theory, sir,' he said smugly. 'Hello, Mr Trowerbridge? I have Detective Inspector Trevellyan of Hopbridge CID for you.' Nick picked up his own extension.

Alison had telephoned Jake Trowerbridge just that morning. He had in any case seen the first newspaper reports. He had offered to come straight down but she had refused, giving him the same reasons she had given Thomas. But she had instructed him to be co-operative if questioned. After a few polite preliminaries, Nick came to the point.

108

'Did you draw up the original partnership agreement between Alison and Aidan Hope?'

'No, but I'm familiar with it. I still have Miss Hope's copy on file.'

'What are the terms of the partnership?'

'Well, it's quite complex. I can't go over it all on the phone. In any case, as Miss Hope has told you, the partnership was terminated by mutual agreement.'

'But not in writing.'

'That's so.'

'Can you tell me what the agreement was for the business in the event of either of the signatories dying?'

Jake Trowerbridge hesitated.

'The survivor took everything,' he said finally. 'It's like joint ownership of a house or a joint bank account. A lot of people think that means that you each own half but it doesn't. It means that you both own all of it – a concept which non-lawyers sometimes have difficulty in grasping.'

'It's quite clear, thank you,' Nick said tartly. He could do without being patronised by Jake Trowerbridge.

'*Totum tenet et nihil tenet*,' Jake said relentlessly. 'Broadly speaking that means – '

'He owns everything and owns nothing.'

'Um, yes,' Trowerbridge agreed, not used to being beaten at his own game.

'Isn't that rather an unusual arrangement in a business partnership?'

'Mmmm . . . it's not *the* most usual arrangement but it's not unknown. In a very small business, struggling to get off the ground, the partners are all active – people who know the business and work in it. You want to avoid any say in the running passing to someone quite unconnected with the trade or profession, perhaps even a minor. That could bring the business to its knees in no time.'

'But Mr Hope already had a wife and child.'

'As I say, I didn't draw up the agreement. I probably wouldn't have advised its being drawn up like that. I imagine that when the business was off the ground and in profit the terms of the partnership would have been varied to allow each partner to provide for his or her dependants. But the matter didn't arise since Mr Hope sold his share to my client and disappeared.'

Nick noticed that Alison Hope had become *my client* all of a sudden. Jake Trowerbridge was as well able as himself to grasp the implications of this new information.

'So what was your advice to Miss Hope when she consulted you?' he asked.

'That she should come to some sort of arrangement with her cousin.'

'Pay him off?'

'If you want to put it that way.'

'Thank you very much for your time, Mr Trowerbridge,' Nick said, with disarming politeness. 'So there can be no doubt, now, that Miss Hope owns the whole of the business?'

'Exactly,' Jake said, 'or rather,' he amended hurriedly, 'there never was any doubt.'

They hung up.

Chapter 13

'Shall I have her brought in, sir?' Bill said after some minutes had passed in silence. Nick did not reply at first. 'Sir, we can't put off arresting her much longer. Normally with this much evidence we'd have picked up a suspect by now.'

'We've not got a shred of evidence. Motive and opportunity but no evidence at all. No one saw her at the pub that night. If she was ever in the room, she's left no trace.'

'It's early days yet. There are still plenty of people to question and someone may come forward as a result of the press conference. If you arrest her she may simply admit to it and that'll be the end of it.'

'Have her brought in but don't arrest her yet,' Nick said at last. 'Unless she refuses to come,' he added, as an afterthought.

He didn't get up as Bill showed her into his office an hour later. How pale she was! Was the shock of her cousin's death beginning to tell or was she afraid? She looked round the dreary room and managed a thin smile. He did not smile back.

'Please take a seat, Miss Hope.' She sank down on the chair opposite him. He reminded her of the caution, watching her closely. Body language was supposed to indicate if a suspect was telling the truth or not. Hers told him nothing except that she was emotionally exhausted.

'Does all this mean I'm under arrest?' She spoke quietly and without expression, as if it hardly mattered to her one way or the other, but Nick noticed that her fists were tightly

111

clenched. Alison despised weakness in anyone, but especially in herself.

'Not at present,' he reassured her. 'If you are arrested you will be immediately informed of the fact. You are here voluntarily and are free to leave should you so wish.' Since she was co-operating there seemed no point in telling her that if she tried to leave he would indeed arrest her. He also reminded her that she had the right to legal representation during the interview.

'Are we to sit here for hours while my solicitor gets down from London?' Nick proffered the duty solicitor. 'No thanks. If I have a solicitor he will just tell me to keep quiet. I have nothing to hide and can answer your questions perfectly well, inspector.'

'Good. I've been making enquiries into the partnership agreement between you and Mr Hope. Why didn't you tell me that you stood to inherit his half of the business on his death?'

'Because it isn't true.'

Nick glared at her in annoyance. He wasn't going to have her treat him like an idiot. He snapped at her. 'Don't lie to me! I'd better warn you that I spoke to your solicitor on the telephone just an hour ago.'

'Yes, I know.'

'Then you must see that it's pointless to deny it.'

'No. I mean that was the original agreement but, as I've told you over and over, he didn't own half the business. I bought him out five years ago.' She banged on Nick's desk. 'The partnership was terminated by mutual consent.' Bang. 'His death has made no difference to my position at all.' Bang.

Nick stared at her in exasperation. Could anyone be so naive? Was it a sign of her innocence or was it just a good act? She was leaving him no choice but to arrest her.

'Get me Sergeant Appleby right away,' he said to Bill. Appleby was the custody officer. Bill put on his about-time-too face and reached for the phone.

There was a knock on the door at that moment and Carol Halsgrove came in. She looked pleased with herself.

'Have you got a minute, sir? It's urgent.'

'Leave that call for a moment, sergeant.' Nick followed her out. 'It had better be good, Carol.'

'I've made all those enquiries about Ian McCarthy. E & D haven't heard from him today, which they would normally expect to do.'

'Is that all?' Nick said impatiently. It wasn't like Carol to interrupt an interview with a suspect for anything so trivial.

'No, sir,' she rebuked him. 'I checked out his references. The company in London he was supposed to be working for before this have just rung me back. They had an Ian McCarthy there all right.' She paused for dramatic effect and took out her notebook. 'Here's the description they gave me: tall, dark hair, about thirty-five, smartly dressed . . .'

'But that's nothing like the man who called on Miss Hope!'

'No, sir, it's nothing like the man who arrived at the Dawlish depot last week either.'

'Well done, Carol,' he said enthusiastically. She flushed with pleasure. 'I think we'll get Miss Hope to do us a Photofit of Ian McCarthy. Meet me downstairs in a minute.'

He burst back into his office. Alison started nervously.

'Downstairs,' he said. 'I've got a little job for you, Miss Hope. I want a Photofit of Ian McCarthy, so start racking your memory.'

Alison was quick and positive in picking out the components that made up the features of Ian McCarthy.

'You said he had a Scottish accent,' Nick said.

'I thought it was Scottish. I'm not very good at regional accents but my mother was of Scottish stock.'

'Could it have been Northern Irish by any chance? They can sound similar and he may have been putting it on and thought a Scottish accent was his best bet.'

'I don't really know. It's possible, yes.'

'You said he smoked roll-ups?'

'Yes, is it important?'

'It might be.'

He handed the Photofit to Carol Halsgrove.

'Get this copied for the house-to-house. Then fax a copy through to the Yard. See if they recognise him. Go straight to the anti-terrorist squad.' He turned back to Alison. 'All right, Miss Hope, thank you for your help. Constable Halsgrove will drive you home in a few minutes.'

'You mean I'm free to go?' she said faintly.

'Yes, certainly.'

To his consternation she sank back on her chair and let out a strangled sob. Carol Halsgrove, always prepared, moved forward with a packet of tissues but Nick waved her away.

'Stop it,' he said sharply. 'If you break down in front of a load of coppers, you'll never forgive yourself.'

'No,' she sniffled, getting up. 'Thanks.'

'We should have arrested her,' Bill said, after the two women had gone. 'She might have admitted it. She nearly broke down there.'

'I thought you said she was cold and hard,' Nick reminded him.

'Well, even the tough ones can be worn down.'

'We're not here to make women cry. Her cousin has been murdered – the shock has probably just come home to her.'

Nick rapped out a series of orders:

'Get all the ports watching for McCarthy. Get the number of his van from the security firm and get all forces looking out for it and him. Get that Photofit in all the papers. Give it to the men on the house-to-house and tell them to start all over again. I want all the people who were at that disco interviewed again. I want a positive sighting of McCarthy in Little Hopford on Saturday night.'

'Steady on, sir, you can't go putting evidence into people's heads.'

'*Can't?*' Nick said dramatically. '*Can't* is not a word to use to . . . to detective inspectors,' he finished lamely.

'You're in a good mood all of a sudden.' Bill gave him a sour look.

'We've got a suspect, Bill.'

'Yeah, a bloke who's disappeared. So we can spend all our time looking for him. I was quite happy with Alison Hope as murderess, thank you.' Nick did not reply. He had not been at all happy with Alison Hope as murderess. 'What's all this stuff about roll-up cigarettes anyway?' Bill went on.

'An RUC man once told me that it's an almost infallible sign in the province that you've been inside. And what do people go to prison for in Northern Ireland?'

'All the usual things.'

114

'Yes, and a few more.'

'What makes you think Hope was mixed up with terrorists?' Bill objected. 'He doesn't seem the type.'

'He told Miss Hope he was in funds at the moment. Does that sound like the Aidan Hope we are growing to know and love?'

Bill shrugged. 'Just bluffing, like she said.'

'I wonder. Get the all-ports call out first.' Bill picked up the phone. 'And get them looking for the real Ian McCarthy while you're about it,' Nick added, to keep him nice and busy.

'Nothing on that black dress.' Nick was leafing through a pile of reports which had turned up in his in-tray. 'But they say Miss Hope must have a remarkably efficient washing machine.' Very likely.

'If there'd been any blood you'd expect them to find it none the less,' Bill said.

'Quite,' Nick agreed cheerfully. 'Therefore there is no blood. No asphalt to be seen on any of the shoes we brought in, hers or Jack's. The Land-Rover's completely kaput and probably has been for some time. Hope hasn't got a police record. Quite a number of judgements against him for debt, though, largely unenforced. I should think he just moved on when things got too hot.'

'Everything we're getting in is negative,' Bill grumbled. 'Time we got some positive evidence.'

'Too right. Come in! Oh, it's you, Paul. How are you getting on?'

Detective Constable Penruan came into the room. Nick pointed to a chair and he collapsed on it thankfully.

'We've finished the pub-party guests who live in Hopcliff, sir. I'm on my way up to the other end of the valley now, to see how they're getting on there, so I thought I'd better report in. I get the impression that, by eleven o'clock, most of them wouldn't have noticed if Hope had been shot down in front of them.'

'Big celebration?'

'That's right. Complete blank on sightings of Alison Hope and Jack Ashcroft.'

'What about Leighland?'

'I interviewed the regular barmaid this morning. She's adamant that he didn't leave the bar at all between eleven and twelve. They were rushed off their feet and wouldn't have been able to cope without him.'

'So if Leighland did it he was cutting it pretty fine.'

'He could have gone straight up there at twelve,' Bill put in. 'No one would have thought anything of it, since his own bedroom was up there.'

'It still gives him only a few minutes to kill Hope and ransack the room before he gave the alarm. And why raise the alarm then? Much more sensible to wait until morning – obscure the time of death even more.'

'I'll get on with the rest of the guests, then,' Penruan said wearily, getting up.

Nick gave him a sympathetic look. 'Not quite as simple as that, I'm afraid, Paul. I've got another photo for you to take out. Or rather Photofit.'

'Does that mean what I think its means?'

'You'll have to go back on the ones you've already done.'

'Yes, sir. Thank you, sir. Cancel the squash game for this evening, then?'

'Oh, I don't know. It's quite a late booking, isn't it?'

'Eight-thirty.'

'Do us good, clear the mind.' Paul made a face. His mind was fairly clear at the best of times.

'Of everything except physical pain,' he said. 'See you there, then.' He went out.

'After all,' Nick said, to no one in particular. 'If he's that tired, I might even beat him.'

The phone was ringing as Alison arrived at Hope Cottage. She rushed to answer, knowing that it would stop if she didn't.

'Alison?' said a voice she didn't recognise. 'I've been trying to get you for ages. It's Tom Howard.'

'Who?'

'Tom Howard, we met at Lady Armitage's last night.'

'God, I'm being really stupid. You were introduced as Thomas and I didn't make the connection.'

He laughed. 'Thomas is such a pompous-sounding name, isn't it? Never mind that. Will you have dinner with me tonight?'

'Oh, it's really nice of you, Tom, but . . .'

'I know . . . you've got a lot on your mind. I hoped I might be able to help you forget it, that's all. Just a quiet little dinner – you needn't talk to me if you don't want to. I shall just sit there and rabbit on about the weather, and films, and the scenery, and . . . oh, anything at all.'

She hesitated – it was nice of him and she did want to see him again. He coaxed. She agreed.

'I'll pick you up at – '

'No, don't come here,' she yelped. 'I've got hundreds of reporters on my doorstep. I don't want you to be involved in all this.'

'They won't stay all evening, will they?'

'Don't bet on it. I'll meet you in town. I can give them the slip.' The reporters had to leave their cars along the road a bit, where the grass verge began. So she knew if she just drove off in her Jaguar they'd never catch her.

'Anything you say,' Tom said amenably. 'Do you know of a decent restaurant?'

'No, I'm virtually a stranger here myself.'

'There's a little place just off the Market Square. I don't suppose the food will be wonderful but it's candlelit so it'll be nice and dark. It's in Sheep Street, the Leg of Mutton, OK? I'll book us in for eight o'clock. See you later.'

Reg Grey got back from his meeting at County Headquarters at half past four and summoned Nick to his office. He was standing by the window, holding an account of Nick's conversation with Jake Trowerbridge that morning. He waved it at Nick.

'I understand you had Alison Hope in for questioning this afternoon.'

'Yes, sir.'

'But you have let her go without arresting her. It seems to me that we have enough evidence to justify detaining her. People are saying we're not arresting her because she's related to Sir Anton. They're implying she's still at large because she's got powerful friends.'

'She's co-operating, coming into the station when asked.'

'You've got a nose for it, Nick. You don't reckon the Hope girl for this one, is that it?'

'I didn't say that. As far as known motive goes she's head and shoulders above the rest. But there's been a new development, sir.'

He told Reg about Ian McCarthy. Reg sat down and listened. 'Why didn't you tell me this before, Nick?'

'It's only just come up.'

'All right then, pursue this line of enquiry. It certainly looks very suspicious, I grant you. I told the ACC that an arrest was imminent and he agreed not to send anyone else in for the time being – he's a bit short-handed anyway.' Nick caught Reg's eye and managed a grateful look. Reg would call the debt in soon enough. He went on. 'But I'd like this case wound up. It's causing gossip. The fact that you and I were at that party doesn't look too good.'

'Aren't policemen allowed to have any friends?' Nick asked wearily.

'You know what the *Valley Voice* is like. Ashcroft won't hesitate to allege police corruption. He'll be dragging Tim Lingfield up from the grave before we know where we are.'

'I think you'll find that Ashcroft won't be too quick with his allegations this time, sir,' Nick said dictatorially. 'He doesn't come out of the whole business too well either.'

Which showed how wrong you could be.

Carol Halsgrove burst into Nick's office at five o'clock.

'The Yard say he's a wanted terrorist, sir, an Irishman called Gerard Doherty. He was last heard of in Belfast but he went to ground a few weeks ago, just as they were about to pick him up. The word on the grapevine is that he crossed over to England. They think that's his real name. He also calls himself Gerard Murphy and John Doherty. They're already watching the ports for him.'

'The Irish connection!' Nick said. 'Now we're getting somewhere.'

Chapter 14

Alison roared past the reporters in her Jaguar at twenty to eight. One or two of them started to make for their cars, then realised the futility of it and wandered off to the pub.

To be on the safe side she left her car near the bridge and walked the short distance to the Market Square. She couldn't help wishing for once that she had a less obtrusive car. One of the reporters might have told a colleague in town to look out for her. As she rounded the Cornmarket into the Market Square she ran straight into Nick Trevellyan. It was hard to say which of them was the more surprised and embarrassed. Alison tried to pretend that she didn't know hers was the first name on his list of murderers: underlined in red, probably.

'Hello, where are you off to?' she said gaily.

'I live here.' He pointed to an elegant, early-Victorian building just across the square.

'Goodness, is that your house?' she said, in surprise.

'No, the top floor is my flat. And where are you off to, Miss Hope?'

'Is that an official or an unofficial question?'

'Call it unofficial. Unless that means you're going to tell me to mind my own business.'

Alison reddened. It occurred to her that candlelit dinners for two might not seem very appropriate at the moment with her cousin lying dead in the mortuary. Not everyone would realise that Tom was just a kind friend. She prevaricated.

'I'm meeting a friend for supper. Must dash or I'll be late.'

She did not look back but she could feel his eyes on her as

she crossed the square, turned into Sheep Street and entered the restaurant.

Although it was only five to eight Tom Howard was waiting for her inside the door. He led her to a table for two in a secluded alcove. Alison discovered that she was hungry. She ordered, picked up a bread roll, spread it liberally with butter and began to eat. Tom smiled approval at her across the table.

'It's nice to see you've got your appetite back. You hardly ate a thing at the Armitages' last night.'

'Didn't I? I don't remember.'

'There you are then. You had no appetite at all.'

'That's not like me. I always thought I was such a rational, unemotional person but this business has really shaken me up.'

'Don't talk about it if you don't want to,' he said gently.

'No, I'm ready to talk about it now – if you're ready to listen. It will make a change to talk to someone who doesn't keep questioning my version of events and trying to trip me up all the time.'

As they ate their dinner she went over the events of Saturday night. Tom listened attentively, putting in a sensible question here and there. She told him the whole sorry story – about Aidan and the partnership and their verbal agreement of five years ago and the stinking, lousy trick he had tried to play on her. She drank a little wine and began to feel like a human being again. Tom was a good and sympathetic listener.

'So these policemen, the inspector and the superintendent, were actually there at your party?' he said incredulously. 'They're friends of yours?'

'Not really, I hardly know them. I don't think they're going to be my friends after all this, do you?'

'Have the police been giving you a hard time?'

'They had me in for questioning today. The inspector – he looks at me so coldly, I can't tell what he's thinking. I was so sure he was going to arrest me this afternoon.'

'No!' Tom was horrified. 'I just can't believe it.'

'I was sure of it. I'd almost geared myself up to it. You know, so I wouldn't crack up when it happened. But then he got some new information, about that security man I told you about, and he got me to do a Photofit picture of him.'

'That's great! They've got a real suspect. Now perhaps they'll leave you in peace.'

'Then he said I could go. My God, the relief! That was when I nearly broke down and cried.' She twisted her spoon round and round in her hand, remembering the scene. 'The humiliation of it!'

But it would have been so much more humiliating if she *had* cried, and he had known that and had not let her.

'I don't think I could bear it if he arrested me,' she said miserably. 'Being locked up in a cell, treated like a criminal.'

'It won't come to that. Here.' Tom leant across and wiped a trickle from her cheek with his napkin.

There's some beer in the kitchen,' Nick said. 'Help yourself.' He sat down on the sofa.

'Thanks.' Penruan reappeared a minute or two later with two cans of beer and two tumblers.

'I've put some coffee on as well,' he said. 'I think I'm dehydrating. That was a dirty trick, wasn't it? Making me traipse round the valley all day just so you could beat me at squash.'

'That's why I did it.'

Penruan sat down in the armchair and opened one of the cans. He put the other down in front of Nick, who ignored it. He was too busy staring out of the window across the square.

'I dare say you're worried about your electricity bills, Nick,' Penruan said at last, 'but are we really going to sit here with the lights out?'

'It gives a better view of the square,' Nick told him.

'Oh, good. That explains everything.' Paul peered down into the deserted streets. 'Hopbridge on a Monday night – why do we stay?'

'I like it here.'

'I can't see anything. Only if I'm doing some detecting, I like to know what it is I'm detecting.'

'What's the time?'

'Quarter to ten.'

'Good, about right. Shouldn't have long to wait.'

'Oh, I give up. Be mysterious then.' Penruan leant back in his armchair and drank his beer.

121

'I heard quite a bit about this Trevellyan from Lady Armitage last night,' Tom said. He paused and Alison looked at him expectantly.

'She was full of the murder and before Sir Anton joined us she was telling me all about him. She said he had a pleasant manner but that underneath he was really very clever and pretty tough. It seems his subordinates think the world of him, but his superiors are a bit less keen. He gets results but he's too independent-minded for their taste.'

Tom glanced round, cloak-and-dagger, and lowered his voice. 'She was telling me how he nearly blotted his copybook a couple of years ago, when he first moved back to Hopbridge. He took up with a girl, a schoolteacher from the comprehensive, who was some sort of subversive.'

'What!' Alison said. 'You mean a criminal or something?'

'Well, no,' he admitted. 'There was nothing actually known against her but she had some very dubious friends, political extremists. Anyway, it seems the superintendent gave him a friendly warning about being careful who he associated with and Trevellyan virtually told him to mind his own business.'

'Good for him. His private life is his own affair.'

'But it isn't, Alison. A policeman must not do anything to jeopardise his impartiality and, almost as importantly, nothing that the public would perceive as jeopardising it.'

This struck Alison as a bit pompous but all she said was 'So what happened?'

'Well, the affair just fizzled out and no more was said. Bit of an anti-climax really.'

Alison was thoughtful as she sipped her coffee. She decided to say what she was thinking.

'Molly had no business telling you something she must have heard in confidence, through Anton's being on the Police Authority. Anton would be furious if he found out. You'd better not repeat it.' She realised that she sounded like the school prefect and Tom looked annoyed for a moment.

'I wasn't gossiping for the sake of it! The point I'm trying to make is that you mustn't be taken in by his pleasant manner. In a case like this, where there's a lot of publicity, the police are under pressure to make a quick arrest. So be very careful what you say to him. In fact, don't say anything to him at all. If he hauls you in again sit mute and ask for a solicitor. I'll write my number down for you.' He scribbled on a piece of paper and she stuffed it into her pocket. 'I'm not starting work in the practice until the end of the week, not properly, I can come at a moment's notice.' Alison mumbled her thanks.

'I think he takes it hard that a murder should be committed almost under his nose like that,' she said.

'He could hardly have been expected to foresee it.'

'All the same, I think he feels very personally involved.'

'There!' Nick said triumphantly. 'There she is. Who the hell is that with her?'

'She? Who?' Penruan joined him at the window.

'Alison Hope.'

'So that's her.'

'I'd forgotten you hadn't seen her – in the flesh.'

Penruan watched intently as the two figures passed under a streetlamp. 'Her photo doesn't do her justice.'

No, Nick thought, no photograph could capture the sheer energy of the woman.

'Bit of all right, if you ask me,' Penruan went on.

'I don't remember asking you,' Nick said sarcastically, 'but my memory isn't what it was.' He knew from experience that trying to put Penruan down was like trying to flatten a rubber ball with a hammer.

'Only the way Bill was going on about her, I was expecting the Wicked Witch of the West,' Paul said, unflattened.

'She's not Bill's sort, that's for sure. And it's Sergeant Deacon to you.'

'Yes, sir.'

The two walkers turned under the Cornmarket and the two watchers could now see them clearly.

'Very nice. Moves well. Bit of class,' said Penruan, the connoisseur of the female form.

Nick gave him a vinegary look. 'Like older women, do you?' he enquired.

'How old is she?'

'Twenty-nine, thirty.'

'Oh, as old as that.'

'One foot in the grave,' Nick agreed.

123

'I don't mind, though, older women are more experienced
. . . and more grateful.'

'If you could just stop drooling over her and have a look at
the man . . .' Nick suggested.

'Have done. Never seen him before.'

'Sure?'

'Yep.'

'Nor have I. Somebody's introduced a joker into the pack.'

The two walkers stopped under a streetlamp, waiting to
cross the road. He took her arm protectively.

'Wouldn't kick her out of bed,' Penruan said, recklessly
piling straws on the camel's hump.

Nick gave him the smile which brought housebreakers out
in goose pimples.

'Rehydrated yet, Paul?' he asked sweetly.

'Oh no!'

'I'd go myself, of course.' Nick was all wide-eyed innocence. 'But she knows me.'

'You callous bastard!' Penruan affected a limp as far as the
door, then sprinted down the stairs. A few seconds later Nick
saw him cross the square, loping with apparent nonchalance,
but in fact at high speed, towards the bridge. He pulled the
blinds, switched the lights on and made a fresh pot of coffee.

The doorbell rang a mere twenty minutes later. When Nick
opened the door Penruan came in and gave him the thumbs-
up sign. 'He saw the lady back to her car – flashy job, isn't it? –
and gave her a peck on the cheek. Then I followed him to East
Park Road and he opened the door of number eight with a key
and went in. Well done, Penruan!'

'Not bad, Paul,' Nick paraphrased. Now at least he knew
where to find his joker.

Chapter 15

Judith Hope came to the station the following morning with a list of half a dozen names. Aidan Hope had not been a popular man in betting circles.

'This is one of the worst,' she said. 'Michael Lynch, he's a small-time bookie in Harlesden and Willesden. After Aidan left in May he, or at least some of his bully boys, took to ringing me up. They wouldn't believe I didn't know where Aidan was. They said to tell him that Michael Lynch would put him in hospital. I don't know his address but his main shop is in Willesden High Street, it's just called Lynch's. They'll know where to find him.'

'Thank you, Mrs Hope,' Nick said. 'That's a great help.'

'Exeter on the phone at last,' Bill said, a few minutes later. 'They've spoken to Mrs Collier and she spent all Saturday evening with Judith Hope and her mother.'

'No doubt that it was Saturday?'

'She was adamant. She and Mrs Cooke watched their favourite game show: *Blind Date*. I checked the TV listings. It's definitely on Saturday.'

'And Mrs Hope was there all the time?'

'Never further away than the kitchen. Certainly didn't leave the house.'

'Marvellous!' Nick said. 'First-rate alibi.' Fake alibis tended to be flashy, overelaborate. This one was simple and convincing.

The reporters soon got bored and by that Tuesday morning only a handful of local ones remained outside Hope Cottage.

125

Alison stood in the kitchen watching them watching her as she ate her breakfast. She wondered what they were after: the chief suspect had two slices of toast, a boiled egg and three cups of tea – hold the front page. The others had got fed up soon enough, she thought. There they were with their lives turned upside down – her, Aidan, Judith, Daniel. But they were yesterday's news now. The reporters were off after the latest novelty. Until Nick Trevellyan arrested someone – they'd be back then.

The phone rang. This time she recognised his voice.

'Alison? I hope I didn't wake you. It's Tom. I wanted to say thank you for a lovely evening last night.'

'No, no,' Alison said automatically. 'It's I who should be thanking you.'

'Can I see you again this evening?' He was keen, she thought. Did he see her as a lucrative client if they got her into the dock? 'I could come to your house,' he went on. 'Don't worry about the reporters. There's been a bank robbery in Taunton and most of them have gone off to cover that. You can always say I'm your solicitor anyway.'

'All right, come about eight. I'll cook you some supper.' She hung up.

The phone rang again almost immediately. It was Nick Trevellyan. He identified himself and said, 'Have you seen today's *Valley Voice*, Miss Hope?'

'No, I've only just got up. It's probably on the doormat.' The *Voice* was a free sheet delivered to every house in the valley.

'Do yourself a favour and chuck it straight in the bin.'

Alison considered the implications of this, then said, 'I've always preferred to face up to unpleasant facts, but perhaps you'd like to break it to me gently.'

'OK. Don't say I didn't warn you. They more or less accuse you of the murder and accuse me of dragging my feet over arresting you. They imply that the only reason you have not been arrested before this is that you are related to Sir Anton Armitage. It also mentions the fact that Reg Grey and I were at your party and accuses us both of, at best, incompetence, at worst – well, you can guess.'

'But . . . but that's libellous!' Alison's voice achieved an effortless coloratura.

126

'They don't mention anyone by name,' he went on. 'That doesn't make it any the less libellous, or course, since everyone knows who they mean – as they are supposed to. But there isn't much we can do. Taking out a writ will only give it more publicity on the no-smoke-without-fire maxim. If we had only known about it we could have got an injunction preventing publication. It's too late now, the damage is done.'

Alison sat down on the windowsill and wound the phone cord feverishly round her wrist as she listened.

'I'll get even with Ashcroft for this one day,' he added suddenly. This last outburst surprised her. Could it be that Nick Trevellyan was not as cool and collected as he liked to make out?

'Ashcroft!' she said, amazed, as his words sank in.

'Jack Ashcroft. You know, got into that fight with Aidan Hope.'

'I know who you mean! I just don't understand where he comes in.'

'Sorry, I keep forgetting you're new round here. Ashcroft owns the *Valley Voice* and although he's got an editor called Gordon Dangerfield, he just does what Ashcroft tells him. The story is anonymous but Dangerfield will be the author of it for sure.'

'But why should Ashcroft turn on me like this?' she asked, her voice still sounding unnaturally high, even to her own ears. 'I've never done him any harm.'

'It's not you he's after, it's us. He's got it in for the police.'

'But he was chatting to you and Reg Grey on Saturday night.'

'He's two-faced and completely unpredictable.'

'Thanks for letting me know.' She hung up in a daze. It was nice of him to warn her, although she wondered if he was playing some game of his own.

She picked up the *Valley Voice* from the doormat. It was all there on the front page. Under the headline HOPE MURDER – NO ARREST YET was the smaller headline: ONE LAW FOR THE RICH? The main story was anonymous, as Nick had said, but in the bottom right-hand corner of the page, under the heading BLAZING ROW CULMINATES IN MURDER – AN EYEWITNESS REPORT was a word-for-word account of the row she had had with Aidan in the summerhouse a few days ago. The column was signed J. A.

Alison sat and stared at it, reading it over and over, until the words began to jump out of the page and claw her eyes out. She tore the paper across, threw it into the kitchen waste bin and went out of the front door. She stalked over to the gate. The reporters fell silent.

'Is any of you Gordon Dangerfield?' she asked loudly.

They looked at each other shiftily – unused to direct challenge. A large, ill-shaven man finally emerged from the small group. 'I am Mr Dangerfield.'

Alison stepped forward and punched him straight in the face with all her force. Dangerfield, taken completely by surprise, staggered back in disbelief, holding his nose, which was beginning to bleed. The other reporters tittered nervously. None of them had been quick enough to get a picture of the incident but several of them took shots of Dangerfield, who swore at them viciously. Alison turned on her heel and went back towards the house.

'I'll have you for assault!' Dangerfield yelled, thickly, to her departing back.

'I'll have you for libel,' she yelled back. 'I'm going to call my solicitor. Now!'

She got into the hall and started feeling in her pockets for the piece of paper on which Tom had written his number. It was only when she had dialled it that she realised that Tom had somehow become *her* solicitor.

He arrived in fifteen minutes. The reporters had not dispersed, hoping for more excitement. Only Dangerfield, who had retired to tend his wounds, was missing. Some of them took photos of Tom and his car. Alison hurried to open the front door.

'Tom, I'm so glad to see you. I'm really sorry to drag you into this, though.'

'I'm delighted you called.' He was carrying a copy of the *Valley Voice*. 'I've never seen such appalling libel. He must be quite off his head.'

'He has some sort of vendetta going on with the local police force. It's really them he's getting at rather than me. I've been caught in the cross-fire.' She explained sheepishly about her attack on Dangerfield. Tom roared with laughter.

'Well done! I say . . . what guts you've got.' He stood looking at her with frank admiration for a moment. Then he cleared his throat. 'Right, down to business. I think we should put out a statement denying this libel and demanding a complete retraction. Ring Trevellyan and tell him we want to talk to him. We can make a joint statement to the press.'

Nick stood up to greet them as they were ushered into his office. Well, well – if it wasn't last night's dinner date. Now he'd have a name for his joker. She had said on the telephone that she wanted to discuss the libel and bring her solicitor. She introduced them and the two men shook hands.

'I thought Trowerbridge and Colman were your solicitors, Miss Hope,' Nick said. She looked a bit taken aback.

Tom said, 'Miss Hope has asked me to represent her as a local man. I am the new partner in Waddington's in Hopbridge, you understand. It isn't really practical to bring her usual solicitors all the way from London.'

'So Trowerbridge's have asked you to act for them locally?'

'I represent Miss Hope personally,' Tom said firmly. He held a chair out for Alison and sat down, uninvited, next to her. Nick sat down too and launched into his speech.

'You must understand that it is very difficult for me to make any statement to the press while a murder investigation is going on. I can only make simple statements of fact such as I gave at my press conference yesterday.'

'A simple statement of fact is all we require, inspector. A denial of the implication that Miss Hope is under suspicion of murdering her cousin.'

Nick stared at him steadily. He couldn't be serious. 'You know very well that I cannot make such a statement. Miss Hope is one of a number of people whose actions cannot be satisfactorily accounted for at present.'

'What about your own libel? They're as good as accusing you of corruption.'

'I have a very thick skin,' Nick lied. 'So does the police force in this county. We can wait.' Revenge was a dish best eaten cold and he intended to savour every mouthful – when the time came.

'As for this column signed J. A. . . . ' Tom continued, pointing.

'I was about to come to that,' Nick said. But it was silly of you to draw it to my attention, he added silently.

'I've never seen such rubbish!' Nick wished people would stop banging on his desk. 'It's pure fabrication from start to finish.'

'No it isn't,' Alison said quickly. 'It's true.'

'Alison!' Tom was outraged. Even Bill looked stunned. Only Nick did not react but continued to watch her closely.

'Well, it is true,' she said angrily. 'I did quarrel with him in the summerhouse, though I didn't know we had an audience. I didn't kill Aidan, so I am not afraid of telling the truth.' She glared at the three silent men, all equally her enemies now. 'I apparently have more faith in justice than any of you lot, who are paid to uphold it. So there!'

She leant back, folded her arms and looked at them defiantly. She was a little flushed and her green eyes were wide with indignation. Nick had to put a hand up to his mouth to hide a smile. Really, she was superb – the way she tossed her head.

'Why didn't you tell me about the quarrel?' he asked, when he thought his features were sufficiently composed.

'I honestly hadn't thought about it. You already knew I'd quarrelled with him about the business, which is what this was about. That was the day he sprang it on me. It must have been Tuesday of last week. I can't see what difference it makes.'

'Is this newspaper column accurate then?'

'Let me have another look at it.' He handed her his copy and she scanned the paragraphs quickly. He got the impression that she knew it off by heart and was just gaining a little time.

'Interesting,' she said, as though engaged in an exercise in literary criticism. 'It falls into two distinct parts, if you notice. The second half is all quotation, which is reasonably accurate as far as I remember. But the first half is much more woolly. That bit is made up. Our eavesdropper didn't arrive until half-way through the quarrel.'

'And the bit at the end, where you say, "I'll see you in hell

130

first, Aidan Hope"',' Nick quoted. 'Is that accurate?'

'Spot on, I'd say.' Alison refolded the paper and put it down on the desk. She looked him straight in the eye.

He said, 'Is there any part of your previous statement you would like to change, Miss Hope?'

'No.'

'That's two occasions on which you are known to have threatened your cousin.'

'I'm hot-tempered. I get angry quickly but it doesn't last. You should know that – you've been on the receiving end yourself.' She smiled at him suddenly. He did not respond.

'If you killed him – '

'I didn't!'

'If it was an accident, say, or self-defence, then it wouldn't be murder.'

Alison clenched her fists and gave a rapid demonstration of her hot temper. 'It says in the paper he was battered to death from behind! Funny sort of accident or self-defence. Bloody cowardly murder, come to that.'

'That's enough,' Tom said. 'Sit down and stop shouting, Alison.' She subsided obediently back on her chair and Nick stopped fearing for his own life. 'Miss Hope is not answering any more questions, inspector. Now what about this libel?'

After a moment's thought Nick said, 'Until an arrest is made in this case, my advice to Miss Hope is the same I gave her on the telephone this morning before you interf – before she called you in. When I have got a conviction for this murder, then nothing will give me greater pleasure than to see Ashcroft dragged through every court in the land, having his nose rubbed in his own dirt. But until then . . .' He spread his hands in a gesture of futility.

Alison looked from one man to the other, at a loss which of them to trust. Then she said, 'Let's do what the inspector advises, Tom, at least for the time being.'

'What do you make of Thomas Howard then, Bill?' Nick asked.

'He certainly seems to have got into Miss Hope's confidence, sir. I thought it wouldn't be long before she was shouting for a solicitor.'

'He has the bloody cheek to refer to himself as a local man.'
Nick banged on his desk – the habit was obviously catching.
'He's been in the valley since last week. She can't have known
him more than three days or he would have been at her party.
How on earth has he managed to worm his way into her good
books in that short space of time?'

'He seems pleasant enough, sir.' Bill gave him a startled
look, wondering why the inspector had taken this irrational
dislike to Thomas Howard. 'So we're still not arresting her?'

'Not until Ian McCarthy has accounted for his odd
behaviour to my satisfaction. Particularly now they've found
his van abandoned in Bristol. It's quite true what she says,
Bill, we did already know that they'd quarrelled. It's also to
her credit that she admitted it like that.'

'She's got guts, I'll give you that. Which is precisely what
makes her the most likely suspect.'

'If Hope had been stabbed in the chest or . . . I don't
know,' Nick gestured wildly, 'shot in the face, I might agree
with you. Hot-tempered people don't attack from behind.
They charge in with battle colours flying. It was, as she so
rightly says, a cowardly murder and, whatever else she may
be, Alison Hope is no coward. Ashcroft now, I can see him
hitting a sleeping man from behind.'

'Speaking of Ashcroft, she probably thought it best to
admit it since we'll soon have it out of Ashcroft's eyewitness.'

'Don't be so sure. Ashcroft won't give him up that easily.
But we'll go and talk to him now. Apart from anything else
he's been quick to point the finger away from himself. Hasn't
he?'

'I've met that Ashcroft,' Tom said, as he drove Alison home.
'J. W. introduced us the other day. He struck me as a nasty
piece of work. It was really quite brave of your cousin to
thump him like that, being a much smaller man.'

'Aidan was just drunk, I think. Anyway Ashcroft's all talk
and bluster. Look, you must think I let you down in there,
Tom.'

'We operate an adversarial system of justice in this country,
Alison. It's up to the police to prove things.'

'But it must be best to tell the truth, surely.'

He smiled at her and took his hand off the steering wheel to pat hers. 'I thought that was a terrific lecture you gave us all.'

He dropped her back at Hope Cottage but she did not invite him in. 'Do you mind if we cancel tonight, Tom, make it tomorrow instead? My head's splitting.'

'Of course I don't mind. You take care of yourself. I'll be seeing you tomorrow anyway. I'll pick you up at eleven o'clock to accompany you to the inquest.'

'Oh, God! I'd forgotten about that.'

Ashcroft was outside in the yard when Nick and Bill reached Threeoaks Farm. The limp body of a chicken – not one of his battery birds – hung in his hand.

'Supper,' he said cheerfully. 'Arrested those ARM people yet, Nick?'

'I'm conducting a murder investigation actually, Mr Ashcroft.'

'Well, those letters were death threats. What do I have to do to get any action out of you lot? Get myself murdered?'

'Rest assured that if your letter writer does murder you, you will get my full attention. Until then I am trying to find out who murdered Aidan Hope.'

'Perfectly obvious, I'd say. Don't you read the *Valley Voice*? It's all in there.'

'That is why I'm here. Apart from the libellous aspect of the whole front page – which we shall leave to a later date – I want to talk to your "eyewitness" to this quarrel between Miss Hope and her cousin.'

Ashcroft smiled smugly. 'No can do, old man. Can't reveal my sources. You know how it is.'

'This person is an important witness.'

'Don't expect me to do your job for you, do you? Find my eyewitness yourself. You've got more resources than I have.'

'It is usual for members of the public to help police with their enquiries.'

'Tough. I notice you don't accuse me of making the whole thing up. Has Miss Iron-Drawers confessed then?'

'Are you going to tell me your source?'

'No, sod off.'

'Then I shall get an injunction forcing you to reveal it.'

Ashcroft was a proficient amateur lawyer but it was always worth a bluff. It didn't work.

'Rubbish!' he brayed. 'Neither I nor my informant has committed a crime. You won't get one and you'll just make yourself look stupid. Go home and read the Contempt of Court Act.'

Ashcroft went back into his house and took the dead chicken into the kitchen.

'You should have made yourself scarce then, Jen,' he said. 'They might have come into the house.'

'They'd hardly come into the kitchen, would they?' Jenny said, not looking up from the sink.

'They would if they had a search warrant.'

'Why should they search the place again, for heaven's sake?'

'Well, no harm done, but let's be a bit more careful, shall we?'

'I am being careful. I put my car in the barn out of sight, didn't I? Stop worrying, Jack. We'll be out of here in a few days.'

Chapter 16

'There's a young woman asking to see you, sir,' Carol Halsgrove said, late on Tuesday afternoon. 'She's come in response to the press appeal.'

'You mean she's got some information about the murder? Anything useful?'

'She won't say what it is. She won't talk to anyone but you.' Carol smiled mischievously, arousing Nick's suspicions.

'Who is it? Do I know her?'

'Yes, sir. It's Miss Fielding from Hopbridge Comprehensive.'

Lucy Fielding!

'Show her up then,' he said.

'Hello, Nick,' she said, as she came into the office. 'I haven't seen you for ages. You're looking well.'

'So are you,' he said sincerely. 'You haven't changed a bit. Do sit down, Lucy.'

She perched on the edge of the chair as if she might make a run for it at any moment.

'I always wondered what your office was like,' she said, peering round. 'At last I have an excuse to get up here and it looks like any other office. What a disappointment.'

She relaxed a little, sat back in the seat and crossed her legs. She was a small woman, waiflike. She looked nothing like her thirty-six years and might almost be mistaken for one of her own sixth-form pupils. She had a pretty, mobile face. When Nick had known her, almost two years before, her hair had been straightened. Now she wore it braided with beads, presumably in some sort of ethnic-solidarity gesture. It suited her. He smiled at her, kindly. He had nothing but pleasurable memories of that compact brown body.

'I believe you have some information for me,' he prompted.

'I hesitated about coming. It seems so trivial.'

'It's the little facts that eventually make up the full picture,' he said, for perhaps the thousandth time in his career.

'And Bob said I should mind my own business, said to leave the machinery of state oppression to its own devices.' She smiled conspiratorially at her lover's jargon. Lucy was very active in left-wing politics – pretty much a lost cause in the Hop Valley. She was also active in women's politics, trade unionism and black politics. While she was completely law-abiding, some of her friends were less scrupulous.

'Arresting the wrong person would epitomise the oppression of the state,' Nick said seriously. He half expected her to call him a pompous prat but she didn't. She just shrugged her shoulders.

'Women like her, Alison Hope – rich, middle-class, white – they can look after themselves. They know all the right people. Still, I'm here, aren't I?'

'Then I'd very much like to hear what you know.'

'I saw her in Little Hopford that night – Alison Hope.' Carol looked up from her notebook. Nick stared at Lucy dry-mouthed.

'Yes?' he croaked.

'We were driving through Little Hopford on Saturday night just before eleven. It had come on to rain very heavily and Bob was driving slowly. You know how he dotes on that car of his – won't let anyone else drive it, so much for property being theft. As we came round the corner I saw two people appear at the side of the road. When I say appear, I mean they literally seemed to materialise out of the hedge. I realise now that a footpath begins there but at the time they gave me quite a shock and I looked at them pretty hard.'

'You could see them clearly?'

'Yes, they were in our headlights for a few seconds. It was Aidan and Alison Hope.'

'You knew them?'

'I knew who she was. I didn't know who he was at the time.'

136

'Can you describe him, describe them both in fact?'

'The man was small – short and very thin. His hair looked dark but it's hard to tell in that sort of light. He wore dark trousers, probably black, and a checked shirt. When I saw the photograph of Aidan Hope in the paper, I recognised him at once. The woman was tall and well built – what they call junoesque, isn't it? She had on a dark dress. Her shoulders were bare and I thought she must be freezing standing there.'

'Excellent. What happened?'

'Well, that's why I say it was trivial. They came out on to the verge and he looked as if he was going to step straight into the road. I almost shouted to Bob to watch out but she put a hand on his arm to stop him. Then, when we'd gone past, I looked back and she gave him a little push, as if to say it was OK to cross now, and he lurched across the road and into the pub.'

'And the woman?'

'She turned and disappeared back into the hedgerow.'

'Are you sure of the time?'

'Yes. We'd been to a political meeting in Taunton. Bob switched on the radio for the eleven o'clock news on Radio South West to see if there was any mention of it. The pips went just as we left Little Hopford. I told you it was very trivial.'

'On the contrary, it's a very useful confirmation. I can't thank you enough for coming forward.' Nick beamed at her, this bearer of good tidings.

'I probably wouldn't have come if it hadn't been you,' she said candidly.

'I shall need your statement in writing. No point in asking Mr Shepherd for his version, I suppose?'

'None at all. Anyway, he was busy watching the road.'

'Miss Halsgrove here will take your statement down in writing if you can spare us half an hour. She'll also arrange for you to see some rather better photos.'

'Now I'm here I may as well get it all done.'

'Damn!' Carol said. 'Sorry, sir. I've broken my last good pen. I'll just nip out and get another before I take Miss Fielding downstairs.' She disappeared without waiting for an answer. Catching efficient Carol Halsgrove without a pen was like finding Mrs Thatcher without a ready retort at prime minister's question time. She didn't fool Nick. He could tell Lucy wasn't taken in either.

'So how are you, Lucy?' he asked dutifully. 'Still living with Bob, I take it.'

'No,' she said quickly. 'That's all over, long ago. It was a mistake ever to go back to him.'

'Sorry. When you said you were with him the other night, I assumed . . .'

'He still takes me to political meetings, as I don't have any transport. That's all. I live alone now, back in my old flat.'

Nick could think of no reply to this. There were some obvious ones which he might have made a week ago. So they sat in silence until Carol got back.

'This way, please, Miss Fielding,' she said.

'See you around, Nick,' said Lucy.

'Yes, see you.'

Carol Halsgrove was back in half an hour with the statement, some coffee and several rounds of sandwiches. Nick had that lean, hungry look which made women want to feed him.

'I thought you could do with something,' she explained. 'Ghost from the past, Nick?'

'Yes, I suppose so,' he said lightly. 'Thank you, Carol.'

She hovered for a bit as if she was going to make sure he ate it all up before she let him have any cake, so he gave her another job to do to get rid of her. After she had gone he realised that he was, in fact, quite hungry and he began to eat the sandwiches thoughtfully.

Lovely, uninhibited Lucy Fielding. Had she dropped a hint that she wanted him back? He remembered the first night they had spent together. He had asked her if she wanted the light left on. He could hear her quiet voice with an assumed West Indian drawl saying, 'Sure, sugar. You won't find me in the dark, else'.

Then six months later she had left and gone off with Bob Shepherd. He had tried to talk her out of it. She had said, matter-of-factly, 'You don't love me, Nick.'

He had protested. 'Yes I do. If what we've shared – friendship, affection and terrific sex – isn't what people mean by love . . . then I don't know what is.'

138

'That's just it. There is something more, and you don't know what it is.'

Since the weekend Nick had begun to suspect that she was right: that there was a higher circle of heaven which he had yet to visit.

'It doesn't mean she didn't hang about for a minute or two and then follow him,' Bill said after he had read Lucy Fielding's statement.

'True,' Nick said. 'But as far as it goes it confirms her statement almost word for word.'

'Miss Hope could have hired a hit man,' Bill said suddenly.

'You've been watching too much television,' Nick said in disgust.

'You said yourself she was ruthless. I think she would have acted really quickly when Hope started trying to get money out of her. She took Hope as far as the end of the footpath, made some sort of signal to the man she'd hired and got home in plenty of time to change and bump into you at eleven-thirty.'

'What about this tape-recorder plan? If that had worked she would hardly have taken the risk of having him killed, would she?'

'That was Plan A. If that failed – which it did – she would make the appropriate signal to the man hiding at the pub.'

Nick looked at him in silence for a moment, turning the idea over in his mind. To be fair, he couldn't rule it out. But damn it! This was Little Hopford, not Chicago.

'It's going well,' she said that night.

'I wish I could be so sure. If only we knew who burgled his room after I left. That's what really worries me. To think that someone else was hanging around there that night. He might even have seen me! It's giving me bloody nightmares, I don't mind telling you.'

'Don't be so feeble. Whoever it was has good reasons of his own for keeping quiet. I must go now.'

'Stay a while,' he said, embracing her. 'I see so little of you. I want you.'

'No. It's vital that we shouldn't be seen together.'

Darkness; rain; sky starless and overcast. Tarmac underfoot. Noise of music and laughter from the pub. This is the place. So dark on that footpath, better to do it there – too dark. How long must I wait? Can hardly breathe. I didn't mean it. I didn't mean to be taken so literally. When I said we should kill him, I didn't mean it. I've never killed anyone. How can I stick a knife into another human being? Keep out of sight. I must go back. Walk back the way I came. I must go back and say it's no go. Church clock striking, eleven o'clock. I can't. I must say. . . . *What's that*? Someone in the passageway. *It's him.*' What's that light? That's his room. Feet moving towards the passageway. I must go back. Can't breathe. Feel sick. Light gone out again. It's now or never. No one will come out in this torrential rain. Gloves on, knife ready. Now or never . . . never . . . never.

Awake with a jerk – sheets soaked in sweat.

'Jesus! Why didn't I go back? Why did you make me do it?'

Chapter 17

Molly rang Alison the next morning to ask if she wanted company at the inquest. Alison explained that Tom would be there to hold her hand – metaphorically. Molly laughed and said in that case she would steer clear. Then she muttered something incoherent about gooseberries which Alison affected not to understand, saying merely that she hadn't realised they were in season.

The inquest was well attended as the murder was the most exciting thing to hit the valley in months. Alison and Judith came face to face outside the town hall under the interested gaze of Nick, who was lingering on the steps for that very purpose. Alison was standing outside the building with Thomas Howard when Judith stepped out of an unmarked police car and began to ascend the steps. She did not at first seem to notice Alison.

Alison saw her at once and stepped forward. Judith looked startled as Alison took her by the arm and kissed her on the cheek. Judith was looking drabber than ever in a dowdy black dress and black headscarf. Alison was elegant in a charcoal-grey suit and a small black hat – obviously what the well-dressed woman wore for an inquest, Nick thought. It was a windless day and he could hear Alison's clipped voice perfectly.

'Judith, it's been years. How are you?'

'Alison, you're looking so well.' Judith's voice was more of a mumble.

'Um.' Alison could not really return the compliment since Judith was not looking well. Nor did she waste breath on expressions of sympathy. 'Come and meet Tom Howard. He's been a real friend to me.'

Thomas Howard shook Judith's hand, bending over it with a little bow. If he'd been wearing a hat he would certainly have raised it. He was the sort of man who prided himself on always being polite to women, Nick thought crossly, however old or plain. Slimy creep.

The trio came up the steps. They all nodded coolly to Nick and he turned and followed them into the building.

Jos Leighland followed Nick out of the courtroom when the inquest had been adjourned.

'Mr Trevellyan, there's something I wanted to talk to you about. Something I forgot to tell you the other day.'

Nick turned round sharply. 'Something about Hope?'

'I didn't tell you about the girl he was talking to on Friday night.'

'For Christ's sake! Look, come round to the station, Jos.'

'What, now?'

'Yes, bloody now.'

'Well, that wasn't so bad,' Alison said, as she stood with Tom on the steps outside the town hall.

'It's just a formality at this stage,' he said. 'Let's get off, shall we? Or would you like to go for lunch somewhere? It's a bit early.'

'Lunch, but let's wait for Judith.'

Tom looked less than enthusiastic. 'If you say so.'

Nick Trevellyan passed them with Bill Deacon and Jos Leighland. They disappeared back towards the police station without a second glance at Tom and Alison.

'Sure you don't want to invite them too?' Tom whispered. They both giggled guiltily.

'Shh, here she comes,' Alison said. 'Judith, can I buy you some lunch?'

They went back to the Leg of Mutton in Sheep Street. Judith and Alison went into the cloakroom and Judith took off her headscarf, combed through her short hair and put some powder on her face. She looked a little less pale. Alison had been shocked by her appearance. They were the same

142

age, but Judith looked about forty. For a moment Alison found herself at a loss for words.

'You haven't brought Daniel with you, have you?' she asked in the end.

'He's staying with Mum, back in Exeter.'

'Oh, it was Exeter. I told the police to start looking for you there.' Alison took her hat off and shook out her hair. 'Wish I hadn't worn it,' she said, with a little laugh. 'I felt very overdressed. I've never been to an inquest before. It was all over so quickly.'

'You look so smart,' Judith said wistfully.

It was only twelve o'clock and the restaurant was deserted. Tom stood up as they reached the table.

'I took the liberty of ordering you a gin and tonic, Alison.'

'Well done, that man.'

'I didn't know what you'd like, Mrs Hope.'

'I'll just have a tomato juice. And please don't keep calling me Mrs Hope. It's Judith.'

'Right. Sit down and I'll go and find the barman.'

'He seems nice,' Judith said, sitting down in the corner. Alison sat down next to her, opposite Tom's seat.

'Yes, he is. I hardly know what I'd have done without him all week.'

'You've been having a really rotten time, haven't you?'

'Oh, Judith! How typical of me to go on about what a time I've been having. You're the one who's been widowed.'

They sat in silence for a moment until Tom came back with the drinks.

'I asked you if anyone had come to see him,' Nick said, in annoyance.

'You asked if anyone had come in *asking* for him,' Jos said indignantly. My God! Nick thought. The awful literalness of the public. Interrogation was a game of twenty questions where they just answered yes or no and you had to find the right question to ask.

'I didn't think she had come specifically to see him, anyway,' Jos said sulkily. 'What I mean is, a girl came in on Friday night, quite early. She sat at the bar and I wondered if she was after a pick-up – because I don't encourage that sort of thing.

143

She sat there for ages with just one drink before Hope came in. She started chatting to him at the bar, then they went off to a table together, over in the corner. So I thought I'd been right about the pick-up. But they just talked for about a quarter of an hour and then she left. Hope stayed there the rest of the evening, so he wasn't meeting her later.'

'But you don't know who she was?'

'Never seen her before. She's not from the village.'

'What did she look like?'

'Quite short, plump. Spiky hair, dark but with blond tips, bit punky. Not bad-looking.'

'How old?'

'Early thirties, I should think.'

'Let me know at once if she comes in again, or if you see her anywhere about. At once, do you hear?'

'OK.'

'And you didn't hear any of the conversation?'

'That corner's out of earshot.'

'Who would have thought we'd meet again like this?' Judith said. 'Aidan always caused so much trouble when he was alive. It's hard to believe he can cause even more now he's dead.'

'You don't think I killed him, do you, Judith?' Alison blurted out.

'Of course I don't. The police have had me in twice since I got here. I told them you weren't a murderer.'

'Why are they pestering you so?'

'They wanted a list of all Aidan's enemies.'

'*Enemies*!'

'Well, that's rather a strong word but he did run up a lot of debts. I got some phone calls after he went off, while I was still in London. There was one man in particular, a bookie. He said to tell Aidan that if he didn't come up with the cash he was set for a nice long spell in hospital. Luckily I knew his name so I was able to give it to the police.'

'Nice to know the police are doing something constructive instead of making poor Alison's life a misery,' Tom said, with considerable warmth. He took Alison's hand across the table and squeezed it. There was a certain, recognisable look on his

144

face, which she found slightly irritating. Then he caught Judith's eye, blushed and released Alison's hand. Judith gave them one of those little, knowing smiles. Rather like the way Molly had been looking at them on Sunday night – bless-you-my-children. Tom looked embarrassed.

'Have you come up from Exeter today, Mrs . . . Judith? It's quite a long way, isn't it?'

Judith frowned. 'No, I'm staying up here until the funeral is over. I didn't realise I was going to have to stay so long. I thought I could just bury Aidan and get off home. It looks as if I shall be stuck in the bed-and-breakfast place for at least a few more days.'

'Why don't you come and stay with me?' Alison said. 'I've got masses of room at Hope Cottage. I should have thought of it before. But of course today was the first time I'd seen you. I forgot.'

It seemed strange to her now that she and Judith had not met for so many years. They had been so close at Cambridge, those first two terms. A female David and Jonathan. 'I'd love to have you,' she said, meaning it. 'You shouldn't be alone at a time like this.'

'It's very good of you. I really appreciate it.'

Alison noticed an odd look on Tom's face and suddenly remembered their date that evening. Tom obviously didn't want Judith hanging around, in her widow's weeds, cramping his style.

'I'll get a room ready and pick you up tomorrow then,' she said hastily, taking out her Filofax. 'What's your address?' She wrote it down and jotted down her Exeter address too. 'Shall we say midday then? Is that OK?'

'Fine, thanks. I should give Mrs Penhaligon a day's notice anyway. It's only fair. Will you be coming to the funeral, Alison?'

'When is it likely to be?' Alison asked, stalling for time. She loathed funerals.

'Early next week probably. At the Catholic church at Hopcliff. That seems to be the only one in the valley.'

'He wasn't what you'd call a practising Catholic, was he?' Alison said doubtfully.

'Once a Catholic. It's what he would have wanted.'

145

'I'll come if you'd like.'

'You're his only blood relation, except Daniel, obviously. Come if you can.'

'Of course I will.'

Tom dropped Alison off at Hope Cottage. He walked her to the door and said, 'Do you want me to come in for a few minutes? I can make you some tea or something. I'm really quite house-trained.'

'No, I've got things to do. See you tonight as arranged.'

'You're sure you're up to it?'

'Yes, of course. Don't keep talking to me as if I were an invalid, Tom.' If there was one thing Alison hated it was being fussed over. 'It will do me good to occupy myself with something absorbing like cooking,' she said. 'I'll find a nice complicated recipe.'

She waved him off and went into the house. She had a quick look round the cupboards, which were Mother-Hubbardish. She would have to look out a recipe and go and do some shopping. She glanced out of the kitchen window. At least those poxy reporters hadn't come back after the inquest – given up hope of her committing any more grievous bodily harm, presumably. She hoped they weren't harassing poor Judith since they had now learnt of her existence. Judith looked as if she might be near the end of her rope. Alison poured herself a mug of coffee and took it out on the terrace.

She sipped her coffee sadly as she looked out at her overgrown gardens. She had lost heart in making any plans for them now. Would she even stay at Hope Cottage when all this was over? Trust Aidan to go and spoil everything. Her mind slid back inexorably to Saturday night and the picture of him – bloody Aidan Hope – standing over Jack Ashcroft like a cockerel on top of a dungheap.

Nick's phone rang that Wednesday afternoon. He was alone in his office and he answered it and gave his name.

'It's me,' she said. 'Alison,' she clarified unnecessarily. 'I want to talk to you, off the record.'

'I don't think that would – '

She broke in impatiently. 'Don't give me all that po-faced

146

crap. It's important! There's something I must discuss with you. In private. I'm coming into Hopbridge to do some shopping this afternoon. Will you meet me somewhere? Please.'

Nick sighed. 'Against my better judgement. Meet me at my flat at five o'clock. The street door isn't locked. Wait outside my door at the top.' He hung up.

He told himself that he was going crazy.

At half past four the phone rang again. It was the police in Swansea. They had arrested Gerard Doherty trying to board the boat to Cork. He had nearly twenty thousand pounds in his luggage. They were holding him there and transferring him to London in the morning. If Nick wanted to talk to him urgently he'd have to go and interview him in Swansea.

He told them to expect him that evening. He tried to ring Hope Cottage but there was no reply. She had already left.

'You hold the fort here,' he said to Bill. 'I'll get home and pack an overnight bag.'

Alison was already waiting on the landing. Nick picked up her carrier bag, which was full of groceries, and unlocked the door. He stood back to let her in and, as she brushed past him, he caught a faint trace of her scent.

She looked round his flat with interest. The front door opened straight into the sitting-room. Two sash windows overlooked the Market Square on either side of the fireplace, and a skylight filled the room with light. There were shelves full of books along one wall but few personal objects.

'Fashionable garret living,' she said cheerfully. 'Bit spartan. I see you favour minimalism in decoration. That's all a bit *passé* now, you know.'

'I'll try not to lose any sleep over it,' Nick said solemnly. She was a mercurial woman, he thought; unpredictable, irrepressible. Nothing seemed to dampen her spirits for long.

She had crossed to the window and was looking out over the square. It was market day and down below all was noise and bustle.

'Why, you can spy on the whole of Hopbridge from up here,' she said in amazement.

'I hadn't quite thought of it as spying, but it's true that if I sit there long enough I see almost everyone pass by.'

147

'Very useful in your line of work.' She turned from the window and smiled at him.

He said, 'I can only give you a few minutes. I've got to go to Wales tonight. I shouldn't really be talking to you like this at all. By the way, is it true you punched Dangerfield on the nose?'

'Who told you that?'

'It's all over town. He's not well liked. Feared rather than loved and respected. His "friends" were only too pleased to put the story round.'

'Yes, it is true. I gave him a bloody nose.'

'Well done,' Nick said, with approval. 'Not that I can condone assaults,' he added hastily. She gave him an odd look but had the good manners not to call him a hypocrite.

'It should really have been Ashcroft, of course, if it's true that Dangerfield is just his monkey. But let's not waste time if you're in a hurry.'

She perched on the edge of the sofa. Nick leant back against the door in case he needed a quick escape route. The trouble was that he couldn't think of anywhere he could hide from what he was afraid of. He looked at her face and wondered how he had ever thought she was not beautiful. She was watching him with a puzzled frown.

'Are you listening?' she enquired kindly.

'Er . . . yeah, sorry.'

She told him why she had come. He heard her out without interruption. When she had finished he said:

'There could be a perfectly innocent explanation, of course.'

'Of course. I thought you ought to know all the same.'

'You did right.' He felt she deserved something in return. 'Off the record, we've traced this Ian McCarthy – he's a wanted terrorist. I'm going to interview him. The case may be sewn up by tonight. You're not to tell a soul I told you that.'

Alison looked unconvinced. 'I can't see Aidan mixed up with terrorists. The only cause that interested Aidan was Aidan Hope.'

'We shall soon know. You'd better go now, I've got to pack a bag for tonight. That's what I told Bill I was coming home for.' He handed her the groceries and opened the door. On

148

her way out she picked up the only photograph in the room.

'Your family? Do they still live round here?'

'My parents are dead and Gwen, my sister, married an Australian shortly after that photo was taken. She doesn't get back often.'

'So you're alone in the world, like me.' She looked up from the photo and smiled at him again. He turned away, unwilling to meet her eye. She took a last look round the room. 'I get the impression you don't care much about possessions.'

'No, I suppose not – a few books, a few decent meals, a comfortable chair.' And a warm bed and someone warm and soft to share it with. And if that someone was a loose-limbed, red-haired goddess with sea-green eyes, might not Paradise be regained in that warm bed? A few strands of hair had drifted across her face and he stuck his hands firmly in his pockets to stop himself from reaching out to brush it back.

'You must go,' he repeated. 'Tomorrow morning you may wake up to find it's all over.'

'I hope so. Bye, Nick.'

He closed the door behind her and leant against it again, listening to the sound of her feet going down the stairs.

He crossed to the window. She appeared in a few seconds and he watched her as she threaded her way between the market stalls, her shopping cradled in her arms. She walked with a spring in her step, like a young girl. Surely she was innocent, dear God.

Chapter 18

Alison got back home and busied herself preparing a chicken *parmigiana* and green salad. She fetched a bottle of red burgundy up from the cellar and opened it to let it breathe.

Tom arrived punctually, armed with several small sprigs of jasmine.

'I would have brought roses but I know you have a garden full of them.' He kissed her cheek.

'I love jasmine,' she said, 'it's one of my favourites.' She told him to make himself comfortable while she put them in water. 'We won't eat just yet, if that's all right with you. Let's sit out on the terrace and enjoy the last of the daylight. It's through the drawing-room. You haven't been past the front hall before, have you?'

'It's a lovely house,' Tom said, looking round. 'I hope I can find something half as nice. Lot smaller, of course.'

'I won't be a minute,' Alison said.' She had finally got her answering machine installed that day and she switched it on so they wouldn't be disturbed.

She joined him on the terrace a few minutes later and they chatted happily until dinner was ready.

Nick was having a less enjoyable evening. Driving, particularly motorway driving, was not his favourite pastime and he was beginning to wish he had got Bill to drive him. There were tailbacks at the Severn Bridge and the road works on the M4 outside Port Talbot seemed interminable. It was after ten when he reached Swansea and found the police station. They took him straight to an interview room and brought Doherty to him.

'He's not dangerous, sir,' the young sergeant said, 'but he's a tough customer. Don't worry about soiling your hands. He's been cautioned, of course. I can give you a constable to take notes.'

Nick thanked him and looked at Doherty. He didn't look dangerous. He was watching Nick silently – Nick sensed that he was an old hand at this game. So was Nick.

Doherty said, 'I've told you everything I'm going to. This is a waste of bloody time.'

'I'm not from this force. I want to talk to you about something quite different.'

'Which mob are you? The Met?'

'I'm stationed in the Hop Valley.' Doherty gave no obvious sign that the name meant anything to him but Nick could almost feel his muscles tensing.

'Never heard of it,' he said.

'No? How odd. Do you recognise this Photofit picture?' Nick held out a copy of the Photofit Alison had made up. 'Looks a lot like you, doesn't it?'

'Lots of fellers look like me.'

'This picture was made for us by Miss Alison Hope of Hope Cottage. Ring any bells? Yes, I can see it does.'

'Never heard of her,' he said stoutly.

'No? Don't you read the papers? It's been in the news. Her cousin was found murdered. A Mr Aidan Hope, whom I believe you knew.'

'I don't know anything about any murder. Never heard of him either.'

Nick put on his complete-bastard expression and snapped at him.

'I'm not wasting any more time on you, Doherty, or McCarthy, or whatever you want to call yourself. Miss Hope can identify you so we know you were in the Hop Valley last week. Several people at E & D will be able to identify you. Someone saw you at that pub in Little Hopford where you murdered Aidan Hope and burgled his room. That's where the twenty thousand quid came from, isn't it? Your picture has been hawked, door to door, all over the valley. Several people caught a glimpse of you that night.'

'You're a bloody liar then! They're all bloody liars.'

Doherty was a professional. He'd made damn sure no one saw him. He was ninety-nine per cent certain of that.

Nick pressed on. 'You're small fry, Doherty. Your organisation won't do anything to help you. I'm arresting you for the murder of Aidan Hope and don't think I won't make it stick.'

If Doherty had killed Hope, Nick could have sat there until Christmas without getting an admission out of him. But as he hadn't, he weighed up the alternatives and opted for the lesser of two evils.

'Look, mate,' he said reluctantly. 'You're making a big mistake. I'll tell you what I know. I'm bloody glad Hope is dead – he only got what was coming to him – but it wasn't me that killed him and I'm not going to go down for it. It was the other feller.'

'Let's hear it then,' Nick said, 'and get a move on.'

'Aidan Hope, he was always short of cash. My boss thought he'd make a good courier. He had no record, you see. They fixed up that Hope would take a suitcase over to an address in Belfast, via the republic. A hundred thousand pounds there was in it. They paid him two thousand and his expenses. But he was a greedy bugger. He figured he'd double-cross us. He did a deal with the police to pick up our people as soon as the money was delivered. Then he took twenty thousand of it for himself. What he didn't know was that we had a man with the police. He didn't find out about the raid until it was too late to stop it but he knew they'd only got eighty thou out of it and he put the finger on Hope all right. Three of our men picked up and all that money lost!

'So we were out to get him. We wanted the money back too. A hundred thousand gone just like that! We wanted to salvage what we could. I tracked him down and followed him. I lost him at Exeter but I found an address he'd written down – the one you said, Hope Cottage. I fixed up to go there and get a good look round.'

'How did you know about Ian McCarthy?' Nick asked.

Doherty sneered. 'We've got supporters everywhere, contacts everywhere. You lot like to think we're just a tiny band of extremists but we're not. Ian McCarthy was persuaded he'd like to take a nice long holiday, all expenses paid, and I took his place and his references.'

'Get to Saturday night.'

'I found out where he was on the Friday and I'd been scouting the place out. There was a big party on at Hope Cottage that night. I figured Aidan Hope was going and I figured he'd take that footpath that leads from the village there and back: it stood to reason. I saw him leave, quite early, it was still light. I hung around. I was in luck as there was some disco on at the pub. There must have been eighty or ninety people there. I just hung around, out of sight, behind the storeroom and waited, because I figured Hope wouldn't be home until really late. But then I saw the light go on in his room about eleven o'clock. It went off again almost at once and I figured he'd gone to bed. So I waited a few minutes; there was a thunderstorm and I didn't want to risk being seen in a lightning flash.'

'Wouldn't it have been more sensible to look for the money earlier in the evening while he was out?' Nick asked.

'Oh yeah! Then when he came back, he'd have seen the mess and run for his life. I wanted to get him too, remember.'

'OK. Go on.'

'Well, the thunderstorm ended, though it was still pissing down. So I climbed up on the storeroom roof. But then I heard someone moving – down in the car park – so I lay flat, the way he wouldn't see me. When the noise stopped, I went up to the window really quietly. I could make out Hope lying face down on the bed. He was obviously pissed out of his mind. I was just about to cut the pane when the door opened again. I nearly fell off the bloody roof, I can tell you.

'I edged back away from the window and waited for who-ever it was to go. A good few minutes went by, then the window opened and a bloke looked out. I made myself as small as possible in my corner but he was pretty preoccupied. He took a few deep breaths. Not surprising – he made quite a mess of Hope, didn't he? Almost made *me* throw up. I reckon he was wondering if he could get out that way but the window was too small for him, and he went back into the room.'

'You're sure it was a man?'

'I may not be as young as I once was but I can still tell the difference.'

'A tall woman, maybe?' Nick persisted.

153

'Not unless she was over six feet. I tell you he was a great big bloke.'

Ashcroft! Nick thought gleefully. Got you!

'Tall, I mean. So he shut the window again. Pity, I thought. I crawled up to the edge of the roof on my stomach and saw him come out of the door and into the car park. Then he disappeared into the darkness. I waited a few more minutes, then cut the pane and climbed in. Aidan Hope was lying there with his head caved in. So I didn't bother about him. Somebody had done me a big favour as everyone would think that I had killed him – my bosses, I mean – and I hadn't even had the trouble.

'The money was quite well hidden. I was on the point of giving up, what with the body lying there. But I found it in the end, after about ten minutes, sewn into a pillow. I left the pillows until last, what with having to pull them out from under his head.' Doherty unexpectedly made a moue of distaste, but it was only the disdain of the master craftsman for the fumbling apprentice. 'Bloody amateurs! I got away as fast as I could. That's it. That's all there is.'

'But you got a good look at this man. You'd know him again?'

'Maybe.'

'I suggest you think about it more carefully,' Nick said. 'There's only your word at the moment that you didn't kill him yourself. And I can still charge you with attempted murder.'

'Mother of God!' Doherty snapped. 'I've told you, he was already dead.'

'But you went there with the intention of committing murder. Therefore you are guilty of attempted murder. The fact that the crime you contemplated was, by then, impossible is irrelevant.' Nick knew it sounded stupid but it was true. No one ever believed it. Doherty didn't believe it.

'You can't be serious, mate. You can't try to murder a dead man!'

'I assure you that the law says you can. So would you know this other man again?'

Doherty looked sulky. 'Well, he's nothing to me, for all he did me a favour. I reckon so. I saw him clearly enough. Yeah, I'll know him again.'

154

Nick fumbled in his pocket book and produced a photograph of Jack Ashcroft. He handed it to Doherty.

'Ever seen this man?' Not *is this him*? That would be a leading question.

Doherty glanced at the picture. He knew what the real question was, of course.

'No, it's nothing like him. Much too heavy and the hair is all wrong.'

Nick stared at Doherty. 'So what did he look like?' As if he didn't already know what was coming.

'Tall, over six feet, like I said, but much more athletic than this one. Very fair hair, very straight, what's the word? Lank. Sort of fell in his eyes as he looked out the window. He had to brush it back.'

Tom Howard brushed the hair back out of his eyes once more and yawned.

'That was a fabulous supper, Alison. I don't know why I'm so sleepy. You must think me very rude.'

'Of course not. It's been an exhausting time for everybody.'

'You're a superb cook, in addition to all your other talents.'

'*Cordon bleu*, no less,' she said, attempting modesty without noticeable success. 'I did a course. Have another brandy.'

'No, I mustn't. I'm already over the limit and I must get off.'

'It's only just gone eleven and it's less than five miles to Easterbank.'

'No, I'm supposed to set an example in the community. What's old JW going to think if I get hauled up for drunk driving? He'll think he's chosen the wrong partner. I'm seeing my first clients tomorrow – they don't want to meet a bleary-eyed, hung-over solicitor.'

'OK. I'll get your coat.'

At the front door he turned. 'Thanks for a lovely evening, Alison.' He leant forward as if to kiss her on the mouth. She turned her head away at the last moment and his lips merely brushed her cheek.

After a short pause he said, 'There isn't really any chance for me, is there?'

'No, I suppose not.' What made her say that? She had not thought it until then.

155

'It's Trevellyan, isn't it?'

'Nick!' she said, startled. 'That's preposterous. Where did you get that idea?' The sentence was hardly out of her mouth before she knew it was the truth. 'You're very perceptive,' she said slowly. 'More perceptive than I am.'

Her mind wandered away from Tom, who might as well not have been there. She was thinking about Nick and wondering what was going on behind those guarded eyes.

'Good night.' Tom reminded her he was there by going. He walked away towards his car.

'I'd like us to be friends,' she called after him.

'I'd have liked that too,' he replied oddly, turning back.

It was well past midnight when Nick got his statement out of Gerard Doherty. The young sergeant offered to find him a bed for the night but he shook his head. The traffic jams would be worse during the morning. They could pick Thomas Howard up for questioning tomorrow – he would keep for another few hours. Nick didn't want to miss the arrest himself. This let Alison off the hook, didn't it? He pictured her as he had last seen her, clutching her bag of shopping in one hand, the photo in the other. Why had she had so much shopping? Was she expecting company? Fear ran through him like errant electricity. He dived for a phone.

He knew the number of Hope Cottage by now as well as he knew his own. He dialled it as quickly as his ten thumbs would allow. It rang four times and then answered. Thank God!

'Alison! Is that you? Are you all right?'

Alison's voice said, 'Hello this is Alison Hope. I'm afraid I can't answer the phone in person at the moment. If you'd like to leave a message please speak . . .' Nick swore violently and hung up.

He got through to Bill's house. Susie answered, sounding sleepy. Bill took a week to come to the phone. Nick drummed his fingers on the desk in impotent fury.

'Listen, Bill. I'm on to something. Get out to Hope Cottage first, see if Miss Hope is all right. If she isn't . . . all right, or you can't get an answer, get out to that Howard bloke's house right away and arrest him. . . . What? Oh, God! It's in East Park Road – number eight. If she's all right then wait until

156

morning and I'll come with you. Yes, I've got an eyewitness. I'll ring into the station at hourly intervals on my way back. Leave messages for me, starting at one a.m. Get going. Now!'

He drank three mugs of black coffee; wasted some time arguing to no great effect that his need of Doherty took precedence over the Met's; and set off back towards the motorway. He stopped in a village just after one and rang into the station. There was no message yet. He was furious. He considered waiting for fifteen minutes to try again but decided to press on back towards the valley. He drove at breakneck speed for another hour. This time the desk sergeant put him through to Bill in person.

'Miss Hope is fine – but puzzled and annoyed at being dragged out of bed in the middle of the night,' said Bill, implying that he knew just how she felt.

Nick leant his hot forehead against the cold glass of the phone booth and sighed.

'Are you still there, sir?' bellowed Bill, who was inclined to yell on long-distance calls. Nick reassured him. 'So we're waiting until morning to pick up Mr Howard, like you said. I've detailed someone to keep an eye on the place in the meantime. You sure you want to come? Sounds like you'll be up half the night.'

'I'll be there, Bill. I want to be there when we pick him up. Get me up at seven. I may be hard to wake.'

Nick got back to Hopbridge shortly after three and fell into bed for four hours. He arrived at Howard's rented cottage at seven-thirty with Bill and two constables. The house was in darkness. A dawn raid.

There was no reply to their knock.

'Try round the back,' Nick commanded. 'See if he's left the back door or a window open. Otherwise we'll have to break in.'

Detective Constable Penruan clambered over the side gate. A moment later his head reappeared.

'I think we shall have to break in, sir. Everything's locked up and I can't make him hear.'

'Go ahead, then.'

They heard a smash of breaking glass from the side of the

157

house and a certain amount of cursing from Paul Penruan. The front door did not open for a minute or two.

'Come on, Paul,' Nick shouted impatiently. He banged on the door again. Penruan opened it.

'Too late, sir.'

'Don't tell me our bird has flown.'

'He's in there.' Penruan pointed to a door at the end of the hall. 'In the sitting-room. He's not going to be talking.'

Nick brushed past him, running along the hall and into the room.

But Thomas Howard has passed beyond Nick's jurisdiction. He was seated comfortably in an armchair, his head slumped to one side. He had been dead for several hours.

Chapter 19

'I can't see any obvious marks on him,' Nick said.

'Poison of some sort, you think, sir?' That was Bill.

'Well, a drug anyway. It could be suicide, I suppose.' Nick said this without much conviction and was not surprised when Bill gave a snort of derision, But he made an effort to support the theory.

'He killed Aidan Hope, you see, Bill. That's what I found out in Wales last night. The man Doherty says he saw him and I believe him. Howard probably didn't know he'd been seen but he did know that the room had been ransacked after he left, so he must have suspected that someone was watching him. He may have decided on suicide.'

'He also knew that whoever ransacked the room had his own reasons for not going to the police. The more time that went by, the safer he would have felt. Why should he suddenly do himself in now? Besides, I still don't see what possible motive he could have had, sir. As far as we know, he and Hope never even met.'

'As far as we know. We shall have to do some delving into Mr Howard's past.'

'There's one possible motive he could have had that I can see.'

'Namely?'

'Alison Hope paid him to do it.'

'Still clinging to your hit-man theory, Bill?'

'You said yourself that they seemed to have got friendly in a very short space of time. But if they already knew each other, that would account for it. He's from London too. It's quite likely that they met there.'

'Eight million people live in London,' Nick said patiently.

'They were the same sort of age, though, and both professional people. It's perfectly possible that they knew each other. He may even have taken this job with Waddington's to follow her down here – if he's her boyfriend, say, or ex. Then when Hope turned up asking for money she just rang this Howard up, tipped him off that Hope was staying at the pub and told him to find a good time to get him. Miss Hope might well have known that there was going to be a birthday party at the pub that night. She made sure that Hope had plenty to drink and Bob's your uncle. Like you say, no one would have suspected him since he didn't even know Hope – as far as any of us knew.'

'Pity she didn't have the sense to get herself a better alibi then, isn't it? She'd hardly have walked him back to the pub alone if she knew he was about to be done in.'

'But she might have needed to signal to Howard that the tape-recorder plan hadn't worked and that he should go ahead with plan B. Perhaps Howard was meant to wait until a lot later when Miss Hope would be safely back at her house. Only he panicked a bit and decided to get it over with, or he thought the rain might cause footprints, or any one of half a dozen reasons.'

'There's one thing which makes your theory unlikely, though, Bill. I had a talk with Miss Hope yesterday before I left for Wales. She told me that Howard had said something which worried her. It was after they came to see me about the libel in the paper. He said that he had met Ashcroft and didn't think much of him. Then he said that Aidan Hope was quite brave to throw a punch at him as he, Aidan, was a much smaller man. But he had supposedly never met Aidan Hope, so how did he know that he was short and slight? If he murdered Hope at her instigation she'd hardly be trying to put the finger on him now. If we arrested him he would certainly have talked about her involvement.'

'Except that he's not going to be talking about anything ever again,' Bill said meaningfully.

'Go on.'

'If she paid him, or blackmailed him, or seduced him into killing Hope, there are several reasons why she might want to get rid of him subsequently. She might have been afraid that he would panic and give them both away. Or if he was her boyfriend, she might have got fed up with him, and realised that this crime they'd planned and committed together meant that she was stuck with him for good.'

'Do you have to use stupid euphemisms like "boyfriend"?' Nick demanded angrily. 'If you mean he was her lover then say so.'

'Bill looked at him in surprise. It was not at all like the inspector to be rude to subordinates. He said reproachfully, 'Why didn't you tell me what Miss Hope said, sir? I should have been present at the interview too.'

'She wanted it kept off the record. She wasn't sure, you see. There might have been a perfectly innocent explanation. One of the papers might have got hold of a full-length photo of Hope and printed it – instead of the head-and-shoulders one most of them carried. I was just leaving for Wales, anyway, so I didn't get a chance to tell you.'

'Where did this interview take place, sir?'

Nick shuffled uncomfortably. 'At my place.'

Bill was silent for a moment, then he said, 'Was that altogether wise, sir?'

Mike Brewster arrived at that moment. Nick was rather glad to see him.

'Found another body, Nick? Starting to get out of hand.' He gave Howard the once over and agreed that there were no obvious marks. He lifted his right eyelid and stared into the dead eye.

'In the absence of any mysterious South American poisons turning up in the p.m., the most likely thing is some sort of barbiturate – sleeping pills, to you. They're easily available and can be very effective if washed down with alcohol. Let's get him on to the table and I'll be able to tell you exactly what it was.'

'Time of death?' Nick asked. Mike shook his head.

'No witnesses this time? I doubt I'll be able to pin it down within two hours. Try to find out when he had his last meal. That'll give me something to go on at least.'

'Let's hope he didn't eat it all alone here then.'

'Is that his car on the hard-standing outside – the Golf with the soft top?'

'I think so. Yes, now I come to think of it I saw it on the morning of the inquest. Yesterday, I suppose. Seems like weeks ago.'

'Then I saw it parked outside Hope Cottage last night,' Mike said. 'When I was on my way to a home delivery in Hopwood. I should start there.'

'So 'I was right after all,' Nick said to Bill. 'He was there. Why the hell didn't I have him picked up last night? I could kick myself. Just because I wanted to be in at the arrest.'

'I reckon it was already too late,' Bill said. 'He's been dead a few hours.'

'Thanks, Bill, but I still can't help feeling I screwed up.'

Alison answered the door to them.

'You look awful,' she told Nick. 'You look as if you've been up all night.'

She led him and Bill into the drawing-room. They told her about Tom Howard. She showed no surprise.

'I knew something was up when Sergeant Deacon was banging on my door at one o'clock in the morning, wanting to know if I was all right.'

'We know for certain now that Thomas Howard killed Aidan Hope,' Nick said. 'The man you know as Ian McCarthy saw him.'

Alison shook her head in disbelief. 'It just doesn't make sense. He can't even have known Aidan, surely?'

'Would you repeat to Sergeant Deacon what you told me yesterday?'

She did so. Then she said, 'He was a frightfully amateurish murderer, I'm afraid. He gave himself away again last night. He made some reference to my garden being full of roses but he'd never been past the front hall and you can't see them from the road. He must have walked up the footpath that night to see if there was any sign of Aidan. He might even have considered killing him on the footpath if he got the chance, safer than risking being seen at the pub. But of course when Aidan came away from the party I was with him. If he was paid to do the murder, the person behind it may justifiably have thought he was becoming a danger.'

'Quite so, miss,' Bill said woodenly.

'What I can't understand,' Nick said, 'is why you let him come here last night if you suspected him – even half suspected him – of murdering Aidan. Closeting yourself away alone with a possible murderer is not my idea of sensible behaviour.'

'You didn't know him. I couldn't believe that he was capable of killing anyone. He's just not the type. And even if he had killed Aidan, why should he harm me?'

'We don't know yet why Hope was killed, so we don't know who else may be under threat.'

'I felt perfectly safe with him and I was,' she said defiantly. 'He's the one who's lying dead today, not me.'

'He ate here with you, last night? What time?'

'It must have been about quarter to nine when we sat down and about quarter past ten by the time we finished.' She described exactly what they had eaten.

'Ring that information through to Dr Brewster, sergeant. Is it all right for the sergeant to use your phone?'

'Of course. Use the one in the hall.'

When Bill was safely out of the room, Nick leant towards Alison and said very quietly:

'Look, I have no right to ask this, I know, but will you be more careful in future? Two people have been murdered now. Take a few precautions, if not for your own sake . . .'

She met his eye. He wore the same look that Tom had worn in the restaurant after the inquest but it wasn't irritating on him. Then she knew. She laughed out loud. He reddened, misunderstanding her reaction.

'Please, Alison, don't make me grovel,' he muttered.

She looked at the floor to spare his embarrassment and nodded. 'I didn't realise.'

'That you might be in danger?'

'That you . . . that it mattered to you.'

He didn't answer.

'Poor Nick!' she blurted out without thinking. 'It must be awful for you.'

He shook his head in exasperation, unsure if he wanted to laugh or to shake her. 'You're the one who's having a hard time.'

'But it's not the same. I mean . . . I know I didn't kill him

. . . either of them. Whereas you . . .' She wanted to convince him – needed to convince him. But how?

They sat in silence until Bill came back a few minutes later. By that time Nick had resumed his usual inscrutable face and began to ask her quick-fire questions.

'What time did Mr Howard leave here last night?'

'It was just after eleven. He said he was sleepy and had to work tomorrow.'

'We're making house-to-house enquiries in that part of Hopbridge, but it seems likely that you were the last person to see him alive.'

'Except the murderer,' Alison said, for the second time that week.

'Did he say anything odd at any time in the evening?'

It was Alison's turn to blush. She wondered what Nick would say if she repeated Tom's last remarks to him. She pictured Bill Deacon's reaction and suppressed a smile.

'Nothing but the slip about the roses. Except that, just as he was getting into his car, he did say something which struck me as oddly expressed. I said I wanted us to be friends and he said something like "That would have been nice" or "I would have liked that". The choice of tense seemed odd.'

'The conditional mood, as though it could not now happen. I see. Didn't you wonder what he meant at the time?'

'I thought I knew what he meant, but now I see he might have meant something quite different.'

'What did you understand him to mean at the time?'

Alison leant back in her chair and looked at the ceiling, wondering how best to express herself.

'I got the impression that he wanted us to be more than just friends . . . and I thought I might want that too. Then last night I realised that there couldn't be any more to it than that. I enjoyed his company but I didn't want anything else to come of it. I didn't say anything but he sensed it and raised the subject himself. So when I said I'd like us to be friends and he said that, I thought he meant that he wasn't interested in a platonic relationship, that's all.'

'Then he left?'

'He just turned back to kiss me goodbye . . .' She grinned

164

at Nick, who returned her gaze impassively. 'On the cheek. Then he drove off.'

'Do you keep any barbiturates or similar drugs in the house?'

'Sleeping pills?' She laughed. 'I don't have any difficulty in sleeping, I assure you.' Not until this week anyway.

'Please answer the question.'

'No, I don't keep any barbiturates in the house.'

'Have you recently been prescribed any barbiturates?'

'Certainly not. I've never taken a sleeping pill in my life.'

'Can I have the name and address of your doctor, please?' Bill said, scribbling steadily.

'I'm registered with the health centre in Hopbridge in case of emergency but I shall continue to go to my man in London for the time being.'

'Then I'll take his name and address.'

She gave the details. Nick recognised the address as being just off Harley Street.

'How long have you known Mr Howard?' Nick went on.

'Since Sunday evening. I met him at Lady Armitage's. She had already invited him to dinner and didn't like to cancel him at the last moment.'

'Just four days. You seem to have become very friendly in such a short space of time.'

'I've seen him every day since then. I liked him. He was very easy to get on with.'

'But you didn't know him in London?'

'Goodness, no. London's a big place.'

'Did he ever mention having known Aidan Hope?'

'No. I had no reason to suppose that he did know him.'

'What made you invite him here last night?'

'He bought me dinner on Monday, in Hopbridge. I wanted to return his hospitality. I thought it would be easier here. The last thing I needed, after the *Valley Voice*'s little attack on me, was a photo of me wining and dining so soon after the murder. You can see how it might look.'

'Had you been to his cottage in Hopbridge?'

'No.'

'But you knew where it was?'

'He gave me the address and phone number and vague directions as to how to find it if I ever wanted to.'

'Did he mention the name of the firm he worked for in London? Or where he lived there?'

'Mmm . . . No. Definitely not the firm. I expect James Waddington would know that. He lived in Clapham, but I've no idea whereabouts.'

As they were about to leave, a thought struck Nick.

'You don't happen to know a short, plump woman, do you? Spiky hair with blond tips. About your age, or a little older.'

'Why, yes. It sounds like Jenny Tilney,' Alison said. 'Christ almighty!'.

'What?'

'Jenny Tilney! She was here that day I quarrelled with Aidan in the garden. I think we've found our eyewitness.'

'Who is she?'

'Interior designer. I've got her address somewhere. Hang on.'

She ran upstairs and reappeared two minutes later, waving a business card in her hand. 'Tilney Interiors, Bridge Street.' She handed the card to Nick.

'Did she have a car?' he asked.

'Yeah, a sort of souped-up Mini.'

'Colour and registration number?'

'Red and don't be silly.'

'Well, it was worth a try. I thought you'd be good with numbers, being a computer programmer.'

'Computing's got nothing to do with numbers. I don't know why everyone thinks it has. I have enough trouble remembering my own registration number.'

Nick and Bill sat in the police car in the courtyard for a moment. Nick was thoughtful.

'What an amazing coincidence,' he said. 'Jenny Tilney was talking to Aidan Hope in the pub the day before he was murdered and she is an acquaintance, at the very least, of Jack Ashcroft's.'

'If it was her, in the pub.'

'Ashcroft has let his spite get out of hand this time. He couldn't resist printing that attack on Alison but doing so has exposed his connection with Aidan Hope.'

Bill looked round at Nick. Not one of his sidelongs. A full-frontal.

'Be careful, Nick,' he said.

Nick gave a start of surprise and let go of his seat belt, which hurtled back into its reel. Bill was an old-fashioned sort of copper and he nearly always called Nick 'sir' or 'Mr Trevellyan', even outside work. When he called him by his given name he meant business.

'What?' Nick said feebly.

'Be careful,' Bill repeated.

'I don't know what you mean.'

'I think you do.' He started the engine. 'I know you like to think you're unfathomable but I've known you a long time, remember.' Nick felt like telling him not to worry. She had laughed at him. Bloody laughed at him.

'Which of them do we see first?' Bill asked, having said his piece.

'Neither. They can keep until this afternoon. Radio in and have an eye kept on her shop until then. First we'll go back to Hopbridge to see James Waddington. We know Ashcroft didn't kill Hope. What we really want now is a connection between Ashcroft and Thomas Howard. So let's find out as much about Mr Howard as we can, shall we?'

'Just a sec. Here's Miss Hope, coming out.'

Alison tapped on the passenger window. Nick wound it down.

'I just remembered.' She rested her arm on the car roof and leant in. 'I thought there was a man following me and Tom on Monday night.'

'What!'

'I can't be sure. But I got the impression he was following us after we left the restaurant. I noticed him particularly as he was rather good-looking. He was behind us as we left the square. Then we stopped on the bridge to have a look at the Hop in the moonlight. He walked past us and stopped at the sportswear shop, looking into the window, until we'd passed him again. Then he walked quite slowly past my car and round the corner.'

'What did he look like?' Nick asked unnecessarily.

'Tall, fair, early twenties, rather decorative.' She smiled sweetly.

'OK. Thanks.' He wound up the window.

167

'What d'you reckon?' Bill asked when Alison had gone.

'I reckon Penruan needs more practice at tailing people. God! She's a sharp one.'

Alison's phone rang shortly after they had left.

'Alison, it's Judith. I just heard about Mr Howard. The whole town is buzzing with it. He seemed such a nice man. He was a great friend of yours, wasn't he?'

Alison found herself shaking her head. 'I hardly knew him. I met him only a few days ago. It is a bit of a shock, though.' Actually she had more important things to thing about than poor old Tom.

'When I met him with you at the inquest I thought you seemed very friendly.'

'That was just his manner. He was affable to everyone. Or so it seemed. The thing is, you see, the police say he murdered Aidan.'

'But that's incredible. How did he know Aidan? Aidan's never mentioned him.'

'I can't imagine. But someone saw him at the pub that night. Another Irishman. I don't know the details.'

'I just can't see why, that's all.'

'The police think he did it at someone else's instigation – a sort of hit man. It all seems too ridiculous for words. They were just about to arrest him, too.'

'Looks like he died just in time, then. For the murderer, I mean.'

'Yes.' Alison sighed. 'This is becoming more nightmarish by the moment.'

'I really rang about the funeral. It's been fixed for half past eleven on Tuesday. It'll be such a relief to get it over with. Then I can get back home to Exeter and try to pick up the threads.'

'I wish I'd been more help to you.'

'Don't be so silly. You've had enough on your plate, with the police pestering you and treating you like some sort of criminal. Are you sure it won't be any trouble me coming to stay? It'll just be for a few nights.'

'I'd love to have you.' You'll be doing me a favour. Until this murderer is caught, I'm not sure I feel safe all alone here. Tom was here last night, you see.'

168

No!'

'Yes, he was killed within hours of leaving here. It's frightening, isn't it?'

'Don't!' Judith said, with feeling. 'You're making my flesh crawl. See you at midday as arranged then.'

'Why don't I pick you up now? I'll get us a cold lunch, if that's OK. Then tonight we'll make ourselves a slap up dinner and chat about old times.'

'Lovely. See you soon then.'

Chapter 20

Nick and Bill went to see James Waddington at his office in Hopbridge. The old solicitor was badly shaken by the news of Thomas Howard's death. He gave them the name of Howard's London employers and his old address. He was unsure if Howard had any relations still living. He began rambling disjointedly.

'His father's dead, I know that. Puffy Howard. I was at school with him, you know. He was the same age as me. Dropped dead this winter. Went to the funeral. My turn next. Then Waddington's will be finished. After a hundred and fifty years. I think he mentioned an aunt. That would be his mother's sister. Poor Puffy married a rather unsuitable woman – married beneath him, as the saying used to be. You don't hear that said much these days, do you? We're all supposed to be equal now. Goodness knows where the aunt lives or what her name is.'

'Can you tell me how you came to offer Mr Howard a job?' Nick asked.

'Met him at the funeral in February. Puffy and I hadn't really kept in touch after his wife died about ten years ago, so I hadn't seen Thomas since he was at university. But we'd sent Christmas cards with a few lines of news, so I knew he had trained as a solicitor, so that gave us something in common to talk about. I was pretty shaken when I saw him, I can tell you. He looked like his own ghost. I gathered he'd had some sort of breakdown. Partly the strain of Puffy's last illness, which was long and painful, and partly, I gather, woman trouble.'

Bill looked up from his notes. 'What was the woman's name? Did he tell you that, or describe her?'

'Gentlemen don't discuss these matters.' James Waddington put plebeian Bill down in the politest possible way. 'Especially not when there is a generation's age gap between them. And they certainly don't mention names.'

Bill looked disappointed.

'I told him a bit about the firm,' the old man went on. 'How I was the last of the Waddingtons and the firm would soon be defunct. Then we said goodbye. Well, a few weeks ago I had a letter from him out of the blue, saying that he was completely better now but he had decided not to go back into a City firm and would I consider taking him on as a junior partner? I was a bit dubious, but when I met him he looked like a different man. He had obviously made a full recovery. I rang the senior partner of his old firm, who said that they had no complaints about his work and would be glad to give him a reference.'

'So you saw him? When and where?'

'About a month ago. He came down here to see me and I offered him a job on the spot. Couldn't promise much money, of course, business has got a bit run down. But Puffy had left him enough to buy a little house and we all live quite quietly around here, don't we? Well, we used to.'

'Let's get back to the station,' Nick said, as they left the solicitor's office. 'Penruan can go up to London and interview Howard's former friends, flatmates or colleagues. I want to know if there was any previous link between him and either Aidan or Alison Hope. Or Jack Ashcroft. Ring the Met and make the right noises.'

'You ring 'em,' Bill said in his best West Country burr. 'You're better at making the noises than I am.'

'Just do it!' Nick snapped. 'Hello, that was Miss Hope's car which just went past.'

'I didn't see, sir.'

'Yes. She had Judith Hope with her, in the passenger seat.'

'I expect she feels the need for a bit of feminine sympathy.' Bill said. He began to practise the soothing noises needed by a provincial flatfoot trespassing on the Metropolitan Police's ground.

171

When they got back to Nick's office they found Inspector Colin Burcombe sitting in Nick's chair, his feet on Nick's desk, rifling idly through his in-tray. He was also smoking – and using Nick's coffee mug to stub his cigarettes out.

'Make yourself at home, Burcombe, you filthy slob,' Nick said.

Burcombe took his feet off the desk but did not vacate the chair. He folded his arms and glared at Nick.

'I've been after you for ages, Trevellyan. What's this crap about you giving Jack Ashcroft an alibi? Isn't my life hard enough without people who're supposed to be on my side alibi-ing arseholes like Ashcroft?'

'If I knew what you were talking about I might have an answer for you. And if you get out of my chair I might even give it to you.'

Burcombe conceded defeat and stood up. He perched on the edge of the desk instead, knocking over the coffee mug as he did so and leaving a pile of ash.

Nick dusted the chair off deliberately and sat down. 'So when and for what am I alibi-ing Jack Ashcroft?' he asked.

'Saturday night. For the petrol-bomb attack on the offices of those animal-rights people.'

Nick stared at him with a slightly sinking feeling. 'Petrol-bomb attack?'

'Don't you read the daily bulletin?'

'Not this week.'

'It happened in the early hours of Sunday morning. It's not really an office, just somebody's council flat in West Hopbridge. It was burnt out. Luckily the owner managed to get out, otherwise it'd be a murder inquiry. Of course, it's really your job but Reg dished it out to me on Monday – said he'd told you.'

'Crossed wires.' Sometimes Nick wondered if Reg did it on purpose. 'What time?'

'About half past midnight.'

Nick shook his head. 'Ashcroft's not getting an alibi from me.'

'He says you took him home that evening, tucked him up nice and cosy in bed, read him a bedtime story and can confirm that he had no transport.'

172

Nick shook his head again. 'I left him before half past eleven and I think I can confirm that he did have some transport. Probably a souped-up Mini.'

'Well, that's a relief. I'll haul him in then.'

Nick gave him Jenny Tilney's name and address. 'I want a word with both of them when you've finished with them,' he said. 'Now don't let me keep you.'

Burcombe turned as he reached the door. 'You're taking your time on this Hope murder, aren't you?'

'What's it to you?'

'You've pinched most of my men is what it is to me. You know what I always say: in the absence of any evidence to the contrary, it has to be the husband or wife.'

'Even when she has no motive for killing her husband?'

'She must have. I expect she had him insured.'

'Believe it or not, we did check up on that.'

'Just wanted rid of him then – another bloke.'

'Divorce would be less messy, don't you think?'

'Mine wasn't. He was a paddy, probably Catholic – wouldn't agree to it.'

'Where have you been for the last twenty years?' Nick asked impatiently. 'She wouldn't need his agreement. He'd deserted her. All she needed was a good solicitor.'

'Contradiction in terms.' Burcombe, who recognised a good exit line when he heard one, left the room. He was half a second ahead of the coffee mug, which shattered harmlessly against the door jamb. Bill began to pick the pieces up in silent reproach.

'That'll teach me to make time to read the daily bulletin, won't it?' Nick said. 'Still, Burcombe can make himself useful for once by finding out exactly what Ashcroft was up to while Aidan Hope was being killed. Should save us quite a bit of time.'

'Bit of a turn-up, isn't it?' said Bill, who favoured meiosis.

'No wonder Ashcroft was so shocked when I told him Hope had been murdered. It must have been a nasty moment for him. He had been setting himself up an alibi but not for a murder, for a revenge attack on the rights group. So he could have proved he was elsewhere at the time, but he didn't dare,

173

because it meant admitting to another, very serious crime. It's almost funny.'

   . . . Except that bang went the Ashcroft-as-murderer theory.

Chapter 21

Mike Brewster had finished the postmortem and his report landed on Nick's desk in the middle of the afternoon. Nick telephoned him to get it straight from the horse's mouth.

'Phenobarbitone – is that what it says? How does the pharmacist ever read your writing?'

'You said you wanted it quickly so I didn't get it typed up. It's a powerful hypnotic. It used to be popular as a sedative. GPs were always prescribing it to neurotic women who reckoned they were martyrs to insomnia – too often, in my view. A placebo would do just as well for most of them.'

'So you'd prescribe it for sleeplessness or as a tranquilliser?'

'*I* wouldn't. I said it used to be popular. It's been superseded by other drugs now, the main reason being precisely that it was so easy to overdose on. If you can't sleep, Nick, my prescription is a brisk walk and a glass of warm milk before bed – or a nice buxom girl in it is even better.' It seemed to Nick that Mike Brewster took an unhealthy interest in his sex life. Like a lot of long-married men, he seemed to assume that bachelors were putting it about all over the county. He went on.

'I only prescribe phenobarbitone these days as an anticonvulsant. That doesn't mean, of course, that hundreds of old buffers all over the country aren't still dishing it out. Where was I? He died, strictly speaking, of respiratory failure – barbiturates depress your breathing. It wouldn't take much to do someone in. Howard had had quite a well-measured dose, so someone had been doing their homework. You only need a good reference book. It was washed down with brandy – almost certainly dissolved in it beforehand.'

'Wouldn't you be able to taste it in that sort of dose?'

'Probably not in something strong like brandy. It has a slightly bitter taste but then so does brandy, and if you'd already had a few drinks – bit of wine with dinner, say – no, you wouldn't spot it.'

'Would it come in soluble form, though? Surely these things are prescribed as pills?'

'When did a doctor last prescribe you a pill?'

'I don't know. I haven't got time to be ill.'

'Most drugs these days come in powder form in slow-release capsules, that's those gelatin things. They're easier for the patient to swallow and they break down in the gut, releasing the powder little by little. All you have to do is break open the capsule and you've got a powder to mix with your brandy. It dissolves OK in alcohol, bit of stirring – you'd need a couple of minutes. The alcohol has a two-fold purpose of disguising the drug and making its effect far more certain.'

'Would a suicide take the trouble to break open the capsules? Wouldn't it be easier just to swallow a load of them?'

'Maybe, but if he wanted to get it over with quickly then powder is better. After all, if you've made up your mind to do it then you want to get on with it – I should think.'

'What time did he die?'

'As I told you, I couldn't tie it down to within two hours. Some time between eleven and one. His dinner was hardly digested at all. It's put me off aubergines for the next month.' He really was disgusting, Nick thought, and felt no reluctance about telling him so.

'You really are disgusting, Mike. How long would it take to kill him?'

'It's slower acting than other barbiturates. Anything from half an hour to about two hours, depending on metabolism and build. A little old lady would be gone in no time. But a big chap like him . . . best part of two hours, I should think. He'd had a big meal not long before so that would slow down the action of the drug. But he'd be unconscious before that. He might have realised something was wrong, but by that time he'd have felt unable to move to phone for help.'

176

'Could he have driven four or five miles, say a quarter of an hour after taking the dose?'

'In theory. He might already have felt a big groggy by then.'

Nick thanked him and hung up.

'So,' he said to Bill, 'it sounds more likely that he took the drug once he got home. There was a bottle of brandy in the sideboard in his sitting-room, wasn't there?'

'Miss Hope's got cupboards full of drinks, including brandy,' Bill objected. He added something under his breath about dinner with the Borgias which Nick pretended not to hear. 'And she admitted he felt sleepy,' he concluded, playing his ace.

'Quite,' Nick said, trumping it and claiming the trick. 'She would hardly have said that if she'd drugged him, would she? She'd have said he was bright-eyed and bushy-tailed.'

'You think criminals are much cleverer than they really are, Mr Trevellyan,' Bill said mutinously. 'Telling lies consistently requires practice, and a good memory.'

'Haven't got your experience of that, I'm afraid, not being a married man. Let's hope Penruan gets a move on up in London. We seem to be going round in circles here.'

He wondered if Lucrezia had been a red-head.

Penruan rang at about four o'clock.

'Mr Howard left his old firm in February, sir. So there was a gap of six months before he came to the Hop Valley. The partners say he had a nervous breakdown but they don't want to discuss it any more than that. They claim not to know the details.'

'Sod the partners!' Nick said. He wasn't going to forgive Penruan in a hurry for letting Alison spot him on Monday night. At this rate he'd have him out directing traffic by the end of the week. 'Get back there and talk to the secretaries or clerical staff, especially any middle-aged women. They'll know the details. Use those blue eyes of yours and that sickening charm you exercise on the WPCs. I'll wait here until you ring back.'

'Yes, sir. Sorry, sir.'

Paul rang again at half past five.

'You were right about the secretaries. They fell over themselves to tell me about it. I don't know how much of it is fact and how much conjecture, though. Mr Howard was having an affair with a woman. She gave him the elbow at Christmas. He kept going for about six weeks but he was in quite a state, apparently. Then his father died and that was the last straw. There was a nasty incident when he punched a client. The partners hushed it up, compensated the client, accepted his resignation and got him off to a sanatorium. He was there for three months, then he went to stay with his aunt in the west somewhere for another few weeks. When Mr Waddington approached them the partners were happy to give him a reference because he'd always been a good employee until his health cracked up.'

'Never mind all that,' Nick snapped. 'Did you find out who this woman was?'

'Her name was Muriel. She was married to someone else – hence all the trouble. She was a client of the firm, so they were a bit cagey about her. I persuaded one of the secretaries, a young girl, to look it up for me and meet me for a drink after work. I'm seeing her at six.'

'Very enterprising,' Nick said approvingly.

'I showed them Miss Hope's picture but none of them recognised her. Or Aidan Hope either, or Mr Ashcroft.'

Nick accepted this news – or lack of it – with equanimity.

'Miss Wilmington, that's the senior partner's secretary, she said Thomas Howard was very susceptible to women. That they could twist him round their little fingers. Those were her very words.'

'OK, Penruan, don't make a night of it with your typist. When you've got the details of this woman, get down to Clapham and ask the same sort of questions there. You can get me at my flat later if anything comes up.'

'Shall I go and see the woman, sir?'

'No, I may have to go myself since it's a bit delicate.' Nick had found that husbands had an odd aversion to policemen asking them about their wife's infidelities.

He hung up. So they had learnt one little thing about Thomas Howard's personality. He gave Bill the gist of the conversation.

178

'Penruan's finding out who the woman was,' he said.

'Jealous husband, just the job.'

'Only if you think Aidan Hope was knocking her off too.'

'Um, see what you mean. The two have to be connected.'

'Right.' They sat in silence for a moment. 'Sod it,' Nick said. 'Sod everything.'

'Why don't you go home, sir?' Bill said. 'We can't do anything more tonight and you were up half of last night.'

'You know, you may be right.'

The phone rang at that moment and Nick answered it.

'It's me,' said Reg Grey's voice. 'I've had the ACC bending my ear now that there's been a second murder. He's decided to send Detective Superintendent Seymour over tomorrow with Inspector Cartwright. You can expect them some time in the morning.'

'Oh,' Nick said coolly.

'So you're taking your orders from him until further notice.'

'I see.'

'I shall expect your full co-operation, of course,' Reg said sharply.

'Of course.'

'Sorry, Nick.' Reg sounded as if he meant it. 'It's out of my hands.'

Nick hung up without further comment.

'What's up?' Bill asked.

'The ACC has put that fat bastard Seymour in charge of the case.'

'Oh no!'

'Oh yes.'

'I think I can feel a bout of summer flu coming on.'

'Me too. Let's spend a happy couple of hours making sure the paperwork is up to date, shall we? Then at least he can't bawl us out over that. Get Carol up here.'

Nick knew just about everything by then. But he was too busy getting the red carpet dry-cleaned for Det Supt Edward Seymour to sit back and think it through until later that night.

Well, that's his excuse.

179

Chapter 22

Alison took some steak out of the freezer and grilled it for Judith – she looked as if she needed building up. She opened a bottle of her best Châteauneuf du Pape too but Judith drank very little of it.

'The more Aidan drank, the less I fancied it,' she explained. 'I rarely touch the stuff now. It's lovely, but you finish it.'

They took their coffee into the drawing-room after dinner.

'It's raining again,' Alison said. 'That heatwave is well and truly over.' She checked that the french windows were locked and drew the curtains. 'Let's shut out the world.' Judith sat down in a chair in front of the empty grate, her hands folded primly in her lap. Alison sat down opposite her.

'How about a liqueur for medicinal purposes?' she said. 'I feel as if I could do with some anaesthetising this evening – I don't know about you.'

'I feel numb already,' Judith said. 'But some brandy would be welcome, to help keep out the cold.' Judith wrapped her cardigan more tightly round her. 'If you'll join me, that is.'

Alison fetched the half-full bottle and two glasses. She poured them both a generous helping and handed one glass to Judith.

'Is Daniel coming up for the funeral?'

'Better not. It's too much of an ordeal for a little boy. He's not strong.'

'He still suffers from the epilepsy? Only sometimes it clears up as they get older, doesn't it?'

'His gets worse. Oh, it's kept well under control. He hardly ever has fits. But I wouldn't inflict a funeral on him.'

'What will you do now?'

'Stay with Mum for a bit. Try to find a job, I suppose. Pity I never finished my degree. We're going to be a bit short of funds. I had no idea funerals were so expensive.'

There was a meaningful pause. Alison realised that it was her cue. She said, 'If you need . . . If I can . . . I'd be glad to help tide you over for a bit.'

'It's kind of you, Alison. I'm very grateful,' Judith said with simple dignity.

'I'll get you something now before I forget. I keep a little bit of cash in the house and I can give you a cheque as well.'

'A cheque would be a bit awkward. I'm overdrawn at the bank, you see, so they'd just take it to pay off my overdraft. Cash would be very welcome at the moment.'

'I can let you have a bit now and we'll go to the bank tomorrow. Coming right up.' Alison hurried out of the room up to the study where she kept a few notes in her safe in case of emergency.

Nick pulled the blinds to block out the view of the Market Square and sat down heavily on his sofa. He was still exhausted from lack of sleep the previous night. But he didn't want to go to bed – he knew he would not sleep that night either.

Ted Seymour would arrest Alison as soon as he arrived. That is to say, he would send Nick to arrest her. He pictured her face as he heard himself saying, 'Alison Hope, I am arresting you for the murder of Thomas Howard. You are not obliged to say anything . . .' Bill would have to make the arrest, he could not bring himself to touch her – that restraining hand on the arm to bring home the nature of their action, the deprivation of liberty. Within the hour – long before her solicitor could arrive – Seymour would have her broken down, weeping and ready to confess to every unsolved crime in the valley. Then he would turn to Nick with his usual sneer and say, 'You're too soft, Trevellyan, I keep telling you. You and all the other bloody graduate coppers.'

He toyed with the idea of getting drunk. But he didn't drink spirits and wine or beer would be too slow. He gave up the idea and made himself a cup of coffee instead and sat staring

181

into space and thinking. Thoughts jumbled themselves inside his head. It would have made more sense if it had been Alison and not Aidan Hope who had been murdered . . . Why did that sentence stick in his mind? Was Alison keeping her promise to him to be more careful? He dare not ring her. At least when she was in custody he would know she was safe.

Thomas Howard: he had fallen for Alison, that was obvious . . . but then he was 'susceptible' to women. Penruan had said something about Howard which might be important. What was it? Red hair and green eyes . . . Aidan Hope liked red hair and green eyes. Had there been anything between him and Alison? She had seemed jealous of Judith Hope. Her description of Judith as a strong-willed, tough woman had been quite out of keeping with the mousy creature who had crept into Nick's office on Monday morning . . . Why had she lied about Judith? Jealousy, sexual jealousy? Jealousy, the green-eyed monster . . . Alison was hot-tempered. Perhaps it was the red hair. Red hair and green eyes sounded like a dangerous combination.

Alison handed Judith a hundred pounds in cash. Judith put the notes in her bag.

'It's really kind of you. I can't tell you how grateful I am. Cheers!' She raised her brandy glass.

'Cheers,' Alison responded, sipping from hers.

'This is a lovely big house,' Judith said. 'Do you have a cleaning lady coming in at all?'

'Not yet. I've only just moved in. I shall have to find someone soon.'

'Who has the keys to the house, then?'

'Well, no one now the builders have all finished. Just you and me.'

Alison wondered why she asked.

If it had been Alison who had been killed – as seemed more logical – what then? She had no close family from what Nick could make out. No, she had said that she was now alone in the world. So if she had been killed, Aidan would have been her heir. No, that made no sense either. Had she made a will? Surely she would have done so – a woman in her position. It

182

would be absurd not to. She might have left her fortune to almost anyone. Why hadn't he asked her or her solicitor before now who her heir was? He must be going mad, that was one of the first things you always did when someone was murdered . . . No. Wait a minute. It wasn't Alison who had been murdered but Aidan and Howard. Could he legitimately ring her up and ask her who she'd left her money to?

He reached for the phone and dialled her number, not giving himself time to think better of it. He heard the clicks as the connection was made. Then there was the long bleep of the engaged tone. He tried again two minutes later with the same result. There was no reason why she should not be making a long phone call . . . He rang the operator. She reported back that the line was open but that no one was speaking on it. Probably the phone had been left off the hook. Did he want her to send a warning blast down it? No? Sorry she couldn't be more help. But why were the hairs on the back of his neck pricking?

He dialled another number. This time he got a reply.

'Mr Waddington, Detective Inspector Trevellyan here, sorry to trouble you. Just a brief question. You said that Mr Howard wrote to you out of the blue a few weeks ago. Was that from his flat in Clapham? . . . I see. . . . He was staying there, was he? Have you got the letter still, or do you remember the address? No, it's not urgent. When you're next in your office I'd be much obliged if you'd look it out and ring me. Thank you very much.'

Nick hung up and thought for a moment. Then he got up, put his coat on and went out into the drizzly night.

'Do you remember that first autumn at Cambridge?' Alison asked gaily. She felt a little drunk so she poured herself some more brandy.

'It was such a long time ago.'

'Punting on the backs, parties, getting horribly drunk, earnest discussions into the small hours. You wanted to try everything. You were going to be rich and famous. We both were.'

'But only one of us made it.'

'I was quite envious of you,' Alison said. Judith gave a

183

high-pitched laugh which went on rather too long. Perhaps she felt drunk as well. 'You were the one that the men flocked round. You twisted them round your little finger. Love them and leave them.'

'Until you introduced me to Aidan, yes.'

Twenty minutes later Alison's head was swimming. 'God!' she said. 'No more brandy for me. I'm going to make some coffee. Want some?' She tried to get up but her limbs felt heavy and she fell back on to the chair. Judith stood up and walked over to her. She took Alison's chin in her hand and lifted her head up. Her face wavered in front of Alison's.

'I don't feel well,' Alison managed to say, 'Give me a hand, will you?' Judith didn't move. 'Judith?'

'It won't last long, Alison. You won't feel any pain. You'll be unconscious soon. Tom didn't feel anything. He just went quietly to sleep. He looked quite sweet, sitting there with that lock of hair fallen over his eye.'

Alison made a determined effort to get up but Judith easily pushed her back into the chair.

'You're not going anywhere.'

'Why? Judith?'

Nick left his car at the Bird in Hand. The footpath was still closed off but he clambered easily through the barbed wire and picked his way up the dark tunnel. Needless to say he had forgotten to bring a torch. He stumbled several times. He wondered what sort of a wild-goose chase he had brought himself out on. Now he had found a very tenuous link between Howard and Judith Hope. So what? So Thomas Howard had been staying down in Exeter for the last three months? Exeter was a big place. So Judith Hope had been with Alison that lunchtime? She would surely have gone home by now. Why the hell hadn't he called out Bill and got a squad car? Because he had nothing concrete to go on – that was why. He would have to wait until tomorrow to start a long weary process of enquiry in Exeter. And tomorrow just might be too late.

'Why? Do you know what it's been like for me all these

years?' Judith's voice was calm but there was a glassy look in her eyes. 'While you were swanking round getting richer and richer. What do you think it was like for me and Daniel? You could have helped us. Just a tiny proportion of your annual income would have made all the difference to us. You selfish, greedy bitch!' Her voice rose. 'Then tonight you have the gall to offer me your charity.' She spat the word out.

'Charity! "Thank you so much, Alison, you don't know how grateful I am!" That was what you wanted to hear, wasn't it? What you expected me to say. No, you didn't know how grateful I was. Well, Daniel and I will have all of it now. You thought you'd get round that idiot Tom, didn't you? You thought you could take him away from me just as you took everything else away from me. Worming your way into his affections. Well, if I couldn't have him no one was going to.'

At last Nick reached the garden of Hope Cottage. He passed the summerhouse and peered round the gap in the hedge at the rain-soaked house. The lights were on in the drawing-room but the curtains were drawn and the windows closed. He edged round the rose garden until he was on the terrace. Alison would be safe and sound, alone in her drawing-room, and he could creep quietly away again. A small window above the french windows was open wide enough for him to make out voices.

'Tom was cracking up anyway. He couldn't take it. It was only a matter of time before he gave us both away. He had to go.'
    Alison mumbled, 'It's not too late. Get an ambulance. You're ill. I can help you.'
    'No one saw me go to Tom's place last night. No one notices dowdy Judith Hope. When you're dead I shall wash my glass and put it away, just like last night. Only this time I shall leave your glass and the brandy and the last of the phenobarbitone on the table beside you. The police were about to arrest you, you know. So you committed suicide rather than face it.
    'You were very depressed this evening, talking to me. I got the impression that something was preying on your mind. A guilty conscience. I was upset thinking about the funeral so I went up to bed and left you here soaking up the brandy. Who

185

could have imagined you would do such a thing? Poor Alison! Who would have thought she would have gone to such extremes, killing Aidan, then Tom, then herself?

'You can't think how distraught I shall be when I find your body tomorrow morning, Alison. I shall call the police and cry on that inspector's shoulder.

'When Tom told me you didn't have an alibi for the time of Aidan's death, I was terrified they would arrest you and lock you up where I couldn't get at you. Then on Monday night Tom told me they nearly had arrested you. Luckily I came up with a few "enemies" of Aidan's for them to chase after. That would have been ironic, wouldn't it? If they'd given you life and I'd never seen any of the money. I thought, why not make your death suicide instead of accident? Suicide through remorse – murder case closed. Perfect.

'I shall break down at the inquest, sobbing my heart out over my poor, dead Aidan . . . and poor, pathetic Tom . . . and poor, wicked Alison. There won't be a dry eye in the house. I wish you could be there to see me. How are you feeling, Alison? You'll pass out soon.'

Nick was not a heavy man and the french windows opened outwards and would not easily break inwards. On the other hand the panes of glass were quite large. If he could smash them with something, the thin wooden horizontal bars would give way easily enough. He looked wildly round the terrace. At the top of the steps leading down to the lawn were two enormous terracotta urns, filled with earth and plants.

He hesitated. It would be much better to send for reinforcements. For all he knew, Judith was standing there with a gun in her hand. There were an awful lot of dead heroes in the ground.

What had Mike Brewster said? Death could occur in half an hour, depending on metabolism and build? Alison was tall and big-boned, wasn't she? She'd last at least an hour, wouldn't she? Surely she had eaten tonight. Surely she was taking the drug on a full stomach. It was no good – he couldn't risk it. There wasn't enough time. He could just make out Alison's weak voice.

He heard her say, 'No one who knows me . . . will believe . . . that I would kill myself. Nick won't believe that.'

186

Nick picked up one of the terracotta urns; he could hardly believe how heavy it was. He swung it as high as he could and brought it crashing through the french windows. He was right behind it.

The curtains descended in great folds around him. Judith whirled round in dismay, recognised him and headed for the door. He didn't think she was making a run for it. She was more likely going to look for a knife or some other weapon and Nick was unarmed. He grabbed her from behind but she gave him a vicious blow to the stomach with her elbow, winding him. He reeled back, gasping for breath. Judith was almost at the door. He flung himself at her knees, bringing her crashing to the ground. He let out a howl of pain as she kicked him in the face, but didn't lose his grip on her. She fought him furiously, scratching, kicking, biting for all she was worth. They rolled across the room, over and over.

Suddenly she twisted out of his grasp and seized up the poker from the hearth. Nick was now standing a few feet away from her, facing her across the chimney-breast, blocking her way to the door. For an absurd moment neither of them moved. Judith stood with the poker in both hands, measuring the distance between them. He dared not look at Alison – dared not take his eyes off Judith's sweating face. First rule of unarmed combat – use your opponent's weapon against him.

Judith began to advance and Nick backed away ahead of her, thinking furiously. She had time on her side. He couldn't afford to waste a moment if he was to save Alison. Finally she lunged at him. He side-stepped. The poker crashed down on a little round table, smashing it into splinters. She did not lose hold of it. He backed off again, Judith following, nearer now. She lunged forward for another blow and he dodged again, turning his body this time so as to follow the momentum of the poker.

Then he had her by the wrist and was twisting it with all his strength. At last, she dropped the poker and he was able to kick it away across the floor. He forced her arm up behind her back. She screamed in pain. He wanted to hurt her, he wanted it badly. He twisted her arm higher and put his other arm round her throat.

She gasped, 'I can't breathe. You're choking me!'

'Stop struggling then.' But she did not stop. He increased the pressure on her windpipe and she went suddenly limp in his grasp. Was she shamming? He looked around the room for something to tie her with. Among the ruined curtains were some thin plaited cords, used to tie them back during the day. He took the risk of releasing her long enough to grab them. To his relief she slumped to the ground and he bound her hands and feet.

The phone in the hall was buzzing slightly when he picked it up. He rattled the rest but couldn't get a line out. Judith must have left another receiver off somewhere in the house. The bedroom was the most likely place, or the study. He ran up the stairs to Alison's bedroom, where a cordless telephone glowed green in the darkness. He dialled 999 and summoned an ambulance. Then he rang the police station.

When he got back to the drawing-room Judith had regained consciousness and was struggling in her cords. He went through the formula.

'Judith Hope, I am arresting you for murder . . .'

Her only reply was to scream abuse in language which even Nick, with ten years in the police force, found foul. He ignored her and knelt down in front of Alison's chair.

'Alison? It's all right, my angel, the ambulance will be here in a minute. Don't let go. Don't die, my angel.'

He could not tell if she could hear him. Her eyes were closed. Her breathing was shallow but still regular. She felt a little cold to the touch. He fetched some blankets and wrapped them round her. He stayed kneeling at her feet, holding her limp hand until he heard the distant sirens.

Bill Deacon arrived with two police cars, Carol Halsgrove and two uniformed constables a few minutes after the ambulance had left. The two constables took Judith off to the station, still struggling and screaming.

'You did caution her, didn't you, sir?' Bill asked.

'Yes, I did, although I doubt if she took it in.'

'If we'd taken down the things she was saying, the typist's hair would have turned white.'

'She confessed to the murder of Howard. I heard her and so did Alison.'

188

'Are you sure you're OK, Nick?' Carol asked anxiously. 'You look a real mess. I think you're due for a visit to the hospital too. That cut needs stitches.'

'I feel just fine at the moment. Adrenalin, I suppose. You know, there were times when I wasn't certain I was going to win that fight. She fought as if she was demented.'

'She had everything to lose,' Bill said.

'So did I!'

Bill walked out through the shattered french windows.

'Hold on,' Nick said sharply. 'Don't move.' He retrieved his glasses from the terrace and put them on.

'That was a near thing. Come on, let's get to the station, and we'll stop at the hospital on the way. You'll have to stay here overnight, Carol. I'll get someone to relieve you in the morning.'

Nick and Bill got into the remaining police car and Bill pulled out on to the Hopbridge road. He said, 'What made you go out to Hope Cottage tonight, Mr Trevellyan?'

'I couldn't reconcile what Alison had told us about Judith Hope with the woman we met on Monday. There was a discrepancy somewhere.'

'They hadn't met for five years. People change, sometimes they get the stuffing knocked out of them.'

'At first I thought that it was Alison's version that was wrong. I sensed a rivalry or jealousy between the two women. But I'd got it the wrong way round.'

'She did all this out of jealousy?'

'No, no, Bill. It was money. With Alison dead, Daniel Hope would get the lot. He's only nine so Judith Hope would have had control of it for nearly ten years. I suspect she and Thomas Howard would have found a way of siphoning most of it off for their own use.'

'I don't understand that Howard,' Bill said, shaking his head. 'I can't make sense of it. How did he get mixed up in it all?'

Nick paused, trying to sort out the jumble in his head. 'I think he was a very weak man. He'd had a nervous breakdown following an unsuccessful love affair. He was still recovering from it. He fell for Judith Hope. Probably she would have divorced Aidan and settled down to be a solicitor's wife, comfortably off if not rich.

189

'Then something reminded Judith of Alison – she said she'd seen an article in the paper saying that Alison was moving her business down here. She suddenly saw a chance to get her hands on some serious money. Tom Howard wrote to his old family friend, James Waddington, and got a job here. Then Aidan turned up in Exeter and said he was on his way here too. It was too good an opportunity to miss. Judith provided herself with an unobtrusive and unbreakable alibi while Howard killed a man he had never met. And he might have got away with it if he hadn't been so unlucky as to be seen by Gerard Doherty. The thing that was baffling me was that no one had a *motive* for killing Aidan.'

'Except Miss Hope.'

'Except Alison. Anyway . . . Howard was weak enough to go along with it but he hadn't really a murderer's temperament and he was beginning to crack under the strain. So Judith decided to go it alone.'

'You sat down and worked all this out tonight?'

'Not really,' Nick admitted. 'Although when James Waddington told me that his letter from Tom Howard was from an Exeter address, that pointed the finger firmly at Judith Hope.'

'But you didn't know Mrs Hope was at Hope Cottage this evening. Normally we would just have checked up on the Exeter connection tomorrow.'

They pulled into the hospital car park and got out of the car. Nick blushed in the darkness but managed to keep his voice casual.

'I had an overwhelming feeling that Alison was in danger. When her phone was permanently engaged, I just decided to go round and see if she was all right.'

It wouldn't have fooled anyone, least of all Bill. Nick turned through the door of the emergency unit.

'My, my,' Bill said to himself, as he locked the car, 'you've got it bad, haven't you?'

190

Chapter 23

Mike Brewster was still examining Judith when they got back to the station. He did a double take when he saw Nick.

'My God! I was going to put in a report saying this prisoner had been beaten up but now I see she won the fight.'

'No, she didn't,' Nick said grimly. 'I won.'

'I was a bit taken aback when I heard you were the arresting officer. I thought if Nick Trevellyan had started beating up suspects, there was no hope left for the police force. If it had been Burcombe, now – '

Nick broke in impatiently. 'She's not badly hurt, is she?'

'No. I've given her a mild sedative. I don't think you ought to question her tonight, though. Apart from anything else, you need a long sleep by the look of you.'

'Nothing doing, Mike. I want her in court first thing tomorrow morning. I'm not in the mood for another fight so don't give me a hard time, eh?'

Brewster looked at him in astonishment, then shrugged.

'I trust your judgement, Nick. I won't certify her unfit for questioning.'

He took no one but Bill into the interview room with him. They sat Judith on an upright chair in the middle of the floor. Nick was restless and remained standing, pacing round the room, forcing her to turn on her chair if she wanted to keep him in sight. Which she did.

'I want the whole story, Judith.'

'Fuck you.'

'I heard you confess to Alison that you killed Thomas

191

Howard. I was listening outside the window. There's no point in your denying it.'

'You're lying. I'm not saying anything. I want a solicitor.'

Nick ran a hand up his cheek, feeling the swelling now appearing round his left eye.

'No solicitor,' he said calmly. 'You don't need one. Just answer my questions, Judith. You may as well tell me the whole thing. You're not moving from that chair until you do. I can wait all night.'

Judith gaped at him. 'I've got rights, haven't I?'

'Oh? That piece of paper you signed for the custody sergeant said you waived your right to see a solicitor at the moment.'

'I didn't know that!'

'That'll teach you not to sign anything without reading it first, Judith.'

'Well, I'm saying now that I want one. It's the law. You can't just refuse.'

'No? There's only me and the sergeant here, Judith. He will confirm that you repeatedly refused the offer of a solicitor. Right, sergeant?'

'Yes, sir.' Bill reacted as if this was a perfectly normal way for Nick to carry on.

'Aren't you supposed to tape this interview, or something?' Judith said desperately.

'You've been watching too much television, Judith. We're very old-fashioned in the Hop Valley. Sergeant Deacon will take notes of what you say. Right, sergeant?'

'Yes, sir.'

'He hasn't even got a notebook! He's not writing anything down!'

'We'll write it up later, Judith. Now stop wasting my time. Let's start with the plot to murder your husband, shall we? How did you talk Tom Howard into that one?'

He came close up to her and she spat at him. He raised his hand to strike her across the face. She did not flinch. He let his arm drop. He hoped that was the closest he'd ever get to hitting anyone in the interview room. He hated that woman as he'd never hated anyone in his life.

'Go on,' she jeered, 'hit me.'

192

'OK,' Nick said after a moment's pause. 'We'll leave you here for a while to think about it. I'll get you for the murders of Howard and your husband if I can, Judith, but if I can't I'll get you for the murder of Alison. You can't wriggle out of that one.'

He was behind her now and she spun round in her chair to see his face. He caught the fleeting look of panic in her eyes. His own expression was glacial.

'I don't believe you! There wasn't enough time.'

'Alison died on the way to hospital.'

She was silent for a moment, then her expression changed slowly to one of triumph.

'Good!'

'You're going to prison for life, Judith, for one murder or for three. I'll give you half an hour to think over what you want to say to me.'

'I never thought I'd live to see this day,' Bill said, as he followed Nick into his office.

Nick rounded on him angrily. 'How about if it had been Susie, or one of your girls?'

Bill made a placatory gesture. 'Hey! I'm on your side, remember. It's just not like you, that's all.'

'I'll get the details out of her if I have to thump it out of her.' Nick sat down at his desk and buried his head in his hands. 'Don't suppose you've got any aspirin, have you?'

'Yeah, I'll get you a hot drink too.'

Bill was back in five minutes with a bottle of aspirin and a cup of strong, sweet tea. Nick sipped it and made a face.

'Drink it,' Bill said sternly. 'You need the energy.' He sat down on the other side of the desk and looked at his boss with affection as he forced the rest of the tea down.

'You never fall for the nice, uncomplicated girls, do you, Nick?'

'Eh?'

'The world's full of nice, pretty, sweet-natured girls who'd make any man a good wife, but you have to fall for the Lucy Fieldings and the Alison Hopes.'

Nick glared at him angrily for a moment. Then he saw the funny side and began to laugh. In a moment they were both giggling helplessly like a pair of third-formers.

193

'Yeah,' Nick gasped. 'I must be some sort of masochist. Alison's just as sweet as I could ask, though.'

'How long are they keeping her in?'

'Just overnight, I think. They washed her stomach and gave her some sort of injection. Now she has to sleep it off. The nurse bullied me horribly. She'd decided that Alison was an attempted suicide and that it must be my fault. I had to show her my warrant card before she was even civil. And then she wouldn't let me see her.'

'She wouldn't have been in a position to tell you anything, not tonight.'

'I know. I just wanted . . . to see her.'

'I'd made up my mind it was her. You must have got pretty fed up with me.'

'There were times I felt like slapping your fat face. It took you long enough to catch on, anyway. Call yourself a detective? You're fired.'

'Well, you don't give much away at the best of times, do you? You were certain she hadn't done it?'

'Not certain, no. Not certain.'

Bill looked at his watch. 'Is Mrs Hope going to talk?'

'I think telling her that Alison was dead was just what she needed. We'll give her a few minutes, then we'll see.'

'It was all Tom's idea,' Judith began.

Well, of course, Nick thought. He could have written that line himself. Since Howard wasn't there to stick up for himself. If they'd had him in another interview room now, he'd have been screaming out that it was all her fault.

'I told him about Alison and how she'd come to live down here. Aidan had pointed out that paragraph in the paper to me. Tom seemed very interested. He said how odd it was that only she and Aidan stood between me and all that money. He liked money, Tom. He had expensive tastes. He told me about James Waddington and how he reckoned he could get a job here any time he wanted. He said we should kill them both. I thought it was a joke but then I got to thinking about it . . .

'It had to be Aidan first. Tom said there would be two lots of death duties otherwise. One lot on Alison's death and the

194

rest on Daniel's share when Aidan died. He needed to make sure Alison hadn't made a will anyway, or that, if she had, it said the right thing . . .

'One small snag. We didn't know where Aidan was. Then he turned up again, in Exeter. On the way to the Hop Valley. Well, it was obvious that the whole thing was meant . . .

'Tom was supposed to stab Aidan. He took a knife with him. God knows why he had to batter him like that. I realised then that he was the type to panic. But it was a bit bloody late then. The whole point of the thing was to kill Alison . . .

'I was looking forward to killing Alison. We started out the same. Two scholarship girls. I was as good as her. Better, I had a better brain. Where did she get the idea she was so superior? She had it in for me. She introduced me to Aidan just to get me out of her way. So I wouldn't be there to compete with her any more . . . So she could be top dog. She started that business with Aidan. Left me out. Poor Judith is too busy washing nappies. Aidan couldn't see it. Had a soft spot for her, always . . .

'Her death was going to be an accident. But then Tom rang me on Sunday night and told me Alison hadn't got an alibi for the time of Aidan's death and that the police suspected her. So I thought up a much better idea, let her commit suicide and wrap the whole thing up neatly . . .

'Tom was supposed to be ingratiating himself with her. Only it was working the other way round. He was supposed to play the solicitor – tell her not to say anything, make her act suspiciously. But it didn't really work because she trusted you and nothing he said to turn her against you seemed to change that. I'd told him to pretend he liked her, win her confidence, make her think he fancied her. But it was getting just a bit too realistic. It must have occurred to him at that point that marrying Alison would be an even better way of getting his hands on her money – no death duties at all then . . .

'And he was having nightmares . . . I couldn't trust him any more. That burglary was the last straw. He'd convinced himself that someone had seen him. I went to his place that night and asked if he was ready to do it – to kill her. He made excuses. I didn't wait to hear any more. I had the capsules – Daniel takes them for his epilepsy. I had a store with me when

195

I left London and I just went to Mum's GP and said I hadn't got any and he gave me a load more. The doctors always made a point of telling me how dangerous they were. He was unconscious in quite a short time. I just left him. I knew how much to give him – I'd looked it up, ready for Alison . . .

'I slipped back to the guest house, it was only a couple of streets away, through the park. There's no one in the park late at night, I mean, you don't know who you might meet there, do you? Homicidal maniacs and all sorts. I let myself back in the side door. Mrs Penhaligon is an insomniac, she drugs herself up to the eyeballs every night. You might as well try to waken the dead . . . You might as well try to wake Alison . . .'

They got it all down. She signed it. Nick realised when he saw it in hard print that she was mad. He stopped hating her.

'Now she had started she didn't want to stop.

'I'm glad she's dead. She's had everything, ever since I've known her, money, success. Aidan fancied his chances with her at one time. Then she tried to take Tom away from me. Bloody stupid men. She was a prick teaser! Always was.'

She glared at Nick, who looked back stonily.

'You had the hots for her – that's obvious . . . Wouldn't have done you any good. She'd just have eaten you up and spat you out.'

'Perhaps we shall see,' he said. 'Since Alison is making a full recovery.'

They had to call for two constables to help subdue her.

196

Chapter 24

Nick left the police station at about three o'clock and walked through the sombre streets to his flat. He felt as if he had gone ten rounds with a battering ram. He had only just begun to realise that he was covered in cuts and scratches. He hoped he wouldn't run into anyone of a nervous disposition. As well as the bruises on his face, a great bruise was coming up on his stomach where Judith's elbow had jabbed into him. This was the second night in a row he would have to manage on a few hours' sleep. He would have to be in the magistrates' court in the morning to get Judith remanded while they prepared their case for committal. He fell on the bed fully clothed and slept for six hours.

He rang the hospital as soon as he awoke, only to be told that Alison had passed a quiet night, discharged herself first thing that morning and gone home.

After the magistrates had remanded Judith in custody for a week pending committal proceedings, Bill and Nick stood outside the courtroom, kicking their heels with the usual feeling of anti-climax which followed an arrest. From now on it would just be reams of paperwork.

'You get back to bed, sir,' Bill said solicitously.

'No. I'll just go and pick my car up. Then I'm going round to the offices of the *Voice*. I want a word with Jack Ashcroft and he's usually in on Fridays. He'll have to print a retraction now.'

'Odd that,' Bill said. 'Now I come to think of it, Dangerfield wasn't at the magistrates' court this morning. Not like him to miss a juicy story.'

'Perhaps he didn't hear about it in time.'

'Dangerfield! A special court session? He would have known about it before we did.'

Nick got a constable to drive him out to Little Hopford and retrieved his car from the pub. Then he pulled into the courtyard of Hope Cottage. Carol Halsgrove opened the door.

'I didn't realise you were coming to relieve me in person,' she said.

'Shit! I'm sorry, Carol. I forgot you were here.' He went to strike himself on the forehead to underline his absent-mindedness but remembered his bruised face just in time.

'It doesn't matter. I got some sleep on the sofa. Are you all right? Does that eye hurt or what?'

'Not really.' He brushed past her into the hall. 'Where's Alison?'

'She's gone away.'

'What!'

'She turned up at about half past eight – looking a bit rough, I thought. She just stayed long enough to shower and change, then drove off up the valley in her Jag, pausing only to ring an emergency glazier. That's him making all that racket next door.'

'Where has she gone?'

'She didn't say. Sorry. She took a suitcase.'

'Why the hell didn't you stop her?'

'What was I supposed to do, arrest her?'

'You got a statement out of her before you let her go, of course?' Nick enquired witheringly. Then withered himself as Carol handed him a pained look and two sheets of A4 type-script with 'A. M. Hope' spidering across the bottom. He wondered what the 'M' stood for. Mavis, Millicent, Mabel? . . . Maybe not.

'I'm sorry, Carol. Of course you couldn't have stopped her.' He sat down on the windowsill. 'It's all over. Judith Hope's confessed everything.'

'Yeah? Guilty plea, maybe?'

'Maybe. I'm beginning to think it could be Broadmoor rather than Holloway for her.'

'I'm glad it wasn't her, Alison. I like her.'

'Yeah.'

'We're all finished here,' Carol said. 'Scenes of crime and so

198

on. No point me hanging about once the window has been repaired.'

'No, it's supposed to be your day off, isn't it? I'll drive you back as soon as the glazier's finished.'

'Shall I make you some coffee while we're waiting? She said to help myself. I'm sure that applies to you too.'

'OK. Thanks.'

'Not much of a reward for saving her life, is it? Perhaps she can run to a biscuit as well.'

Nick followed Carol into the kitchen. 'Did she . . . mention me?' he asked casually.

'Just – is Nick all right? – something like that.'

'Oh.'

'You should get a commendation.'

He leant on the worktop and gazed moodily out at the silent courtyard.

'More like a right bollocking from Reg for coming out here on my own instead of getting help.'

'At least we're spared the scourge of Seymour.' Carol had once told him that the main reason she transferred out of HQ was so she wouldn't have to watch Seymour doing his Vlad-the-Impaler impersonations any more.

'Yes.' Nick couldn't help smiling at that. 'It was just a pity that no one told him not to bother to come. So he had a wasted journey.'

'No! You didn't!'

'I'm afraid so. I couldn't resist it – I wanted to see his face.'

'Whatever did he say?'

Nick had once seen a road digger – stripped to the waist, tattoos everywhere – blush at what Carol said to him after she nearly fell down his hole. Even so he couldn't quite bring himself to tell her what Seymour had called him.

'A few choice phrases which I shall not repeat to your delicate feminine ears,' he improvised. She made a rude noise. 'I pleaded temporary amnesia owing to a blow on the head. But I suspect Reg will have something to say about that too.'

She poured him some coffee and, sensing his despondency, laid a comradely hand on his arm and squeezed. He considered, briefly, crying on her shoulder. But did not.

Nick walked into the tatty offices of the *Valley Voice*. There was, unusually, no one in the outer room except a young secretary. He ignored her 'Can I help you?' and walked, without knocking, into the editor's office. Gordon Dangerfield was alone there. He was sitting with his great feet up on the desk, his hands folded behind his head.

'What the hell do you want?' was his own greeting.

'I want to talk to Ashcroft.'

'I've just this minute told Burcombe, he's gone.' Dangerfield scratched himself lethargically.

'Burcombe was here? What do you mean, gone?'

'God almighty! Burcombe was here not half an hour ago. I told him. Jack's gone. Left the valley. Sold his farm. Buggered off.'

Nick shut the door behind him and sat down. He looked hard at Dangerfield, who stared coldly back.

'He's scarpered, departed, done a bunk,' Dangerfield continued, like a runaway thesaurus. 'I told Burcombe, he'll have to take his warrant and stick it.'

'Inspector Burcombe had a warrant to arrest Jack?' Nick didn't feel that he was ahead in this conversation.

'Course. For this fire-bombing business. I told the stupid sod at the time he wouldn't get away with it but you know he never listens to anyone.'

'Let's hear the whole story, then.'

'Piss off, I've already had the third degree from Burcombe.'

'Jack obviously confided in you. Do you want to be arrested as an accessory?'

'Funny, that's what Burcombe said. No imagination, you coppers.'

Dangerfield took his feet off the desk, fumbled with a cigarette, made a fuss of lighting it and took a long drag into his lungs before he deigned to speak.

'Jack's been screwing this bird, right? Since about Christmas. Some tart called Jenny, called herself an interior designer – posh name for someone who makes curtains. He was keeping it pretty quiet, though. At first I thought it was just Jack being Jack – not wanting anyone to know some woman had got him under her thumb – but it turned out there

200

was a husband somewhere, not living with her but a violent type by all accounts.'

'Likes a bit of rough, this Jenny?'

Dangerfield gave him a look of something approaching respect. 'First half-way human thing I've ever heard you say, Trevellyan.' He took another deep drag, which sparked off a coughing fit. After some minutes' hacking he resumed. 'So she hears Alison Hope quarrelling with her cousin one day. Nasty temper that stuck-up cow has got – she tried to take a swing at me, you know?'

'I heard she did more than try. I heard she gave you a bloody nose.'

'Yeah, well. Then Jenny found out that the cousin was coming to this party Jack had been invited to. Jack had got it in his mind to get at these ARM people since you weren't doing anything about them. Jenny went to see Aidan Hope and fixed up for this fight to break out at the party, the idea being that someone would take Jack home – leave him all knocked out with no transport. Don't think he'd reckoned on it being you, though. Don't think he'd reckoned on Hope play-ing his part with such enthusiasm either – Jack must have genuinely managed to get up his nose somehow. Well, as soon as you'd pushed off, Jenny turns up in her car, been waiting up on Threeoaks Hill. They did the attack on ARM and Jack was safely tucked up in bed again by one o'clock. Then next day you turn up and tell him Hope's been murdered. God, you gave him a fright.'

'And where's Mrs Tilney, this Jenny?'

'She's gone with him. Beats prison, I suppose – marginally.'

'Sounds like they deserve each other,' Nick said. 'So who's running the paper now? Who's pulling your strings?'

'Ain't no paper to run. It's been making a loss for quite a while. Jack owes money right, left and centre. That's how come he'd found a buyer for the farm on the quiet. He'd been planning to do a bunk. That was why he was so furious about the vandalism – thought the buyer might back out at the last minute.'

'And why he didn't care who he libelled, presumably.'

'That's right.'

'Where's the money gone? He used to be quite a rich man.'

Dangerfield shrugged. 'He wasn't much of a businessman. The paper was just a means for him to settle grudges. The readers liked it well enough but the advertisers were pulling out in droves. Didn't like the tone. It got so it was like tearing up tenners and flushing them down the toilet. So if you've come to ask for a retraction, there's not going to be another edition to print it in. And if you're going to sue the paper for libel, you'll have to join the other creditors.'

'I can sue you for libel personally, Dangerfield.'

'Cobblers!'

'You wrote that front-page story, the anonymous bit.'

'Yeah? Prove it.'

Nick got up to go. 'Let me know if you want a reference for a new job, won't you?'

'Ha bloody ha. I heard you finally managed to arrest someone. I didn't bother to go to court since I shan't be reporting it. Who was it then?'

'Judith Hope, his wife.'

Dangerfield gave a snort of derision. 'God almighty! You're a real bunch of amateurs, aren't you? Everyone knows that when a bloke gets topped it's always the wife did it. Everyone except you, that is, Trevellyan. How d'you get the black eye? Hope's wife give you that, did she?'

'As a matter of fact, she did.'

Nick left the office not feeling particularly downhearted. At least the valley would be free of Jack Ashcroft and his dirty little paper from now on, and Alison wasn't a murderer – just missing.

Chapter 25

'I'm going to Aidan Hope's funeral,' Nick said, on Tuesday morning. 'If you think about it, there's not going to be anyone there. I'm going to pay my last respects – if that's the right word.'

'I'll come with you then,' Bill said. They got into the car and Bill took the Hopcliff road. 'Did you have a nice rest, sir?' he asked.

'Yes,' Nick said without much enthusiasm. 'I'm fighting fit again.'

'I shouldn't go getting into any more fights for a day or two, if I was you. What did the Super say to you?'

'Well . . . he spent about twenty minutes calling me a fucking idiot, then he said well done, then he said if I ever did anything like it again he'd cut my balls off and use them for doorstops, then he said not to come in again until today.'

Bill chuckled. 'One thing you have to say about the Guv-'nor, he's never consistent. You never know which way he'll jump.'

'No,' Nick agreed, 'this time he seems to have managed to jump in both directions simultaneously. I think he was a bit peeved that Alison hadn't done it, though. He'd made his mind up – just like everyone else.'

Bill decided it would be more tactful not to reply to this since he knew that Alison was still absent.

They pulled up in front of the Catholic church outside Hopcliff. It was little more than a hut really, since most of the valley people were low church. There was a small graveyard, though, stretching to the edge of the cliff.

'It seems quite a good resting place for Aidan Hope,' Bill said. 'He can look out to sea, towards Ireland.' He glanced in his rear-view mirror and a very unfunereal smile came over his face. 'Looks like we won't be the only mourners after all, sir.'

Nick turned round in time to see a black Jaguar gliding silently to a halt behind them. He jumped out of the police car, ran back and opened the driver's door for her.

'You look awful,' she teased. 'Do you know you've got a black eye?'

'I thought you'd gone,' he blurted out. 'For good, I mean.'

'Gone? Run away? Not my style.' She stepped gracefully out of the Jaguar. She looked fully recovered: no longer deathly pale as he had last seen her, but restored to the blooming vitality of ten days ago. She wore the same charcoal-grey suit he had seen at the inquest and her glorious hair was coiled up under the black hat. He gazed at her mutely. Bill got out of the car and disappeared discreetly into the church.

'It's only twenty past,' she said. 'Let's take a turn round the churchyard.'

'I've been looking for you ever since . . . that night,' he said, as they turned past the most weather-beaten of the headstones.

'I went to Exeter, to see Mary Cooke and the boy, Daniel. He's an epileptic, you know.'

'I do now. How's her mother taking it?'

'Quietly. I was afraid she would refuse to see me. But she doesn't blame me.'

'She claims not to have known about Judith and Thomas Howard.'

'I think that's the truth. It was so humiliating for Judith to have to run home to mother and admit her marriage was over. She wouldn't have told her mother about her new man until she was quite sure of him. Mary thought he was just advising her about the divorce – his aunt being a friend of the family.'

'I'll take your word for it.'

'I stayed the weekend. The strangest thing happened just as I was leaving yesterday morning. That decorative young man – the one who followed me and Tom that night – turned up on

204

Mary's doorstep. And what do you think? He turns out to be a policeman.' She gave him an amused look.

'Ah . . . Yes.' Sod you, Penruan. Why didn't you tell me you'd seen her?

'Then I got the train up to London to see my solicitors. Mary Cooke will look after Daniel now but I'm setting up a trust fund for him. To pay for his upbringing and education. I've learnt my lesson – he's not going to grow up hating me. I got back very late last night.'

They had completed the brief circuit of the graveyard and stood side by side outside the church.

'I thought I was never going to see you again,' he said softly.

'I should have telephoned you. I nearly did many times. I suppose I wanted to tie up the loose ends, so that I would be free to concentrate on the future. Now I am.' She turned to faced him. 'You saved my life that night.'

He took her by the shoulders and said furiously, 'I don't want you ever to say that again!'

'Why not?' she said, startled. 'It's true.'

'It's not *gratitude* I want from you, Alison. If that's all you can offer me I'd rather you got back in your car and went away again for good.'

They looked at each other for a moment, then she began to laugh. It was the same laugh that had so wounded him the morning he questioned her about Tom Howard's death. Now he recognised it as a laugh of happiness and understanding. He joined in.

'No, Nick. Not gratitude,' she spluttered. 'Come on.' She took his arm. 'It doesn't do to be late for a funeral.'

They walked into the church in silence, arm in arm.

After the interment Bill made off to the far end of the graveyard and took an intense interest in some of the headstones. When Alison had exchanged a few words with the priest, Nick walked her back to her car. She got into the driver's seat.

'Will you come and see me tonight?' she said.

'How early may I come?'

'Not before seven.'

'I'll be there at seven. Alison – '

'Not here, Nick. I have to go and see Molly now, she's been so worried. Save it for tonight.' She started the engine.

'See you tonight, my . . .'

'Angel?'

'Yes.' He blushed. 'My angel . . . I didn't know if you could hear me then.'

'Dimly. I thought I must have died, since someone kept talking about angels. See you later.'

She drove off towards the clifftop road. Nick watched until she was out of sight.

Alison pulled the Jaguar to a halt in a lay-by just before the Armitages' driveway, switched off the engine and sat looking out to sea. She was a coward, she reflected wryly, a coward and a liar. She had indeed run away, snatched a breathing space. She had promised herself last time that she would never care that much about anyone again. He had slipped under her guard, sneakily, by not being her type – he wasn't a big blond; rather the reverse. The intensity of his feelings alarmed her as much as it excited her. He wanted so much from her – and he was not a man to be easily satisfied.

'You're a deep one, Nick Trevellyan,' she murmured to herself. 'I haven't seen the half of you yet.'

She pulled her hat off and tossed it on the passenger seat, shaking her hair loose about her shoulders. Then she left the car by the roadside and walked up the gravel drive to Molly's house.

'Come on, Bill,' Nick called across the graveyard. 'Get a move on. We haven't got all day. I want to get off early.' As he got into the passsenger seat and fastened his seatbelt, he was smiling.

About the Author

SUSAN B. KELLY was born in the Thames Valley section of England. After studying French and English at London University, she worked for twelve years as a computer programmer before making writing her full-time career.

She now lives in London with her solicitor husband and a black-and-white cat called Hope. *Hope Against Hope* is her first novel. She is working on a second novel also set in Hop Valley.